SPEARFINGER

Pete,
Thanks for your support!
Hope you enjoy!

SPEARFINGER

A NOVEL
LAWRENCE THACKSTON

RIVERS TURN PRESS

Rivers Turn Press
617 Rivers Turn Road
Orangeburg, SC 29115

This book is a work of fiction. Names, characters, places, and incidents either are products of the author's imagination or are used fictitiously. Any resemblance to actual events or locales or persons, living or dead is entirely coincidental.

Copyright © 2022 by Lawrence Thackston

All rights reserved, including the right to reproduce this book or portions thereof in any form whatsoever. No part of this book may be reproduced or transmitted in any form or by any means, except by a reviewer who may quote brief passages in a review, without permission in writing. For information address Rivers Turn Press, 617 Rivers Turn Road Orangeburg, SC 29115

First edition, first printing October 2022

Cover Design by Suvajit Das
Author photo by Joni Thackston
Printing by Major Graphics, LLC

Manufactured in the United States of America

Trade Paperback edition ISBN 978-0-9985755-6-8

Also by LAWRENCE THACKSTON

The Devil's Courthouse

Tidal Pools

Carolina Cruel

For the Ani-Yun-Wiya

"There is more to us than meets the eye."

Individually and collectively, Cherokee people possess an extraordinary ability to face down adversity and continue moving forward.

--Wilma Mankiller
Principal Chief of the Cherokee Nation
(1945-2010)

HARVEST MOON
TIME OF THE ANCIENTS

Sundown

Crossing Bear crouched behind the laurel thicket, waiting. He held a heavy, woodland arrow in his left hand, and his bow was slung low on his naked back. It was his grandfather's bow, made from prized Osage wood, carved by the old man's hand—unblemished, smooth, strong. The arrow too was perfect, the flinthead razor sharp, deadly. The brisk, mountain air stirred about Crossing Bear, keeping his senses sharp and intensifying his resolve.

The great Cherokee marksman leaned forward on his knees, peered outward, and found the slightest opening in the laurel. He cut his eyes to either side, saw flashes of movement from his brothers—the other warriors who had made the dangerous journey with him to the white cliffs—they too hidden by foliage, lying in wait. Smoke and the smell of roasting venison rose just a stone's throw distance behind them. All was ready. The trap was set.

Moments later, the Cherokees' prey emerged from the mountain path. She was old and feeble, dragging her limp, right leg behind her. The black cowl she wore hid most of her stringy, grey hair and only the tip of her wrinkled nose poked out from beneath. She shuffled through the leaves as if an elderly member of the tribe who had accidently wandered into the mountain forest.

Her pace quickened as she saw the flames of the fire in the distance. Spittle formed in the corners of her mouth—not at the deer meat cooking on the fire—but at the expectation of satiating a far more nefarious hunger.

"Uwe-la-na-tsiku. Su-sa-sai," she sang out to the silent camp, hoping to lure any children out into the open. No one came forth, but a wind rose from the valley floor and pushed the wispy smoke toward her. She fixed her eyes on the silent forest around her.

Crossing Bear swung the bow around, placing the fletching of his arrow against the taut string. His movements were swift and silent as he leveled his aim through the brush.

SPEARFINGER

"Uwe-la-na-tsiku. Su-sa-sai," her soft, grandmotherly voice sang again. But once more, no one came to her.

Crossing Bear watched her with eyes wide open, willing her toward the fire. She inched forward warily, but with her next step, the fragile, hidden branches holding the patch of leaves beneath her gave way. The old woman's legs buckled, and she fell forward into the pit where thirty sharp spear points awaited her fall.

All of the warriors—save Crossing Bear—emerged from their hiding spots, yelling, and firing their arrows one after the other into the trap. But their hubris would betray them.

The old woman crawled from the pit, undamaged from arrow and spear. She stood on the side and cackled, mocking the warriors' heroics. She would not fall to mortal trickery.

Undaunted, the warriors continued to shoot arrow after arrow at the brazen witch, but again to no avail. Each of their strong arrows bounced away, broken and useless.

She turned to the stunned Cherokees, and from under her cowl; she showed them her dreaded right index finger—nine inches long with the sharpened, deadly point. It was the same finger she had used to rob so many of the Cherokee people of their livers, leaving them to wither and die a painful death.

She continued her malevolent laugh as she slithered her way toward them like some winding, rodent-seeking serpent. The gathered warriors realized they were the ones now doomed. Her trap, so meticulously planned, had quickly become their own.

She cast her spell and the warriors fell to the ground—their legs asleep, their minds frozen in fear. Screams of torment echoed from the high cliffs as she seized upon the closest warrior, cutting him open and feasting upon his liver. The others cried out, awaiting their deaths like helpless flies in a spider's web.

Only Crossing Bear remained unaffected. He held his position behind the laurel, fighting the urge to flee. He knew he must act—he must stop her—but how? He momentarily dropped his bow and searched the sky—a quick, unspoken prayer for guidance. He then took aim once more and waited.

The pleas of his brothers continued. They called out for mercy—begged for an end to this nightmare. Another one of the

Cherokees fell to the witch's wrath, but Crossing Bear held his position. The muscles of his forearm grew hot with pain as he delayed the arrow's launch. His fingers cramped—the tips sliced into the sinewy bowstring and bled. Despite the cool conditions, sweat streaked his face and muscular back.

Show me, Great Spirit... show me! As the witch reached for another helpless soul, Tsi-gi-li-li, the tiny messenger bird, swooped down from high in the clouds and nipped at her right hand—the hand that possessed the vile spear-finger. And right away, Crossing Bear knew what he must do.

He took dead aim again, knowing that he would only get this one shot. He held his breath and closed his left eye. And then with the strength of ten warriors, Crossing Bear stretched his bow to near breaking point. From deep within his soul, he heard a voice: Now, Crossing Bear, now!

With lightning speed, the arrow found its mark and split open the old woman's right hand. The severed spear-finger dropped to the ground and the witch's lifeblood gushed out and onto the forest floor. She cried out in mortal pain, holding up her wounded hand. Black blood spewed from her mouth, and she shed her stone-like skin.

With the spell broken, the fallen warriors rose. They sensed the witch's weakening state and quickly huddled around her to finish her off.

She reached down for her spear-finger, stood before the warriors, and cursed them and her fate. She shook the lifeless appendage at the Cherokee, and then, with a furious blast of wind that shook the roots of the forest and made the mountain tops tremble, the old woman disappeared into a rolling storm cloud.

For many centuries after, those who lived in the Smoky Mountains never saw or heard from the evil witch again....

OCTOBER 17, 1995

7:15 PM

 The grey Lincoln Continental cruised down the unmarked road somewhere in the vast Qualla Boundary. It moved slowly and with purpose—like a prowling wolf stalking its prey. It plowed through a sea of red and gold leaves cast away from the giant oaks, maples and other talking trees found so readily on the Cherokee's expansive lands. The leaves scattered in the wolf's menacing wake.
 The sun had now slipped behind the surrounding peaks. A blue mist had settled into the Boundary's vast acreage, and the temperature began its nightly spiral. It was autumn in the Smoky Mountains. It was the time of the harvest moon—a time of natural endings.
 The Lincoln followed this clay-banked road for several miles until it was safely away from houses, lights, and traffic—far enough away from the eyes and ears of any potential on-lookers.
 It came to a halt beneath a colossal sycamore tree that stretched high into the waxing, evening sky. Both the driver and passenger doors opened, and two heavy-weight men dressed in dark suits emerged.
 The man from the passenger's side opened the back door of the Lincoln and reached in with his meaty paw and pulled out his cargo. It was an older man, a Cherokee, beaten in the face and bleeding from his mouth. The Cherokee's arms were tied tightly behind his back and his clothes were ruffled and torn. They drug the old man to the base of the tree, forced him to his knees and then pushed him back into a sitting position.
 As one took more rope and tied him to the tree, the other pulled out a 9mm and began to roll a silencer on the end of its barrel. The Cherokee man looked up and saw his fate. "Oh… no, no, no. Please don't do this. I swear; I can still make this happen."
 "Little too late for that, Geronimo."
 "No, please, have mercy. Just give me one more chance. I'm begging you."

The white man leaned over and was face to face—his breath reeked. He stuck the silencer into the trembling Cherokee's mouth. "Now, try not to get blood on my new shoes, okay?" The executioner's fat finger went tight around the trigger. He was a second from pulling it when he suddenly backed off. The other assailant standing behind him frowned. "What's the matter, Dutch? Go ahead; get it over with."

Dutch held up his hand to quiet his partner. He then stood tall and looked behind him. "Did you hear that?"

"What? I didn't hear nothing."

But then it came again and this time he did hear it, in fact, all three men heard it. It was faint, hard to make out, but it sounded like laughter. Not the joyful or cheerful kind, but a raspy cackle—an old smoker's laugh. And it was coming from the woods behind them. It suddenly came again, and this time it was much louder.

"Damn it, somebody followed us," Dutch reasoned.

"No way. We're out in the middle of nowhere," the other man said. He then turned to the Cherokee. "You have somebody follow us out here, old man?"

The Cherokee just lowly shook his head.

Dutch waved his gun towards the black forest. "Go check it out, Kenzie. I'll keep an eye on this one."

The one called Kenzie pulled his own weapon from inside his coat and stepped into the thick woods. The laughter continued for a moment and then all went silent. Dutch turned a grim face to the Cherokee. "This better not be any of your tricks, Indian." He then turned back. "Kenzie?! You see anything?!"

His call was followed by more silence. The man nervously inched towards the tree line. "Kenzie?!"

A blood curdling scream stopped Dutch cold in his tracks. He backed off—his excited, frosted breath escaping him. "What the hell?" He paused as he turned and sneered at the Cherokee. "Better not be a trick," he threatened again with a shaky voice.

Dutch tentatively made his way into the darkness, leaving the Cherokee tied to the sycamore. Again, there were agonizing moments of dead silence.

The old man craned his neck trying to see what was happening. His body jerked at the sudden gun shot that rang out. The blast was followed by a tortured bellow that came very close from within the forest. It was high-pitched, filled with terror—another scream of death.

He held his breath; his eyes darting all about. And then he saw what could not possibly be. A childhood nightmare come to life—a living, breathing Cherokee legend of terror. She had emerged from the woods.

Cloaked in a black hood and dragging her right foot behind her, the witch made a snake-like, twisting approach towards him. He dug his heels at the ground before him as he tried to push his body through the trunk of the tree. He pulled at his rope bindings until his wrists bled.

All at once she was right in front of him, hovering, swaying from side to side. From within her cowl, she showed him the elongated finger, covered in the other men's blood. He bit down on his tongue as his muscles went tight.

He wanted to reason with her, beg for mercy. But as she leaned in for the kill, all he could do was scream her name:

"Utlunta!!!"

10:45 PM

Johnny Whitetree sat up in his bed in a cold sweat. His breathing was labored, like he had just finished a mountain mile sprint. The bed sheets were in a twisted mess about him.

The lamp on the opposite bedside table came on. With eyes barely open, Daya sat up and reached over for her husband. "Johnny? You okay?"

"Yeah. Yeah… it was just another bad one."

She waited for him to take another deep breath and then, "Tell me about it."

Johnny rubbed his eyes. "I can't. I mean, I don't remember exactly. It's like the one from the other night. Something was happening to me. It was awful. Felt like I was struggling with someone. But I can't remember any more than that."

Daya patted her husband's sweaty back. "It's probably work-related. You put way too much of yourself into your job, dealing with the Appalachian's most wanted all the time."

Johnny managed a brief laugh. "Yeah. That's true." The faint light then caught his remorseful smile. "I'm sorry I woke you." She caressed his back a little more. "It's okay. But do you think you can get back to sleep now?" She rubbed through her thin nightgown. "We do need our rest."

Johnny leaned over and kissed her pregnant belly. "Yeah, you two get back to sleep. I'll try not to disturb you anymore tonight."

Daya smiled and rolled back over, turning off the light. Johnny leaned back onto his side of the bed. He fixed his hands under his head and stared out into the darkness. Just a dream. He closed his eyes and focused on pleasant thoughts. After a few minutes, his mind relaxed and he gave in to his exhausted body.

Ten minutes later, his eyes shot back open, searching the darkness.

OCTOBER 18, 1995

5:47 AM

Johnny was stirring early in the kitchen. The bacon fat was sizzling in the fry pan and the black coffee percolating. Last night's nocturnal rollercoaster was a thing of the past, and his mind was already focused on the day ahead.

He quickly downed his Tabasco and egg sandwich and even squeezed in an extra cup of coffee before heading to the shower. In ten minutes, he was dressed and ready—his long, black ponytail draped down the back of his tan, tribal police shirt. He took a final glance in the mirror, laid a gentle kiss on his still-sleeping wife, and was out the back door in a flash.

It was a typical mid-October morning in the Smokies. The sky was grainy, and the temperature hovered in the low thirties—it would reach the upper fifties by lunch time. Johnny threw the Dodge 424 patrol car into four-wheel drive and began the slow journey to work. He and Daya had built a cabin up on Deer Gap Hill behind Soco Road, and it took a good fifteen minutes just to manage the treacherous dirt road that led to the highway.

Thirty minutes later and Johnny had driven into the sleepy town of Cherokee. With scarecrows, corn stalks and thousands of pumpkins weaved throughout their signature Native American setting, the town was dressed and ready for the overwhelming number of coming fall tourists—those who would travel to Western North Carolina to catch a glimpse of the changing leaves and then return home with jugs of sweet cider and bags full of mountain-fresh, Pink Lady apples.

After many years of serving the tourist trade, the little town of Cherokee had the hosting game down pat. Found at the crossroads of the Great Smoky Mountain National Park and the Blue Ridge Parkway in Western North Carolina, the home of the Tsalagi, the Eastern Band of the Cherokee, became a favorite stop for those searching for family fun or a get-away adventure. Meandering through her winding roads of the blue smoke mountains and lush, green forests, coming into Cherokee was like coming into a different world. The reservation plied commercial ventures with educational interest in the hopes of attracting all types of wary traveler. Cherokee had made great gains in this area, but as Johnny cruised past some of the worn-out shops and depleted residential areas, he wondered if it would be enough to sustain the home he loved so much.

Johnny skirted down Seven Clans Lane and finally pulled into the headquarters for the Cherokee Tribal Police. He parked the patrol car into his designated officer's spot. At times he still found it hard to believe and smiled at his inserted nameplate atop the post.

Johnny had joined the force as an ambitious twenty-year-old; and now five years later and after several deserved promotions, he had achieved the rank of lieutenant. The parking space was a supposed perk for the officers although the rest of the lot was only spitting distance away.

Lieutenant Whitetree entered the quiet station and surprised at the darkness, flipped on the overhead lights. Patrolman Allan Grogan was seated at his desk with his Walkman plugged in his ears and his eyes closed. Johnny laughed to himself and then went over and rapped Grogan hard on the shoulder, jarring him awake. The patrolman scrambled at his desk and pulled the plugs from his ears. "Oh, good morning, Lieutenant. I was…uh, just…"

Johnny held up his hand. "At ease, Allan. Believe me; I know how difficult the night shift can be around here. I did it myself for three years running."

Grogan smiled thankfully.

"Any calls that you are aware of?" Johnny followed.

Grogan shook his head. "Nope. Quiet as a church mouse, Lieutenant. Just about like every weeknight."

Johnny grabbed at a stack of reports off Allan's desk. He began flipping through the charts. "Did Family Court get our reports on the Metters' dispute?"

"Faxed it to 'em when I first came in last night. It will be waiting on 'em this morning."

Johnny continued scanning the files. "How about Rob Conroy? Any word on him?"

"Uh-uh. Not since he jumped bail the other day. Have no idea who would have posted for him in the first place—can't believe anybody would want that guy back on the streets. Last time we hauled him into court, he had the nerve to tell Judge Ames to kiss his ass. Can you believe that? Right there in the courtroom," Grogan said with a laugh. "I tell you, that son of a gun just ain't no good, Lieutenant."

Johnny smirked. "Yeah, well, if you think he's bad, you should have met his brother Curtis. Now that was one mean snake. I had several run-ins with him my first year on the force. Never knew when to shut his trap. I heard he bought it in a jail over in Georgia a couple of months ago. Had it coming to him, I'm sure."

Johnny paused scanning the files again and then, "Anything else?"

Grogan shook his head. "Just the permits for the Festival of Native Peoples this coming weekend. We need the boss's okay on the paperwork."

"I'll see that he gets that today. And we should probably set up rotations for the fairgrounds to make sure everything goes smoothly. I hear they would like for it to be an annual event for us."

"I'll take care of it," Grogan said.

Johnny handed him the files and headed to the back offices. He yelled back before he reached the hallway. "Haven't seen Squirrel yet, have you?"

Grogan shook his head and tapped his watch. "Are you kidding? It ain't even eight o'clock yet."

Johnny bypassed the small "detention cage" in the hallway used for temporary prisoners and went into his office. He pushed around some folders on his cluttered desk before taking a seat. It was a small room that doubled as a storage area, but at least it was private. Only Captain Mitchell's office was more spacious and, by default, much more accommodating.

Johnny rubbed his tired eyes feeling the pain of the lack of sleep. He tried to remember how that dream had gone—who was involved, all the particulars, but he still just drew a blank. Maybe it was the pressure like Daya said. His recent promotion and new responsibilities, baby on the way, plus Daya's condition, mortgages out of his ears—it was a lot for a man his age to take in.

The station's phone line suddenly rang out. After it went unanswered several rings in, Johnny figured Allan had ventured to the can or maybe had fallen back asleep. He picked up. "Cherokee Police, this is Lieutenant Whitetree. May I help you?"

There was a long silence on the other end and then a guttural voice, "Juko Road."

"Say again? Hello? Hello?" Johnny asked before the line went dead. He hung up the phone and walked back into the main squad room. As he had figured, Allan was away from his desk.

He walked over to the wall map that showcased the entire Qualla Boundary. He ran his finger along Big Cove Road until he found the squiggly annex which the locals sometimes called Juko. It was roughly fifteen minutes away.

Grogan, drying his hands on the back of his shirt, walked up behind him. "What's up?"

Johnny kept his attention on the map. "Just got a strange call. The caller said 'Juko Road' and then hung up on me."

Grogan scratched at his chin. "Juko? An accident maybe? Somebody who didn't want to get involved?"

"Yeah, maybe." Johnny looked at the wall clock. "I've got a little time before the staff meeting. I think I'll ride out there and see."

"Maury is out on patrol. I could call him to check it out."

Johnny shook his head and was already moving to the door. "No, I got it. Something about the call. I don't know what it was. The voice..." He paused as he thought about it, and then with conviction, "I just want to check it out myself."

Grogan shrugged his round shoulders. After Johnny was out the door, he looked around the empty station, went back to his desk, propped up his feet, and plugged back in.

8:03 AM

After many back-to-back twisty turns on the country road, Johnny had almost convinced himself to turn around when he spotted the grey Lincoln near the sycamore. There was no indication of an accident. The car was just sitting there.

He noted Maryland tags and called in the plate numbers to Grogan. A quick scan showed the car belonged to a Reginald Hawthorne of Baltimore. The records also indicated that Mr. Hawthorne had been deceased for six months.

"He's dead?" Johnny fired back.

"Yeah. That's what the DMV shows. No transfer of ownership yet."

Johnny cocked his head and squinted at the car. "Hell of a trick. A dead man driving all the way down here."

Grogan laughed. "You want me to call Baltimore PD? See if anything is up?"

"Yeah," Johnny said, opening his door. "You do that. I'm gonna do a quick surveillance of the area."

"All right. Be careful. I'll inform the captain what's going on. He should be in soon."

"Roger that," Johnny said quickly as he hopped out the cruiser. Although the morning sun was creeping out, the shadows from the big trees kept the temperature cool, and Johnny slid his winter jacket on. He then made a cautious approach to the back of the Lincoln, opening the flap of his holster along the way.

Johnny leaned against the tinted back window on the driver's side, shielding his eyes with his hand. He saw through the bluish tint, but nothing struck him as being out of the ordinary. He took a quick scan behind him, and then using a handkerchief, popped open the door. The interior was dirty and smelled old. And then Johnny saw the stain on the floorboard. He had little doubt—he had seen stains like that before.

"Blood...."

After a further scan, Johnny found traces on the seat and door frame. Troublesome as it was, he decided to look around some more before calling back to the station.

A search around the outside of the car turned up nothing and then the giant sycamore finally drew him in. He kneeled at the base of the tree and carefully checked the wet, kicked dirt around it. The ground was sticky with an odd, iron odor. *Might be blood.* There seemed to be a lot of the substance in the root area. He then took note of a possible blood smear as well as the deep slash markings rubbed into the tree's bark. *Bound to the tree. A struggle. And a hell of a one at that.*

Johnny stood tall and put his hands on his hips. He felt a prick on his neck and slapped at the last of the fall mosquitoes. He then did a 360 on the wooded area around him. The wind picked up briefly and he heard the fallen leaves scattering all about. As the wind died down, it became deathly quiet. At first, there was a sense of isolation—an emptiness. But then Johnny felt there was something more... something in the forest beyond him. Despite his general resistance to paranoia, it was almost as if someone was there with him—watching him.

Johnny rubbed his eyes again and dismissed it as a symptom of his sleepless nights. He should put a call into the agency—get some more eyes, less tired eyes, out here to help him. He checked his watch and then felt another mosquito's tap, this time on his wrist. But as he held up his hand to look at the bite, he noticed it wasn't that at all—it was a blood droplet. Then another one fell on the same spot and streaked down his forearm.

Johnny slowly raised his head, scanning the tree limbs above him.

"Oh my God...."

9:17 AM

Captain Mitchell pulled up and hopped out of his cruiser. He straightened his shirt, adjusted his hat, and marched over to the crime scene. He squeezed past another patrol car and the ambulance van of the Cherokee Emergency Preparedness Team. He furled his brow at the body bag on the stretcher and then signaled to Johnny to join him.

Aaron Mitchell was the no-nonsense leader of the Cherokee Tribal Police Force. An eighth-generation descendant of the Eastern Band, Mitchell had joined the Marines right out of high school. He served for twenty years in the military's leatherneck branch but saw just two days of actual combat—having participated only in the quick '83 invasion of Grenada. After retirement from the service, he returned to Western North Carolina and worked in the Jackson County Sheriff's Office for several years. He then moved back to Cherokee and served as second-in-command to Bill "Red Hawk" Reynolds, the thirty-year, beloved chief of the police. After Red Hawk's retirement in 1991, Mitchell took over as the agency's top cop. Although he was now technically the chief of police, he kept his captain rank in deference to Red Hawk's long-time status and to not cause confusion with the Boundary's political structure. Mitchell became known as a serious, quiet, efficient leader who always seemed to have his people's best interests at heart.

Mitchell looked up and down at Johnny's uniform—all covered in blood. Johnny registered his captain's confusion.

"He was in the limbs of the tree. I had to climb up there to get him down."

"Who was in the tree, Lieutenant?"

"Attle Armstrong…"

"Attle Armstrong?" the captain fired back. "Are you sure?"

Johnny nodded, but Mitchell needed to see for himself. He brushed past Johnny and knelt down next to the stretcher. He unzipped the body bag and looked into the face of the Tribal Council Elder. His eyelids were still open, and his dilated pupils stared back at him as if frozen in fear. Mitchell held his position for a moment and then respectfully closed the bag.

The captain stood with his back to Johnny and scratched at his head. He then turned back to his officer. "You say you found him in the tree?"

"Yes, sir. He was beaten all about the face, gouges on his wrist. And he has a vicious laceration across his abdomen. I believe he bled out from that wound."

Mitchell nodded and then looked at the Lincoln. "This car doesn't belong to Elder Armstong, does it?"

Johnny shook his head. "No, it's a Maryland vehicle. It was reported stolen last week. We think it might have been driven by the other one. We found the keys in his pocket."

"The other one? What other one?"

Johnny pointed across the road and to the second body bag. Two paramedics were prepping this body for transport as well. "A Caucasian male. About thirty years of age. We found him in the woods roughly twenty meters from the road. He's got the same type of slashing cut across his stomach as Elder Armstrong."

Mitchell bit his lower lip and cast his eyes to the ground in disbelief.

"Johnny!" someone shouted from the woods beyond. "Got another one!" Both Johnny and Captain Mitchell took off across the road and ran down the embankment that led into the thick forest. One hundred meters from the road and partially hidden by fallen timbers was the third body.

Standing over the dead man and waving his arm was Tribal Policeman, Corporal Sal Beck. Known to his closest friends as Squirrel, the Cherokee lawman was nothing like his furry, little namesake. He had a large, muscular frame, a square jaw and, like Johnny, kept his long black hair tied in a ponytail behind him. Playful at times and not always the most professional of policemen, Sal was nevertheless a good cop who always did his best when something important was on the line. Johnny called him first after he discovered the body in the tree.

"Another one, Captain," Sal said in his baritone voice. "Ripped open like the others."

Mitchell went again to one knee. He pulled rubber gloves from his jacket and then examined the man's abdomen. "Disemboweled—completely butchered. What are we dealing with here?"

"Look in his hand. He's carrying a Glock 9mm like the one we found on the other guy. I don't think these boys came out here for a little, innocent stroll in the woods with Elder Armstrong," Sal surmised.

Mitchell nodded. "Yes, that point is troubling." He rubbed his chin for a moment. "What the hell am I going to tell his wife?" Mitchell then stood and looked at his two men. "Bag the weapon, get pictures of everything and dust it all down for prints. The person who did this had to leave something behind."

"Yes, sir," Johnny answered for both.

"Then take the bodies to Harris Regional Hospital in Sylva. They have a better forensics capability than what we have here locally. I know the lead pathologist over there. I'll call her and let her know you're coming."

"County and state law enforcement are going to want their say in a triple homicide," Sal added.

Mitchell turned and looked briefly at the carnage around him. "This is our land; it's our problem. If outsiders get involved, they'll just slow down the process." Mitchell did not wait for a response and marched back toward the ambulance.

Johnny knowingly glanced at his friend. "What do you think, Squirrel?"

"Cap's right – our problem." He looked at the dead body at his feet, "Lucky us, huh?"

3:20 PM

Johnny and Sal sat outside the pathology lab at Harris Regional Hospital. Johnny, still wearing his stained uniform, was bushed, and found himself struggling to stay awake. Sal on the other hand was mentally bouncing off the wall, bored with having to wait so long.

"What do they do with the clothes?" Sal finally asked.

"What? What clothes?"

"From the dead bodies. Both the white guys had really nice suits on. It seems a shame to waste them."

Johnny took a long, disbelieving look at Sal. "Jesus, Squirrel, you really are one messed-up individual, you know it?"

"I'm serious. Those guys had some nice threads. Dolce Gabbana, I believe. I wouldn't mind getting my hands on a jacket like that."

"Yeah, you'll start a new trend with the large gash and blood smears."

"You ever hear of dry cleaning, Johnny?"

Through his bleary eyes, Johnny smiled at Sal's wicked sense of humor. He had heard those types of comments from Sal many times before. He just didn't know how his friend could come up with such things.

Johnny and Sal had an easy give and take relationship as far as co-workers go. They both had joined the Tribal Police at roughly the same time and had put in many hours together doing the initial grunt work befitting of rookie patrolmen. They also spent an equal amount of time outside of their jobs just hanging out—hunting and fishing together, playing poker, going to pubs. And both had an affinity for Harley-Davidsons, taking their bikes out on Sunday mornings and racing up and down the Dragon's Tail near Deals Gap or just cruising on the Blue Ridge Parkway.

Sal, at times, could be a bit of a screw-up—coming in late, not filing reports and not following proper procedure. Johnny had to cover for him more times than he could count. But it never became a source of contention for the two friends, and when Johnny was promoted faster up the ranks, nobody was happier for him than Sal.

The doors of the pathology department suddenly sprung open. A doctor in a blood-stained smock walked out. She pulled down her surgical mask as she stood before the two policemen.

"You're the ones with the Cherokee Police?"

"Yes, ma'am. I'm Lieutenant Whitetree and this is Corporal Beck."

"Etta Williams...head pathologist here at HH," she said as she removed the surgical skull cap and shook their hands. Etta was a tall, thin African American with slight features on her oval face. She was a striking woman who looked much younger than her age of fifty. "It's been a while since I worked a case from the Boundary. I hope this isn't indicative of what you guys normally have to deal with."

Johnny shook his head. "Domestic disputes and traffic accidents mainly. This definitely goes beyond our usual day."

"Way beyond," Sal followed.

"The two Caucasians you brought in. They aren't from around here, are they?" she asked, already knowing the answer.

"We don't think so. We were hoping their fingerprints..." Johnny started.

"They don't have fingerprints, Lieutenant," Etta interrupted. "They were removed a long time ago. And by the looks of it, I'd say it was a clinical removal, spotlessly filed."

Johnny paused to look at Sal. "Hired killers—pros."

"I'll check against their dental records, but I can almost guarantee you they've been altered as well. I understand its typical m.o. for persons of interest like these," Etta continued.

"This is part of a goon war then. A Mob reprisal," Sal reasoned "But how the hell does Elder Armstrong fit in to all this?"

"He's on the Tribal Council. You know as well as I what's been on the tongue of every Cherokee for the past two years. I'll bet you anything it's tied to that."

"The casino? Jesus, that's the last thing our town needs to hear." He then added just loud enough for Johnny to hear, "Shit-storm a-coming."

"Still, if this is a mob hit as you say, then you have one savage hit man on your hands," Etta said.

Johnny raised an eyebrow. "By that you mean his choice of weapon?"

"Still undetermined currently. But, no, I was speaking about his dietary preferences." Johnny and Sal gave the doctor confused looks. "Oh, didn't you know?" She began. "All three of the victims were disemboweled in the same manner. And all three bodies had their livers removed."

4:22 PM

Captain Mitchell stood on the steps of Attle Armstrong's home—a 1960's ranch style house located just outside of Birdtown, a small, spill-over community of Cherokee. He took a deep breath and rang the doorbell. Within a few moments, the heavy-framed door swung open. Lynnette, Attle Armstrong's wife of forty years, shuffled her fragile body behind the still-closed screen door.

"Yes?" and then after recognition, "Why Captain Mitchell, good afternoon to you."

"Miss Lynnette…"

"What can I do for you, Captain?"

"Miss Lynnette, I'm afraid I have some very bad news to tell you."

"Oh? What on earth?"

"It concerns your husband, Elder Armstrong."

"Attle? But Attle's not here, Captain. He went fishing with his brother over at Lake Fontana. He said he'd be back tomorrow afternoon."

Mitchell hesitated and then, "Miss Lynnette, may I come in, please?"

Lynnette nodded and opened the screen door. She led the captain down a hallway to the tiny sitting area next to the kitchen. The house was small but clean. Taking care of her home and family had been Lynnette's only concern for the past forty years. The sitting room was a testament to their Cherokee heritage with Native American carvings and artwork on walls and shelves. Deer antlers affixed above the fireplace mantle indicated

Armstrong's bond to the deer clan, and his continued representation of those descendants on the tribal council.

She and Captain Mitchell sat on the flower print couch. He took her hand into his.

"There isn't any easy way to tell you this… but this morning we found your husband, Miss Lynnette. He's dead."

Lynnette kept her chin raised but immediately tears began to run down her cheeks. "Dead? My Attle? But how?" Her voice was breaking.

"From what we can tell, it looks like someone took his life. He and two other men—killed in the same way. They were found on a country road not too far from here. On what they call Juko Road." As the sting of his words sunk in, he then added lowly, "I am so sorry."

Lynnette turned her head away, squeezing the captain's hand. It was too much, and Mitchell realized it. He just sat for several minutes patting her arm and waiting.

"I don't understand. Who would do such a thing?" she finally asked.

"That's what we're trying to figure out. I know this is difficult, but did your husband mention anything that would leave you to believe he was in trouble with anyone? Did he mention any names? Or did he say he was having problems with anyone in town or on the council?"

"No," she said through tears. "Attle is a good man. He never had problems with anyone. You know that, Captain."

Mitchell nodded. "Had he been in good spirits lately? Did he seem happy with everything?"

Lynnette paused. "Well, now that you mention it. Attle had been keeping to himself just a bit lately. Quieter around the house—more than usual."

"As if in deep thought about something? Maybe something that was bothering him?"

"Perhaps. But my Attle is a strong man. He wouldn't tell me if something was bothering him. That's just not like him. We only discussed family issues."

Mitchell nodded and gave a concerned smile. He patted her hand again. "Miss Lynnette, I took the liberty of calling the civic center earlier and some of your friends at the church. They will be here in a few minutes to help you through this. As always, our people are stronger as a unit than as one." Lynnette nodded as the tears fell. "I, on the other hand, must take my leave. Your husband's killer is still at large, and I need to get back to the search. If you think of anything later or need me for any reason, please give me a call."

Again, Lynnette nodded through tears as Mitchell rose from the couch. He leaned over and instinctively gave the old woman a kiss on the top of her head. He then quietly showed himself out.

Lynnette remained on the couch for several minutes; she finally looked to the mantle of the fireplace. She had several pictures of her and her husband, their daughter and of their one grandchild placed along the mantle. She rose and picked up the one of her and Attle near Mingo Falls. It must have been taken thirty to forty years ago. They had been so happy—so much in love—so much promise they had for the future. She cradled the picture, pulling it close to her chest.

Standing there, mending her broken heart with fond memories, Lynnette was unaware that she had come into the room—the deadly spear-finger poised directly behind her back.

5:39 PM

Dr. Etta Williams shoved the body tray back into the wall container and locked the door. "So, as you can see, gentlemen, all three victims were cut precisely with the same surgical emphasis. A thin slice into the upper right quadrant of the abdomen as to not damage the vital organ and then a quick probe of the cavity to find the livers and then another quick slice of the portal vein to remove them. As I said, your attacker knew what the hell he was doing."

Johnny pulled down his borrowed surgical mask and folded his arms across his chest. "And you really believe the livers were removed for consumption?"

"Dr. Lector and his bottle of Chianti notwithstanding, it is not the most common event in homicides, but still... it does happen from time to time. Of course, I have no idea if that's the case here. He may have eaten them or kept them as trophies or perhaps he even took them as some kind of warning to the Cherokee or to you specifically, the police."

Johnny caught Sal's look behind his own surgical mask. He wasn't sure if his eyes were expressing concern over the information or just a symptom of autopsy nausea—more than likely it was both.

Etta took a step toward Johnny. "But I did see how it raised the follicles on the necks of both you and the corporal when I first mentioned it. Does liver siphoning hold a fascination with you, Lieutenant?"

"Just an old Cherokee ghost story, Doctor. Told around countless campfires throughout the years."

"Yes, well, this killer is no ghost."

Johnny nodded. "Thank you for your time, Doctor. I'm sure Captain Mitchell appreciates you working so quickly and letting us in on the results."

Etta smiled. "As long as you stop this killer, Lieutenant, I'm only happy to help."

Within minutes, Johnny and Sal had changed out of their protective scrubs and were walking down the hallway of the hospital. "So, what do you think, Squirrel? Is this the second coming of Utlunta?"

Sal was sliding on his jacket. "I don't believe in witches, Johnny. But I do believe in evil. And as the good poet once said, something wicked this way comes."

As they turned a hall corner, a man and a woman flashed badges in their faces, bringing them to a sudden halt.

"Lieutenant Whitetree? Corporal Beck? I'm Special Agent Davis and this is Agent Wilcox," the burly man with thinning hair said. "We're with the FBI—Arlington office."

Johnny gave a quick nod to both but was immediately drawn to the pissed-off woman dressed in a navy jacket and jeans. She angled her athletic frame into a blocking stance and alternated shooting eye-daggers at Johnny and Sal while her partner held court.

"Gentlemen, we understand you had a little problem over at your reservation. And we think you might be able to use our help."

Sal looked at Johnny. "Bad news travels fast, huh, Lieutenant?"

"Yeah, real fast. Who gave you guys the call?"

"Two of your vics down there in the morgue are known to us," Davis said. "Dutch Anders and MacKenzie Holbert," he continued. "They've been under FBI surveillance for several months now. They're muscle for Joe Ranshaw. Maybe you've heard of him?"

Johnny and Sal both indicated they had not.

"A Baltimore crime lord, Ranshaw and his operation have been building up steam the past couple of years. They've been looking to expand beyond the city."

Johnny nodded as he listened to the quick explanation. He also had a difficult time taking his eyes off the FBI man's partner. Agent Wilcox had short blond hair and high cheek bones that set off her piercing green eyes—very attractive, but more than that, Johnny could sense right away that she was intensely focused and had a high-level of confidence about her.

"Fact is, gentlemen, Ranshaw has been trying to get a foothold into Cherokee now that you people are thinking about bringing gambling to the Smokies. We understand his group has been laying a network of connections throughout the reservation," Davis said.

"Well, if the FBI knows so much about it, then maybe can you tell us people who knocked these guys off?" Sal challenged.

"Obviously it was someone who didn't want Ranshaw to succeed," Wilcox said tersely—finally matching up words to the fire in her eyes. "There are plenty of other groups out there who want into your gaming just as bad. And most of them don't play nice. When you crawl into bed with dirty whores like Ranshaw, you're gonna wake up with all kinds of bugs."

Johnny frowned. He wasn't impressed with the tough talk, and he had had enough of the Feds' lecture. "Hold on a minute. We're not getting into this with any two-bit hoodlums who just want to set up shop in Cherokee. I know for a fact that our Tribal Council is doing everything in their power to ensure that a quality vendor will be brought in to run the gaming operation."

"Quality vendor?" Davis interjected with a sarcastic laugh. "You're talking about casinos here not hot dog stands. It's a pretty rough business, kid. Just ask your red brothers out in California or up there in Connecticut."

Johnny smirked at the racist remark. "I think we're capable of making those decisions, Agent Davis. The point is these crimes were committed on Cherokee land—so we'll take care of it. We don't need your help."

"Sorry, but you got our help whether you want it or not," Wilcox added. "The FBI is now officially in charge of this investigation."

"The hell you are," Johnny said quickly. "Cherokee has autonomy over these matters. We police our territory the best way we see fit. It's called tribal sovereignty—a mandated law of the United States. I suggest you and your partner read up on our agreement with your government."

Wilcox reached into her coat pocket and slapped a folded paper into Johnny's chest. "And I suggest you and your partner read this court order. It allows our investigation to have carte blanche throughout Cherokee and the surrounding Boundary. It supersedes any of your mandates or provisions." She then formed a thin-lipped, go-to-hell grin. "So, I guess we'll be seeing you boys around town then, okay?"

With that, Davis and Wilcox blew past the Cherokee policemen and headed down the hallway toward the pathology lab. Johnny stood there fuming and staring at the paper. He then ripped it to shreds and took off towards the exit. Sal stepped in beside him trying to keep up.

"I stand corrected," Sal said heading out of the door. "Witches do exist."

6:37 PM

Chief Mary Ellen Runingdeer had her Jeep Wrangler zigzag down Highway 19 like a streaking bolt of lightning. As she weaved in and out of Maggie Valley traffic, her thoughts were all over the place. She had left Cherokee that morning to attend a symposium on Native American culture at Western Carolina University in nearby Sylva. She made her presentation as guest speaker and then engaged twenty-five sociology and anthropology majors in a follow-up, ask-the-chief session. A luncheon ensued followed by two more afternoon meet and greets. A viewing of Native American art at the new fine arts wing on the Catamount's campus was scheduled to close out the day.

She started getting worrisome calls just before the start of the art viewing. Cryptic messages from her staff that something had happened with the direst of outcomes. Early reports mentioned a possible murder in the Boundary; later calls raised the ante to a triple homicide and then a final message indicated that Tribal Council Elder Attle Armstrong was somehow involved. Chief Runningdeer finally excused herself and made a beeline for her yellow Jeep.

She tried to put it all together as she whizzed past the rubbernecking tourists. The phone call from Armstrong pleading for an emergency meeting of the Tribal Council echoed in her head. He had sounded desperate, at the end of his rope. *And now he's dead? It has to be tied together*, she thought. She would make sense of it all. That was her talent—to take confusing bits of information and turn it into a logical perception. It was one of the reasons she became the first female Chief of the Eastern Band, and more importantly, it was how she remained as chief for the last six years.

Granddaughter of the great Cherokee leader Edami Sanooke who guided the Ani-Yun-Wiya, the Great Spirit's principal people, through the turbulent sixties and early seventies, Runningdeer inherited her grandfather's ability to lead by example. Throughout her tenure, she became a fixture in the community in all kinds of supportive roles. She sat in on meetings concerning their civic issues, helped to shepherd the ongoing tourist trade, and appeared at schools and centers helping her people end crushing dependencies, both social and chemical. She was progressive yet traditional—a modern day leader of an old-world tribe. She often saw the needs of her people as a delicate balance between respecting their storied past and having a vision for their future. But it was tricky, and she was not always successful.

The casino had been a source of contention throughout her administration. She had always been a proponent for the casino feeling the monetary gains for the Boundary outweighed the negative aspects of possible crime and addiction. Surprisingly, her primary opposition on the council had been Attle Armstrong. When he first addressed the other members, he called for a dismissal vote on the grounds that the casino would ultimately lead to the Cherokees' damnation. He maintained his position for the entire year, until two weeks ago when he did a sudden about-face. When the three finalists' bids for the casino were accepted by Council, Armstrong became upset, demanding that they consider the process all over again. And perhaps now he had been killed because of it.

Runningdeer heard her grandfather's voice as she flew onto Wolfetown Road on the outskirts of Cherokee. He would admonish her to be careful, to be decisive and to be just. To see all sides and to evaluate all the facts before making decisions. And as always, to think of what is best for all the Tsalagi not just herself.

No shit, Grandpa. No shit.

7:22 PM

Johnny and Sal sat in chairs opposite Captain Mitchell's desk. Mitchell leaned back in his chair and ran his fingers through his closely cropped grey hair. Despite his nearing sixty years of age, Mitchell still looked in great shape with his taut skin and solid frame, a holdover from his time in the military. But his present attitude was not as spry as his health; in fact, it was downright sluggish. One he shared with his men.

"They had a court order? May I see it?" the captain asked.

Sal cut his eyes over at Johnny. The lieutenant cleared his throat. "I tore it up," he said sheepishly. "I was... pissed, Captain. Sorry."

Mitchell held his eyes on Johnny for just a moment and then gently brought his hands down on his desk. "I understand, Lieutenant. I will contact our lawyer over in Tribal Affairs as well as Chief Runningdeer's office. I will see what can be done. As for the case, we will continue with our investigation until we are told otherwise."

"Understood, Captain," Sal answered for both.

"I do not want you to engage the FBI, but let's stay on top of their progress," Mitchell continued. "They may have a free pass here but that does not mean they can run roughshod all over our people. Make sure they act according to the law."

"You sound like you don't trust them," Johnny offered.

"No, in fact, I do trust them, the majority of them. It's just that I have seen the way outside agencies at times deal with our people. They get a Wild West mentality, wanting to knock down our teepees and lock up all us savages in their hoosegows."

Both Johnny and Sal smiled at Mitchell's unconventional language. "We'll stay on top of them, Captain," Johnny said.

"Also, continue to draw the connection between Armstrong and Ranshaw's men. Dig deep. I think we all have a good idea of what happened, but I don't want any…." Mitchell's personal phone rang out. "Excuse me…"

He grabbed at the flip phone attached to his belt. "Aaron Mitchell." As he listened, Johnny and Sal noticed a scowl draw slowly across the captain's face. Mitchell then looked up and caught their eyes. "Yes, ma'am. I'll send one of my men right over there to check it out. I'm sure she's just distraught over the news. She may have even been lying down." He listened a few more seconds. "Yes, ma'am. You're welcome."

Mitchell closed the phone and placed it on his desk. "Mrs. Chiltosky," he explained. "I sent her and a few more of the ladies from the center to the Armstrong house to check on Lynnette after I had delivered her the bad news. She said they knocked on the door but did not get a response."

"Might be over at a neighbor's," Sal said.

"Or didn't hear them. She may have been out behind her house grieving. I know they have that gazebo in their backyard they like to use," Johnny added.

Mitchell nodded. "At any rate, why don't one of you run by there and check on her before you head home tonight. We'll draw up more of our plan specifics in the morning."

Sal got to his feet first. "I'll do it. I'll stop by. Give the Lieutenant here a chance to go home and see his pretty wife." Johnny then got up, giving Sal a tired but appreciative glance.

Mitchell stood as well, remaining behind his desk. "Very well. But keep close to your radios and phones. I've got a feeling we're just scratching the surface with this one."

8:05 PM

Daya was seated on the couch in the den of her home. She was leaning over the coffee table, which was covered with old newspapers, carving a face into a small pumpkin.

Johnny came through the back door. She heard him raiding the refrigerator and then popping something into the microwave. After a few minutes, he came into the den, drinking a Budweiser.

"Hey, you're still up," he said with surprise.

"It's only eight o'clock. I've just been doing a little Halloween prep for the house."

Johnny smiled. "Only eight, huh? Feels like its four in the morning." He moved into the den and plopped his worn-out body on the couch next to her. He considered her work on the pumpkin. "Needs a bigger mouth."

Daya squinted at him with her dark eyes and then sat up with alarm. "Oh, my God! What happened to you?" Johnny looked at her with confusion. "Your shirt, Johnny. My God, it looks like it's covered in blood."

Johnny breathed deeply and wiped the tiredness from his face. "It is blood, Daya." He paused. "It's been a difficult and sad day. We had a triple homicide out in the Boundary."

Daya dropped her kitchen knife and sat up on her knees leaning towards him. "A triple homicide? Here in Cherokee? Who, Johnny?"

Johnny moved closer and put his arms around her. He forced a smile and gently rubbed her shoulders trying to keep her as calm as possible. "We don't know all of the particulars yet, but it was two men from out of town… plus… Attle Armstrong."

"The Tribal Council Elder?" she asked to which Johnny responded with an affirmative nod. "What happened? How were they killed?"

Johnny just continued to softly stroke her arms and hair. "We don't know exactly. They were apparently stabbed. We're trying to piece it together now."

Daya grew a pained look and bit her bottom lip. "What is this world coming to? There's too much violence now, too much mind-less killing. My God…"

Johnny pulled his wife close and hugged her. She didn't need to know any more information now. He wanted to protect her from getting too emotional. The doctors had warned them how stress may have been a contributing factor in their past two failed pregnancies.

Daya broke from his hug with sudden concern. "What about his wife, Miss Lynnette? She's such a sweet lady. I'll bet news of this is just killing her."

Johnny nodded and pulled her back into a hug. As he stroked the hair of his wife, he thought about Attle's wife and how he would feel if somebody had informed him of the same horrendous news.

It would kill me too.

11:17 PM

At first, she appeared to him like an old woman, a grandmother, or a favorite aunt. She was aged, brittle, with a careworn yet smiling face, full of warmth and gentleness. Her hair was long and grey, and it floated about her like the smoke swirls of an open fire. She was wrapped in a dark cloak which also seemed to float unencumbered all about her. She then reached her hand out from underneath the cloak and pointed her index finger at Johnny who remained seated against the tree. She called to him, but he was not fooled. He knew instantly who she was and what she wanted. He wanted to get up and run, but she had somehow poisoned his legs, preventing him from standing.

As she moved towards him, her bony finger began to grow. The tip of the finger split on end, sprouting its deadly spear shape. As she came closer to him, wells of blood began to spike on the end of the spear-finger and pour down on Johnny's bare chest. She held the point pressed against the skin of his abdomen. Small cracks appeared in her smiling face which then morphed into a hideous mask of blood, cartilage, and bone. She began her maniacal laugh as she plunged the spear-finger deep into...

"No!" Johnny shouted as he sat up in his bed.

He sat there for a moment, separating dreams from reality. His heart rate was skyrocketing—his breathing, bullish and hard. It was dark in the room but light enough for Johnny to see. Thankfully, Daya was still on her side of the bed asleep. Somehow, she had not heard Johnny cry out.

Johnny remained there for a moment, slowing down his breathing, trying to calm himself. His body ached, and his head throbbed. *Not again. Not more of this. This is just insane.* Johnny threw his legs over the side of the bed in frustration. He got up and walked out to the back porch. The autumn night air hit him hard, but that was just what he needed, a cold slap to the face.

Johnny looked up beyond the slope of trees that served as his backyard and glanced up the hill to the bright stars that hung overhead. He needed to find a way to let it go. His work was eating away at him and not letting him sleep. Utlunta was just the face he had finally put on his problems. And at least that made a little sense.

Ever since he was a child, he had heard the story of the spear-finger witch and it always terrified him. The thought of her ripping and gouging his skin, and then eating his liver while he slowly wasted away, had kept him up many a night, cowering under blankets. And now with the deaths of Armstrong and Ranshaw's men, the horror story had seemingly come to life.

Johnny grabbed at the wooden banister of his back porch and rubbed his hands over its smooth finish. Maybe Daya was right. Maybe his job was too much for him, dealing with Appalachia's most wanted as she put it. Maybe it was time for a new job, a new direction.

Johnny heard the house phone ring and ducked quickly back inside to answer it. He looked at the kitchen wall clock as he grabbed at the phone. "Hello?"

"Johnny. It's Sal. You need to get down here to the Armstrong place right away."

Johnny was taken aback by the heaviness in Sal's voice. "Why, Sal? What's happened?"

"Just come and make it quick."

Sal hung up. Johnny held for a moment and then slowly placed the phone back in its cradle. His anxiety from just moments before had returned in full force. He knew Sal would have more bad news. And he was certain that this long nightmare of pain and death was going to continue—whether he was asleep or not.

OCTOBER 19, 1995

12:23 AM

Johnny whipped the patrol car next to Sal's Harley and hopped out. He ran to the Armstrong's front lawn where Sal awaited him. Squirrel had his hands jammed down into his coat pocket, the cold, mountain air frosting each breath he took.

"What is it? What's up?" Johnny hurried out.

"It's bad, Johnny, really bad."

"What's bad?"

Sal turned and headed toward the Armstrong house. Johnny fell in beside him "I came over to check on Miss Lynnette like Captain asked, but I couldn't get an answer when I knocked on her door. After I combed the neighborhood and checked with everybody under the sun, I decided to go in the house and check for myself. Everything was locked, so I had to break a back window to get in."

"Was she in there?"

Sal came to a stop in front of the porch. "No. But I found blood in the den."

"Blood?"

"Yeah, a bunch of it. All in front of the fireplace."

Johnny was tired and confused. The news was not making any sense to him. "What are you saying, Squirrel? Was Lynnette injured? Did you find her?"

Sal paused. "Yeah… I found her." He stretched his long arm into the air and pointed to the roof.

Sal and Johnny crawled out of the attic window and carefully made their way down the roof to where the stone chimney cornered against the house. Lynnette Armstrong's frail, little body was tucked up against its base. She was soaked in her own blood, a thrashing cut across her midsection.

As Sal took a seat on the angled roof, Johnny moved closer to inspect her body. His gloved hand began to shake as he lifted a fragment of her blouse.

He turned away from the sight.

He brought his now bloody hand to his face and pinched the bridge of his nose. He then pounded his other hand against the chimney.

"God damnit!" Johnny finally shouted. "What the hell...?"

Sal sat emotionless. He had already experienced the same outrage. "The blood droplets were faint, but I tracked them from the den to the pull-down staircase. He must have stabbed her in the den and then carried her all the way out here."

Johnny swung his head around. "Who? Who did, Squirrel? Who could possibly do this?"

Sal shrugged. "I don't know, Johnny. Some devil."

Johnny thought about it for a moment. "Some witch?" Sal didn't respond; he just stared at his friend. "You know, when they inspect her body, they'll find her liver removed just like the others. Whoever is doing this is playing up the Spearfinger angle, big time. Using it as a scare tactic."

This time Sal nodded. "Yeah, well, it's working. It's scaring the shit out of me."

"Me too," Johnny said quickly. "I was dreaming about the witch right before you called me. I felt like I was eight years old again. Whoever it is knows the Cherokee and knows how to get inside our heads."

"Why the roof?" Sal asked. "And why the tree with Elder Armstrong? That was never a part of her legend, was it?"

"Not that I recall. And Ranshaw's men were left on the ground. Why?"

Sal shook his head again. "I don't know. None of this shakes out."

5:03 AM

The Armstrong house was now completely lit up in this early morning hour. Flashing lights of the Tribal Police cruisers were joined by several others from the Cherokee Emergency Preparedness Team, a coroner's ambulance, the Swain County Sheriff's Office and even a first response team of rangers from the nearby Great Smoky Mountain National Park. The house had been yellow-taped, and the investigators were diligently poking around the entire area.

A Crown Victoria pulled up behind the other vehicles and the two FBI agents got out. They both sauntered up to Johnny and Sal who were leaning against the side of the ambulance and sipping on coffee from Styrofoam cups.

"Gentlemen… we meet again," Davis said with loathing.

Johnny gave a half nod. "Apparently so."

Wilcox was a little more forceful. "You had another attack take place and you didn't bother to call us?"

"You didn't leave your number," Sal said dryly.

Wilcox cut her green eyes at Sal and then back to Johnny. "Well, let me remind you gentlemen that the FBI is handling this case. Any information, and I mean any information, that you withhold from this point on will be considered obstruction. Got it?"

Johnny pushed his back off the ambulance and raised his chin to Wilcox. "We're not obstructing anything, Agent Wilcox. But this is our town and our people. In the past twenty-four hours I've had to deal with the senseless deaths of two of our citizens, so forgive me if we forgot to leave out the Cherokee welcome mat for you two to wipe your goddamn feet on."

Johnny snapped his cup to the ground and disappeared into the shadows of the darkened street. Sal leaned off the ambulance and took a nonchalant sip from his cup and smiled. "Damn that caffeine, huh?" He then brushed past both agents, intentionally splitting them apart with his broad shoulders. He followed Johnny out into the darkness.

Inside the Armstrong house, Captain Mitchell was on one knee analyzing the blood splatter in front of the fireplace. Another Tribal policeman, Maury Tobias, was gathering a sample of the same blood. They were gloved and moving at a deliberate pace. Other investigators were scattered around them doing their respective jobs. Wilcox walked in behind them.

"Captain Mitchell?" Wilcox asked. Mitchell stood, turned, and gave a brief nod. "Special Agent Kate Wilcox, FBI."

"How may I help you, Agent Wilcox?"

"A little consideration for starters, Captain. My partner and I have been assigned this case by the Bureau, and we expect the full cooperation of all state, county and other local agencies including your Tribal Police Force. Recently, we've been getting anything but that. As the leads on this case, we demand prompt contact when anything associated with the events of yesterday arises," she paused, waving her hand in the air to indicate her surroundings. "Such as this." She began her own quick observations of the scene as she continued. "Not only do I want to be kept in the loop, but I also want schedules, files, lab work, photos and any and all evidence to go through us first. Is all of this clear, Captain Mitchell?"

Mitchell nodded that he understood. "Forgive us, Agent Wilcox. But our agency will, of course, extend all courtesies and offer full disclosure to the FBI... as is our policy." He ripped the stained gloves from his hands as he moved closer to her. "But a word of caution, if I may." He gently grabbed Wilcox's shoulder and lead her a few steps away from the crime scene. "Cherokee is not New York, Atlanta, or even small-town USA. We are our own entity; and as such, we have our own way of doing things and our own... shall I say... idiosyncrasies."

Wilcox half-smiled. "That's a nice excuse, Captain. But please don't confuse tribal sovereignty with shoddy police work and evidence suppression. That's not going to fly with us," she insisted. "And don't worry about our time on the reservation. We've seen it all before. We know how to handle it."

Mitchell remained stone-faced, only giving her a respectful nod as Agent Davis walked in the front door. "Agent Wilcox," Davis began. "Come out front. You're going to want to see this."

Wilcox raised a quizzical eyebrow and then followed Davis out the door. Mitchell was close behind.

Gathered just beyond the police tape on the front lawn were thirty Cherokees holding lighted torches. In front of them seven clan Elders stood. Each one was dressed in traditional ceremonial trade shirt, sash, and buckskins, and each one was wearing an ornate mask representing their ancient clans. The clan leaders were spread out at arm's length and formed into a semi-circle. They placed their own torches in the ground before them, went to their knees and then began a low, rhythmic chant.

"What the hell is this?" Wilcox asked aloud.

Mitchell moved in behind her and whispered in her ear. "Welcome to Cherokee, Agent Wilcox."

9:23 AM

Daya moved about the den of her home with one hand constantly rubbing her belly and the other holding a stack of ungraded papers. The substitute that the Cherokee Middle School had retained in her absence was adequate, but Daya didn't have enough faith in her to scrutinize most of the assignments she had outlined. It killed her to be here at home and only five months pregnant. She had planned to take her maternity leave after the Christmas break, but the doctors were adamant in her need to remain stress free and teaching seventh grade social studies wasn't exactly the most ideal situation.

Of course, it paled in comparison to what Johnny was going through, she surmised, especially having learned of the terrible situation that happened in the Boundary yesterday. But she knew he would deflect the brunt of his frustration from her. He would be calm and cool with her as always, hiding a seething volcano beneath. It was, no doubt, the source of his nightmares. His inability to express his angst and worry to her had manifested itself into those wicked dreams of late. But that was Johnny. That was who he was. And to be honest, that was probably the reason she fell in love with him in the first place—his strength, his desire to put others before him—even when it was to his own detriment.

The back door swung open and Johnny ambled in. He moved to the small kitchen table next to the bay window and slid into one of the chairs. Daya came in and sat down as well, plopping the papers in the center of the table. She reached over and grabbed his hand. "Didn't see you in bed this morning. Long night?"

Johnny gave a haggard smile. "Yeah. That's all we seem to be having lately, huh?"

"What's happened now?"

Johnny blew out a long breath and diverted his eyes briefly to the ceiling. "Let's just say things have gotten a lot more complicated."

She took another long look at him. She saw the desperation, the tiredness, the frustration. She then got up and went to his side of the table and sat in his lap. She cradled his head, bringing him close. For the moment, it would have to be enough.

10:44 AM

Sal pulled his Harley to a stop along a wooden fence on Old Number 4 Road. He hopped off his bike and took giant strides down the line until he came to an access point. He continued his silent walk across the front yard with purpose—the sickening deaths of the Armstrongs burning deep within.

He walked past several cars up on blocks: old and in ill-repair. Sal noted car parts on the ground—mufflers, axels, whole engine blocks—highway grass growing around their forgotten purpose.

A small trailer sat next to a barn-sized garage. An Open for Business sign hung over the opening of the wooden structure and Sal headed straight for it.

It was dark, but Sal could hear tinkering coming from inside—the distinctive sound of metal being forced on metal. Sal stood in the doorway and noticed a service van sitting high on a lift. He watched from behind as a middle-aged man pried a tire from the van's rim.

The man had long, greasy grey hair which fell to his shoulders. He was stocky, a little over 5 feet, and he wore blue overalls with the moniker Cherokee Auto stitched on the back. He would look to the uniformed as some ordinary mechanic, albeit a messy one. But Sal knew better.

"Spearfinger," Sal finally called to him.

The man swung around and shook a tire iron at Sal. "Don't call me that. Don't you ever call me that." His voice echoed a mix of shame and belligerence.

Sal lifted his chin in defiance. "What's the matter, Montack? Don't care for your nickname anymore?"

"I've paid the price, Sa-lo-li. I've done the time. I don't have to take any crap from you or any of you sons-of-bitches at the stationhouse."

"Keeping your nose clean, I assume," Sal said as he continued his approach.

"Goddamn right I do. Got this job. I make all my appointments. I check in with my parole officer. You should know all this."

Sal nodded. "Yeah, that seems to be the case."

"Then why the hassle? Why come all the way out here?"

"Where were you last night, Montack?"

"Last night? I was at home—watching TV," Montack said bitterly.

"Anybody confirm that?"

"Yeah, I got a girl that comes by occasionally. She was with me last night."

"She legal?" Sal asked.

"Screw you, Squirrel. Yeah, she's legal. And she'll vouch for me. Why? What's happened?"

"Do you know the Armstrongs, Attle and Lynnette?"

"No. I mean I know Attle Armstrong is a Tribal Elder," he paused briefly. "It ain't like we travel in the same social circles."

"He and his wife were both killed recently in separate incidents, but both were done-in the same way."

"How?"

"Their abdomens were ripped open. Someone went inside and removed their livers." Montack remained silent as Sal inched closer. "You know, Montack, like Spearfinger."

"I ain't never killed nobody," Montack said through clenched teeth. "And you know it."

Sal was finally face to face with the mechanic. "No. You just liked to stick your hand down little girls' pants and finger them while pleasuring yourself with your other hand."

"I ain't done nothing like that in three years, Sa-lo-li! Three years!"

"Once a sick-o, always a sick-o. I'm not buying your reform act."

"I'm clean. I got a job. I ain't got nothing to do with this," the man fired back. "You gotta believe me, I got nothing to do with this."

Sal held his position for a moment longer looking deep into the man's eyes and then backed off. "We'll see, Montack. Have that girlfriend of yours call down to the station. We'll need to check out your story. Hopefully it will... for your sake."

Montack smirked at the policeman but kept silent.

Sal turned to leave but swung back around. "Oh, yeah... stick around town for a few days. Just in case we need to have another talk."

"I'm here," Montack said. "I'm always here."

Sal looked around his shop. "Good. Spend some of that time cleaning this place up, why don't you? It's a freaking mess."

1:24 PM

Captain Mitchell met Johnny on the steps of the station. "You get enough rest?"

Johnny nodded although his stifled yawn indicated he had not. "Corporal Beck report back in?"

"Yes," Mitchell stated. "Montack has an apparent alibi for last night."

Johnny shrugged. "Well, it was a long shot, but one I thought we needed to take."

"Agreed. Nothing must be overlooked." He paused for a moment in thought. "The FBI will pursue this case by the book—through all obvious channels. But we can't afford to overlook the very nature of this case. The Armstrongs' murders, the methods of their killer... this speaks to us in a very personal manner."

"Meaning what, Cap?"

"Meaning that we know things the FBI doesn't. Other, less obvious, avenues. Just this morning Agents Wilcox and Davis were taken aback by our tribal mourning customs, the clans' representation, the elders' call and so forth."

"You said it yourself, Captain. Outsiders get a little crazy when coming into the Boundary."

Mitchell grinned. "Yes, and that is the problem. We must show them the ropes, so to speak. Walk them through our ways of doing."

Now Johnny smiled. "Is that your way of telling me to play nice with the FBI?"

"Partly. But also, to remind you that there are considerations in this case of which only the Cherokee will be aware." Mitchell moved past Johnny and down the steps.

"Where are you headed now?"

"Home," Mitchell said. "A late lunch and a little rest. I'll be back this afternoon. You?"

"Think I'll swing by and pick up Squirrel," he answered. "Another avenue we might need to check out."

3:07 PM

Spearfinger squeezed past the opening and was now in complete darkness. Within seconds, the hiss of a kerosene can was followed by a flicker of flame from a lighter and the craggy burrow soon glowed in a soft light.

With the lantern in hand, the witch went through another opening to a larger area and passed by several thin boxes against the cave's far wall. The witch found a resting spot against the cave wall and dug an envelope from within the black cloak.

Utlunta readily tore the envelope open and thumbed through the wad of hundred-dollar bills, holding one of the bills up to the light to admire it. The witch then stuffed the cash into a vest pocket and fished around the envelope again, pulling out a piece of paper and unfolding it to read. It was a list of Cherokee names. Some had been struck through. Others were not.

4:19 PM

The brush was thick and wet, but Johnny continued forward. As he struggled to keep his balance in the ankle-grabbing weeds, he dodged the limbs of the small trees that were coming at him in quick succession. A particularly nasty pine branch suddenly whipped him square in the face.

"Damn it, Squirrel. Watch it, will ya?"

A step ahead of him was Sal who was using his big frame to blaze a trail in this unmarked part of the Qualla forest. "Sorry, Johnny. It ain't much better up here. My arms are torn all to shit." He held up a scratched forearm for confirmation.

"Are you sure this is the way?"

"It's been a while..." Sal said without much confidence.

"How will we know when we get there?"

"You won't. If they want to see us, they will come to us... on their own terms."

"Doesn't exactly sound encouraging."

"It's the best you'll get when dealing with the Nunnehi."

Johnny silently nodded as he understood this, but he had already calculated the risk and decided it would be worth it to seek them out. The Nunnehi were a small group of Cherokee traditionalists who had little contact with the outside world and who did their best to keep the Qualla lands and surrounding areas free from modernization. Their name originated from a race of immortal people who were claimed to have been the mystical guardians of the Cherokee. In the ancient legend, the Nunnehi protected many of the Cherokee people from having to take the forced march to Oklahoma in 1839 on what became known as The Trail of Tears. According to the myth, the Nunnehi warned the Cherokee of the impending catastrophe and hid as many as they could inside a mountain until the white soldiers were gone. Those that were saved by the Nunnehi ended up as the Eastern Band of Cherokee and remained in the area.

This modern group of "Nunnehi" had formed in the early 1970's as a splinter group of the radical national organization AIM, the American Indian Movement. Their sole purpose was to keep the Cherokee people free from the influence of the white man's world. So, it made sense that the casino would be an undertaking they would virulently oppose. As it so happened, Sal's older brother had been a member of the modern Nunnehi years ago. He had taken a young Sal to one of their secret meetings; an act which Johnny hoped would give them an edge in speaking to them today.

"Can we stop for a sec? I've got hundreds of thorns running up and down my leg," Johnny said.

"There's a clearing just ahead. We can rest up there."

As promised, Sal led Johnny to an opening in the brush. It was not much, a few boulder rocks guarded by rows of rhododendron and low-growing box elder. Johnny wearily found his way to one of the rocks and leaned against it. He began picking the barbs from his jeans.

"Amazing how much pain these little bastards can cause," Johnny said as he flicked a thorn to the ground.

"The Devil's Walkingstick," Sal said. "The host plant can grow up to thirty feet tall in some cases. Tons of 'em around here."

"I didn't know you were such a botanist, Squirrel."

"One of my many hidden talents, Lieutenant."

Johnny's smile at the comment quickly faded as he saw movement beyond him. Within seconds, eight members of the Nunnehi emerged from the forest and had them surrounded. Each member had bright red and white war paint hiding their faces, and each held a rifle.

Johnny instinctively raised his hands. "Whoa. Hang on there." He indicated his badge on his belt. "We are with the Tribal Police." The Nunnehi seemed unimpressed and maintained their aim on the two cops. "Did you hear what I said? You're pointing weapons at the law."

As the eight remained silent, another Cherokee stepped into clearing. He too was painted the same as the Nunnehi, but he was much older and without a weapon. He walked up to Johnny and looked him up and down, studying him. The old man was wiry-thin with grey hair about his shoulders.

The elderly Cherokee then turned his attention to Sal. "Sa-lo-li?" he finally asked.

Sal smiled. "Yes. It is good to see you again, U-si-di A-wi-equa."

The old man nodded. "I was sorry to hear of your brother. He was taken from this world much too early."

Sal acknowledged the old man's concern with another brief smile. "Little Elk, this is Lieutenant John Whitetree of the Tribal Police. We'd like to ask you some questions concerning recent crimes in the boundary."

"I know why you are here, Sa-lo-li. And I know of the lieutenant as well." He looked over Sal's shoulder to Johnny. "I will speak with you both."

After a brief wave of his hand, the rest of the Nunnehi disappeared back into the forest leaving the old man alone with Johnny and Sal. But due to Little Elk's authoritative vibe, Johnny felt he and his partner were still outnumbered.

"I have heard of the terrible killings of the Armstrongs and the two white men," Little Elk began with a stony-eyed stare. "And I know of the suspicion of Utlunta in these killings."

Johnny looked surprised. "For a group so separated from

society, you seem to know quite a bit about what's happened."

"It's our mission to know what's happened, especially if it deals with our people."

"Does your mission include preventing the casino from coming to the Boundary? By any means possible?"

Little Elk narrowed his eyes even more. "Are you suggesting the Nunnehi had something to do with these murders?"

Sal frowned at the insinuation as well, but Johnny pressed on. "You tell me. Was it not the Nunnehi who tried to blow up the Fontana Dam in 1972? Or stop the business loop development of Highway 441? Destroyed some road construction equipment that year, I believe. And then there was the '74 riot against the Swain County Sheriff's Department. They had to bring in the National Guard to stop it—with some of your group appearing on the FBI's most wanted list after that. Let's just say, your interference in Cherokee business has long been documented."

"What you call interference, we call protection, Whitetree. I think you should be a bit more grateful for our actions."

Johnny smiled at this. "Okay. So, getting back to my original point then, should I be grateful to you for stopping the casino from coming here, too?"

Little Elk looked at Sal and then back to Johnny. "It is true. We are against the casino coming to Cherokee—and rightly so. We are worried that what has already happened to the Armstrongs will happen to others. The more we embrace the white man's world, and the more we turn our backs on our history and our culture; the more dangerous it will be for us. This pattern has been established since the early days."

"The Council has debated the issue," Sal added. "They are moving forward with it anyway."

"I know," Little Elk said, "and that worries me." The old man glanced skyward as he contemplated it more. "Oh, I am aware of the monetary reasons and the upgrades promised to our community, but dancing with the devil is never a good idea."

"It's progress,". Johnny offered.

Little Elk considered Johnny's words. He then moved face to face with him and took both of Johnny's hands in his. Johnny stood perplexed; he felt the old man look deep within his soul.

"You do not believe your own words, Whitetree." Little Elk

moved his hands to Johnny's shoulders and then backed away as if suddenly struck by something. He pointed at Johnny and mumbled in the Cherokee language, "Ga-tu-gi yo-nv...."

Johnny raised his eyebrows in surprise.

"It will come down to you," the old man said.

"I have no say in the matter. I'm not on the Council."

Little Elk walked to the edge of the opening and hesitated. "I'm not talking about the casino." He then disappeared into the forest beyond.

6:22 PM

Johnny and Sal sat on the hood of the squad car as the day was coming to an end. There was a half-empty 12-pack of Budweiser between them. They had pulled off on a little-known overlook on their way back to town to get a bit of perspective.

"I told you the Nunnehi had nothing to do with this, Johnny," Sal said as he finished another Bud.

"I never would have believed that they had something to do with the Armstrongs' deaths. But I'm not ruling out anything or anyone at this point."

"The Nunnehi don't kill Cherokees. They protect them."

"Agreed, but you know as well as I that their methods are radical and sometimes when you take things into your own hands, it can get messy."

Sal disagreed with a shake of his head but said nothing further.

Johnny took another sip. "What do you think the old man meant by it coming down to me?"

Sal shrugged. "Maybe he was talking in general. You know, how every choice we make has lasting effect and so on."

"Maybe. But it felt deeper than that. Almost personal. He even spoke my Cherokee name."

Sal turned and studied his partner. "Well, then, from now on, Johnny-boy, you better be making some damn good choices."

Johnny laughed and toasted his well-meaning friend as the sun slipped behind the Appalachian peaks beyond.

Out on the eastern horizon, the mountain outlines turned cold and dark.

OCTOBER 20, 1995

8:17 AM

The wind whistled through the tall trees along the Oconaluftee River Trail in the Great Smoky Mountain National Park, sending their spent leaves to the ground and covering the well-worn path below. The sun struggled to break through the morning mist and cooler temperatures prevailed.

Dan Rowland leaped a corner boulder on the trail and carefully dodged a sluice break in the path to maintain his six-minute pace. Dan worked at the nearby Cherokee Civic Center and his daily runs through the river trail helped to energize him for the long workday ahead.

As he rounded another bend, Dan's foot gave way on the slippery rocks, and he tumbled to the ground. He got to a sitting position and brushed off his hands and even laughed at himself. But as he checked out the damage to his ankle, the black and blue discoloration and early swelling indicated he would have to forget about breaking any speed records today.

Dan rose and gingerly put weight on his twisted ankle. It hurt like hell, but he figured he could hobble on back down the trail despite still being quite away from his parked truck.

He made it only several yards when a crashing noise in the woods caused him to stop. Dan turned and looked at the forest around him. He saw no movement, and nothing seemed out of the ordinary. He shrugged his shoulders, quickly dismissing the sound as that of a wayward deer.

But Dan held there for a moment, remaining focused on the natural surroundings. Although he had run this trail hundreds of times now, he often failed to take in its magnificence and beauty. As he stood there, a blue mist seared in and out of the giant rocks, ferns and firs making the woods appear as some forgotten land from some forgotten time. He also became attuned to the melodic sound of the Oconaluftee as it rushed along no more than fifty yards back down the other side of the trail. It was a marvel to behold, and he only wished he could remain in this spot all morning long. But his cooling sweat soon began to chill him, and he once again hobbled off down the trail.

Dan made it around the next bend when he recognized the mammoth granite rock the locals called Sequoyah's Nose sitting high on his left. It was one of his run markers and he knew he was now exactly two miles from his truck. He paused again to study the monolith's mica-flecked surface as it reflected the sun strands now straining to break through the forest ceiling. The reflected light shone bright, and he momentarily diverted his eyes.

As Dan looked back up to start on the trail again, she was there, dressed in her hooded black cloak and swaying from side to side. He was taken off guard by her sudden and strange appearance. "Oh…hello," Dan said with a nervous lilt. "Are you out for a walk today, ma'am? Beautiful morning for it."

The witch said nothing. She continued swaying back and forth, her draping hood hiding her face.

"Are you okay? Do you need assistance?" Again, she did not respond. "I'm injured myself, but I could call someone for you when…"

Dan stopped. He became aware of a faint cackling laughter coming from within the hooded cloak. He felt his blood go cold. This was too strange. And in a flash, it came to him, the childhood nightmare, the old campfire story. Utlunta. Spearfinger.

Dan took a step forward to go on past her, but she quickly brought out her spear-finger from the folds of the cloak. Dan froze.

The laughter grew stronger as she moved toward him, dragging her right foot behind her. With the sloping granite rock to his left, the only exit for Dan was down the right bank toward the river. Although he was now slowly backing up the trail to match her approach, he kept an eye on his escape to the right. He waited for the right moment and then…

Dan leaped hard to the right and sprinted between two spruce pines as he headed down the embankment. He did not feel his injured foot as his adrenaline had kicked in and all but negated the pain. But then a surfaced root caught his other foot, and Dan tumbled headfirst several yards down the embankment, winding up entangled in a laurel thicket on the river's edge.

He shook the stun of the fall from about him and spit dirt and leaves from his mouth. He was locked into the thick brush, but he managed to twist his head around to look. At first, he saw nothing. And then, like an approaching dark fin on the ocean's surface, he saw the top of a black hood. It was a mere twenty feet away and closing.

Dan struggled to pull his arms from the laurel hells, but they resisted like iron shackles. Dan turned again and saw the witch now ten feet from him. He once again could hear the cackling laughter. Dan pulled at the laurel with the desperation of a madman, snapping the deltoid muscle of his shoulder. Finally, he managed to get his right arm free and was able to pull his entire body to where his back was now leaning against the laurel. But it was too little too late. She was already there, standing right in front of him.

"My God... what do you want? What do you want from me?"

Dan Rowland's scream, the last utterance of his life, echoed throughout the Cherokee Forest, past the timbers and rocks, past the birds and the animals of the forest. The echo soon faded, replaced with the trickling sound of the moving Oconaluftee.

10:16 AM

Mary Ellen Runningdeer sat in the far booth in Ma Kettle's Diner having her third cup of coffee. It was all too consuming for the chief. Not only had Attle Armstrong, a Cherokee Elder and member of the Tribal Council been murdered, but now, Lynnette, his wife of forty years, had also been killed in the same manner. Two of her people, two pillars in the community, gone in the flash of some crazed killer's blade.

Mary Ellen reached down and rubbed the gold and turquoise spiritual beads around her neck. They were to bring comfort and guidance in times of need, but she couldn't feel anything positive now. She felt only the sickness of loss and anxiety. And there was nothing she could do about it.

Aaron Mitchell came through the restaurant door, removing his hat. Mary Ellen got his attention and waved him over.

"Captain Mitchell, thank you for coming."

Mitchell slid into the booth. "Chief Runningdeer...."

"Would you like some breakfast, Captain? Coffee?"

Mitchell shook his head. "No. No, thank you, Chief. I believe, as matters rest now, I need to get back to the station as soon as possible."

"Understood, Captain. Then I'll get right to it." She took a quick sip. "Captain, as Chief of the Tsalagi, I need to know what has happened. I must have an understanding so that I may guide the people. All I've been getting lately is the speculation of gossip. And you know how that lends itself to fear and then, of course, more speculation, more fear and so on."

Mitchell shook his head and rubbed his hands. "I understand. And believe me; we are working diligently to find the answers to what has taken place."

"Is this tied into the casino in some fashion? I know Elder Armstrong was vehemently opposed to the casino in the beginning and then changed direction no more than several days ago. He became upset at our last vote. Something about wanting to go with a different vendor."

Mitchell held comment for a moment and then, "I cannot say for certain, but because of some of the evidence involved, I would think that that may have played a role."

Chief Runningdeer shook her head and downed another swallow of coffee. "That's not really helping, Captain. Again, it just adds more fuel to the rumor mill fire. We have asked for our three finalists to submit bids for the casino. I can't have this disrupted now. Millions of dollars are at stake." She paused to add, "But at the same time I can't have my people getting killed."

"I apologize, Chief. But at this time, it is as clear as I can be. The FBI feels the contents of this case are so sensitive that I cannot share them with anyone in the Cherokee community—even our esteemed Chief."

Mary Ellen smiled. "Of course, Captain. But can you at least tell me that the rumor of the Armstrong's having their livers removed is not true? Certainly, that was just someone's idea of a sick, pre-Halloween joke."

Mitchell gave the chief a blank stare. He then grabbed at his hat and quietly stood. "I think I should be getting back to the office, Chief Runningdeer."

Mary Ellen stood with him. "Captain, I am the spiritual, intellectual, and social leader for our people. I need confirmation for a rational response. Please tell me the rumor is not true."

Mitchell fixed his hat squarely on his head. "I am sorry, Chief. But I cannot say anymore."

As Mitchell exited the restaurant, Mary Ellen sank back down into the booth. She fumbled for her cup and then drained the last of the coffee. She sat alone in the booth, lost in her thoughts, anxiously rubbing the spirit beads between her thumb and forefinger.

3:21 PM

The old man eased past the counter and hobbled to the front of Joe's Beer and Spirits, a rundown package store in downtown Frederick, Maryland, a suburb of nearby Baltimore. Wrinkled and snowy-haired, he still had blue, steely eyes that belied his seventy plus years. To most people, he was just that mean old guy who ran the local liquor store, but to those in-the-know, including the FBI, he was Joe Ranshaw, a middle-level crime lord with an itch for grabbing the top ring.

When he migrated to the US from his native Hungary in 1953, Joe left behind a destitute family as well as his original name—Horst Rankinstadt. He slowly built a reputation as a runner and a fixer for several Baltimore crime affiliates throughout the late fifties, and later in the sixties he was given charge of the popular psychedelic drug market throughout Baltimore's more depressed areas. He solidified a name for himself as a ruthless, merciless dealer and made his syndicate bosses very wealthy. But gambling eventually became Joe's primary business. He ran numbers, horses, backdoor casinos, and video slot machines. It was a hot ticket and again made the Maryland fat cats a lot of cash. Eventually, he branched out on his own, and now, even at this latter stage of his life, was looking to expand his empire.

Joe made a quick look out the glass door and then flipped the hanging sign, prematurely closing his shop. He turned off the lights and then turned back to the counter. A large man in an ill-fitting suit and tie stood waiting. He had a round head with jowly cheeks and wore his hair slicked back tight.

Ranshaw gestured with his hands turned up. "So... you've got some bad news for me, Jess?"

Jesse Cooper gave a nod of his melon-sized head. "Yeah. It's pretty damn bad, Mr. Ranshaw."

Ranshaw stuck out his bottom lip. "You know I don't like bad news, Jess. Better give it to me quick."

"Somebody got to our men in Cherokee. Took 'em out."

Ranshaw shot up an eyebrow. "Took 'em out?" He tapped his fingers along the countertop. "Who? Who took 'em out?"

Cooper bumped his shoulders. "We don't know yet. We're still looking into it. Dutch and Kenzie were in the process of pressing the council elder for his failures." He held his tongue briefly and then added, "Whoever it was got the old man too."

Joe Ranshaw paused, thinking it through. "Damn. This little Injun town might be a sweeter deal than I originally thought. We've got to reestablish ourselves and quick." Ranshaw moved behind the counter and retrieved a baseball bat. He leaned back over the counter and stuck the fat of the wood under Cooper's nose. "I want you to take a little trip for me, Jess. I want you down in them blue-haze mountains. Go visit our guy and get him to set you up with another contact on the council. And see to it things go my way this time. Got me? He stung Cooper's nose with a quick upward flip of his wrist before putting the bat in the big man's hands.

Cooper slowly backed away from his boss and then saluted him with a quick wave of the bat as he headed for the door. "I won't let you down, Mr. Ranshaw."

"Better not, Jess," he said. "Like that bitch of an ex-wife of mine who found out the hard way, a busted nose ain't nothing compared to a busted skull."

5:25 PM

The Smokemont Riding Stables in the Great Smoky Mountain National Park was preparing to close for the season and there was a myriad of duties still to be performed before the stables could be officially shut down. Attendant Laine Arant, decked out in rubber gloves and hip boots, was busy hosing down the back stalls when Oconaluftee Ranger Tim Fitzgerald appeared at the stable's main door.

Tim was a rather skinny man with a pale complexion and an angular face. But despite lacking the rugged, woodsman appearance befitting an authority figure in these Smoky Mountains, he was a dedicated and determined ranger. And like most rangers in the park system, Tim had a keen nose for trouble. And today something was definitely pin pricking the back of his neck.

"Hey, Laine. How's it going?"

Laine turned and smiled, quickly turning off the hose. "Hey, Tim. How are things at the station?"

Tim leaned against the door. "Good, I reckon. Y'all getting ready to lockdown for winter?"

Laine wiped her forehead with the sleeve of her sweatshirt. "Yeah. We're about done now. A few more days. Time to start packing it up."

Tim walked on into the stable. "Tell me something, Laine. Y'all got somebody out there riding the trails now?"

"Now? No. We had a family stop by about an hour ago, but their kids were too young to ride. And we didn't have enough people signed up for an afternoon wagon ride, so they left. It's been quiet ever since. Why?"

Tim shot his thumb behind him. "There's a blue Dodge truck out near the entrance. I noticed it on my way in this morning. It's still out there now."

Laine just shrugged. "Might be a hiker… fisherman…. They use our trails from time to time."

"Yeah, but I've noticed that same truck on other mornings when I go to work. It's usually way gone by this time of day."

"Maybe whoever it is decided on an all-day hike today."

Tim nodded. "Maybe…" He walked over to the nearest stall and ran his hand down the muzzle of a beautiful brown quarter horse. "But then, and this sounds weird, I know—we got a call at the station a little while ago. The caller said riding stables and then hung up."

Laine turned down the corners of her mouth. "That is weird."

"Yeah. So, I hope you don't mind if I take a look around. Maybe take a little stroll down your river path. Check things out…"

SPEARFINGER

Laine smiled. "Suit yourself, Tim. Take Zephyr there if you'd like. Just try to be back here in about an hour."

Ranger Fitzgerald had Zephyr, the three-year-old, brown palomino, at a half-quarter gait as he made his way down the river trail. Despite the day's fading light and a sense of urgency, he kept a slow, steady pace to better pick-up on anything that might seem out of the ordinary.

It didn't take long.

As Tim passed the corner angle near Sequoyah's Nose, he came to a stop. The sun was dropping fast now, and the cool, October air was building throughout the forest terrain. He tilted his head back as he followed the water-slick monolith all the way to the top.

That's when he noticed it. Something was hanging just over the precipice of the rock. He couldn't swear to it, but it appeared to be someone's arm. He thought he could make out the individual digits of a dangling hand.

Tim dismounted and walked to the base of the large sheet of granite rock. He cupped his hands around his mouth. "Hello? Anybody up there?"

There was no movement; the arm remained still. He made a brief survey of the rock, looking for a tied-off climbing rope. "How the hell did you get up there?" he whispered.

The smart thing would have been for Tim to call back to the station, alert the other rangers, call in the search and rescue team. But the ticking clock and his curiosity won out.

He made footing on a knee-high ledge and then began a naked climb. He made slow, assured progress, working his way in a diagonal pattern across the face of the rock. He intermittently cut an eye below him and then to the arm above. The closer he got, the more he believed it was indeed someone lying there at the top, possibly injured and unconscious.

It was not an uncommon occurrence for weekend climbers in the park to go beyond their limits and eventually need rescuing. But as Tim now inched closer to the top, he realized this was not going to be a rescue mission—in fact, he feared this was not going to end well at all. Along the wall large smears of blood began to appear. It was as if someone had poured a bucket of red paint all along the rock face. But the pattern of the smear was leading upward which made absolutely no sense to at all.

Tim held it together and made the final ascent. As he pulled himself to the top, he went to his knees and inspected the body. It was a middle-aged man, possibly Cherokee, dressed in running gear. There was no need to check for a pulse; he was obviously gone. The man had a severe rip across his abdomen and bled out from the injury.

Ranger Tim Fitzgerald tried to shake off the shock of seeing someone butchered like this. He sat back and crossed his arms over his legs, thinking it through.

Who could have done this? And how did the body end up here? He had heard about the tragedies in Cherokee, and he had little doubt this was connected. Something decidedly ugly was happening in their beautiful corner of the world. And it was spreading.

OCTOBER 21, 1995

6:47 AM

The morning mist of the Smokies held an icy mix as the westerly winds brought even colder temperatures down from the peaks of the southern Appalachians. Kate Wilcox had on her Quantico windbreaker atop a thin Nike running shirt and form-fitting compression shorts. The exposed skin on her legs had taken on a cold-burnt, reddish color—long since numb to the elements. She had ditched her gloves and skull cap four miles ago and was coming up on the end of her routine ten-mile morning run.

Wilcox was seven years in with the FBI now. Hard-working with a driven ego to match, she had graduated at the top of her class from the Academy and spent her early years as a behavioral analyst for the Bureau. It was important work, and she did well, but she had become a bit restless and eventually converted to a field agent. She moved up the ranks rather quickly and had been given co-lead in the Ranshaw case over a year ago. They had been actively tracing his Baltimore racketeering and gambling operations, figuring him to be a small-time hood with big time aspirations. His muscling into Cherokee had been just the latest example. But now with the recent killings, the ante on the case had been raised big time.

She found most of what had happened to this point bizarre. The hits on Anders and Mackenzie, however, made a little bit of sense to her. They had, in the name of their boss, been moving in on another's territory, and they wound up getting the cold hand for it. She knew it could have been any number of the other sticky finger organizations who put out the hit. Associations in Chicago, Miami and Las Vegas were all vying for the Cherokee casinos. But why kill Elder Armstrong and his wife? And why put them in a tree and on top of a house? And for God's sake, why take out their livers? What the hell purpose does that serve? Wilcox had hoped that her morning run would clear her head and start connecting some of these dots. But the puzzle was just too large and too jumbled at this point.

As she came up on her temporary digs at the Tsali Motor Court in downtown Cherokee, she saw her partner, Davis, out front. He was zipping up his big parker coat over his rumpled shirt and tie, an indicator that he had thrown on his clothes rather quickly. He flagged her down with a wave of his arm.

"What's up?" Wilcox asked, coming to a breathless stop.

"They've found another body last night."

"In Cherokee?"

"In the park. They found him on one of the trails. But get this: the vic is a Cherokee. Male about thirty-five. Probable same cut as the others."

"Pull the car around front," she ordered. "I'll be out in two minutes."

Wilcox headed for her small motel room and a quick change. *Another victim. Another murder. Another piece of the puzzle.* She just blew out a breath of frustration. *Yeah, way too jumbled at this point.*

7:22 AM

Ranger Dell Holloway, a law enforcement ranger from the Oconaluftee Station, was escorting Davis and Wilcox down the river trail to the wooded crime scene. He was explaining the who's and what's of the case, providing them with the blow by blow of Ranger Fitzgerald's discovery.

"When he got to the top, he found the victim with a rather large cut across his abdomen," Holloway said as he drew his hand across his own stomach. "Half the poor man's guts were streaming out."

"Time of death?" Wilcox asked.

"We don't know for certain. Rigor had set in. A couple of hours at least. His truck had been spotted at that gate around eight that morning."

"We'll need to speak directly with Fitzgerald," Wilcox said.

Holloway nodded. "He's back at the station, waiting. I'll shuttle you over there when you finish up here."

Wilcox nodded, accepting the offer. She then turned to her partner. "Nice to finally get a little cooperation around here, eh Frank?" Wilcox said with a slight smile.

"Yeah. And especially without having to go through Cherokee's finest," he agreed, flashing his own long-overdue grin.

Their good mood vanished as they rounded the corner of the trail and set their eyes again on Johnny and Sal. Both men had just repelled down Sequoyah's Nose and were now standing at its base. Sal looked over at the FBI agents.

"Well, what do you know, Lieutenant? The feds work early hours too."

Wilcox put her hands on her hips. "What the hell are you two doing here?"

Johnny calmly turned his attention away from them and scanned the rock face. "We were invited, Agent Wilcox. Oconaluftee gave us a call this morning too." He shot a look back at her. "The park and Cherokee are partners. We look out for each other. Always have."

"You're out of your jurisdiction, Lieutenant…"

Johnny held up his hand. "We're not here to argue or get in your way, Agent Wilcox. We're only here to help." He pointed to the top of the rock. "Dan Rowland. One of our people. He's the events coordinator at the Cherokee Civic Center. A good man." He gave Wilcox a somber look. "He's got two little girls at home."

Wilcox moved forward, craning her neck upward. "Same cut as the others?"

"Yeah. Exact same."

"Placed up there after the fact?"

"Looks that way. Blood smear patterns are leading upward, as if he were dragged up there."

"Liver removed?"

"Hard to tell, but I'd bet on it."

She finally looked over to Johnny. "What's his connection to the casino?"

Johnny blew out a breath. "I don't know of any, Agent Wilcox. And he has no connection to the Tribal Council either. The FBI might want to start thinking outside of that box."

Wilcox cut her eyes to her partner and then back to Johnny. "Okay, Lieutenant, I hear you. So, if this isn't a part of some mob hit, then what is going on?"

Johnny bit down on his lip and then raised his eyebrows as if hesitant to say. "Well, let me put it this way—what do you know about Cherokee lore Agent Wilcox?"

10:09 AM

Angelo Moore brought out three cases of Budweiser from the back-storage room at the Dragon's Breath Saloon. He struggled across the sticky floor and plopped them down on the wooden bar.

Angelo was a paunchy, little man with deep-set, brown eyes and stubby, hairy arms. A twenty-year transplant to the Smoky Mountain town of Deal's Gap, he ran the Dragon's Breath with a combination of down-home Appalachian hard work and the wily sensibilities of his native upper east coast. It was not always easy for him to balance the two, but he somehow found a way to make it work. It gave him favor with the simple mountain folk and bikers who frequented his bar as well as to the bar's invisible but demanding bosses.

He heard the front door to the saloon open and gave an indifferent turn of his head to the new customer. "We ain't open yet, sport. Come back in about two hours."

"Not thirsty, Angelo."

Angelo swung around after hearing the man's icy tone of voice. The customer had his full attention now. "Oh, can I help you?"

The big man nodded. "Ranshaw sent me. We need to talk."

Angelo indicated the closest table with a tilt of his head and then made the first move to sit. Jess Cooper threw his rather large frame into a chair directly across from Angelo. "What can I do for Mr. Ranshaw?" Angelo began.

"Influence, Angelo. We need more of it. Specifically, influence on the Tribal Council."

Angelo leaned forward and went to a whisper despite no one else around. "But he has it. Attle Armstrong…."

"Armstrong's dead. And so are the two men Ranshaw sent down to rattle his ass."

"Dead?" Angelo gave an incredulous look. "But how?"

Jess Cooper smiled as he dragged his finger across the sticky tabletop. "Let's just say the red men got a pretty sweet little deal forming over there. And cutting three guy's throats ain't nothing to those who want in."

Angelo gave a nervous grin. "Well, what does Ranshaw want me to do about it? The vote has probably already gone through by this time."

"You've gotta stop it. We've gotta get one of those bids."

"Impossible. Do you realize what we had to do just to get Armstrong to go along with it?"

"Don't care about your problems. Just make it happen. Delay the vote and get us someone new on the Council."

"But…"

"But nothing. Get me someone influential. Someone who can sway the others." Cooper stood to leave.

Angelo ran his hands through his thinning hair and then pounded them down on the table. "I'm telling you, there ain't enough time!"

The big man adjusted his tie. "No excuses, Angelo. Get me somebody soon. In the next day or so." He turned to leave and then at the door he gave his parting shot. "You'll come through for us. I'm sure you know how Mr. Ranshaw doesn't like to be disappointed."

2:00 PM

While Captain Mitchell had the unenviable task of informing the Rowland household about the latest tragedy, the rest of the investigators had relocated to the squad room at the tribal police station. The place was a study in concern and confusion. Several park rangers, Swain County sheriff deputies, as well as the Cherokee Police were hanging about the desks and chairs while the FBI's Wilcox and Davis were holding the primary meeting with Johnny and Sal in front of the wall map of the Boundary. There was much frustrated talking and gesturing but little consensus among those gathered.

"I'm not buying your ghost story, Lieutenant. Rowland had to have some connection to the casino. This has Ranshaw's dirty hands all over it," Wilcox said.

Johnny shook his head. "There is no connection as far as we can tell. Except that he is a Cherokee. He would, in a minor way, benefit financially from future casino payouts. As would we all."

"What about his connection to the council elder?" Davis asked.

"Everybody knows Attle Armstrong. I'm sure Dan knew him. And I'm sure they've had many forms of contact through the years," Sal replied. "But the point in question is that he is a Cherokee. All the victims were." Sal rolled his big shoulders. "And with their livers removed? Sounds like the work of the Spearfinger witch to me."

"But they weren't all Cherokee, Corporal," Wilcox jumped back in. "Don't forget about Mackenzie and Anders."

"Maybe they just were in the way," Sal followed. "Collateral damage maybe."

Johnny nodded at his partner. "Exactly. The bodies of the Armstrongs and of Dan Rowland, the Cherokees, were placed in a high location for some reason, the tree, the chimney, the rock face. Probably for some ceremonial reason in this sick bastard's mind. But the other two were not."

"He may have been in the process of moving the other two but was interrupted," Davis said. "Someone might have come along before he could get them up in the tree. They also had heavier body weights. May have been too much for our perpetrator to move."

All four went silent for a minute as they contemplated it all. Wilcox finally looked up. "This witch… Spearfinger, you called her. What more can you tell me about her?"

Johnny looked to Sal and then back to Wilcox. "I can only tell you what I've heard around the campfire as a child growing up. Despite my insistence on a connection, I'm no expert on her story by any means."

"Do you know anybody who is then?" she followed.

Johnny took another glance at Sal who returned a knowing grin. He then looked back at Wilcox. "Well, there is this one guy…."

3:07 PM

"Johnny! What a surprise. C'mon in," Eddie Whitetree said, standing and then leaning over his desk to have a look at his incoming visitors. He continued to wave Johnny and the other two into his small office. He waited just a moment taking in everyone until he refocused on his son. "Everything okay? There's nothing wrong with Daya, is there?"

"Uh, no, Dad. Daya is just fine."

Eddie went back to a large grin at that bit of news. "You know how I worry." He looked at the others. "Me being the expectant granddad and all."

"Yeah, I know." Johnny put his hand on his Eddie's shoulder. "Dad, I'd like to introduce you to these people. Eddie Whitetree, these are Agents Davis and Wilcox of the FBI."

"FBI...?" Eddie said, drawing in his brow. For just a moment, there was a sense of apprehension in Eddie's eyes—a resurfaced mistrust and anger. But just as quickly, he forced it to pass.

Davis gave a quick, respectful nod of his head toward the elder Whitetree. Wilcox held out her hand. "It's nice to meet you, sir," she said. Right away, Wilcox could see the similarity in father and son. Eddie Whitetree was almost the exact same height as his son with the same complexion, the same solid build and with the same facial features. Only the streaks of grey that ran though Eddie's long hair and a heavier belly marked him as measurably different.

"Likewise. What's going on, Johnny? This has something to do with the Armstrongs?"

Johnny moved behind Wilcox and shut the door to the office. As he did, the agent took a moment and quickly scanned the heavily adorned walls of the office. She zeroed in on an old, framed Polaroid directly behind the desk. It was a picture of the elder Whitetree dressed in buckskins and an eagle feather headdress with his arm around a dark-haired man in a park ranger's uniform.

Johnny said to his father, "Yeah. Something has come up in the investigation that these agents need to ask you about."

Eddie raised one eyebrow at that and then offered his guests a chair with the wave of his hand. "I will help if I can." Eddie then moved back behind his desk and had a seat.

Johnny remained standing but rested his hands on his father's desk. "This isn't easy, Dad. The facts of the case are bizarre to say the least. But please understand, what we discuss in this office can't be discussed outside these walls."

"Is this about their livers being removed?"

Wilcox leaned forward. "You know about that?"

Eddie gave a muffled laugh. "Cherokee is a small town, Agent Wilcox. And like any small town, gossip fuels the fire." Eddie paused. "So, what's the concern here? Are we looking for Jack the Ripper? Or Jeremiah Johnson, maybe?" He then looked over at Johnny and smiled. "Utlunta?"

Johnny nodded. "Actually… Utlunta was my first thought. And it would make sense. Using Spearfinger would be an obvious tactic to get inside our people's heads."

"It's just an old Cherokee legend, Johnny."

"Yes, but someone could very well be acting on those legends. And there could be something in the old stories that will help us find the real killer." Johnny paused. He took note of the FBI agents' growing impatience. "Dad, I told these agents that as curator of this museum you could shed some light on our local witch. Maybe more so than anyone else."

"As I said, I'll be happy to help. But…." Eddie stopped as he took in his son's pleading eyes. He then looked at the agents for a moment and finally stood. He indicated the door with his hand. "Shall we?"

Wilcox rose. "Where are we going?"

"Our witch, Agent Wilcox…. I thought you might like to meet her."

Eddie led his guests from the back-office areas through the soft-lighted lobby of the Cherokee Museum of Natural History. The museum was a must-see attraction in Cherokee where the Ani-Yun-Wiya (the principal people) had their story told through thousands of highlighted ancient artifacts and extensive dioramic scenes of history and culture.

SPEARFINGER

Besides the occasional staff member darting in and out of the various exhibit rooms, the place was relatively empty. That was generally the case during the latter part of fall and winter. But during the spring and summer, the tourist season, the museum saw as much foot traffic as any other draw in Cherokee.

As they moved toward the main-centered section, Wilcox and Davis slowed, taking in the intricate pottery, stone tools and melee weapons that hung about the walls. A soft, whistling music of Native American origin was being played throughout the entire museum which helped to personify the inanimate objects and bring a sense of mystique to the overall experience.

Wilcox came to a stop in front of the stone statue of Sequoyah. As she studied the pose of the great Cherokee leader and creator of their intricate writing system, she remembered the Rowland man's body had been placed on top of a rock known as Sequoyah's Nose. But having quickly learned of his importance to the Cherokee culture, she dismissed any viable connection with the name. *Sequoyah's Nose. Sequoyah Street. Sequoyah's Flea Market. There's probably no shortage on the use of that name.*

"Over here," Eddie called. All three quickly gathered around the indicated glass case. "Lady and gentlemen... Utlunta, the spear-finger witch."

Wilcox bent down and studied the lighted artifacts. A wooden, booger mask served as back-drop for the small exhibit. Carved in a simple, caricature design with slanted, animated eyes and wicked, open mouth, the mask, made from a reddish cedar wood, had a strip of black deer hair sprouting out of the top. It gave off a creepy yet alluring vibe. But as strangely intoxicating as the mask was, Wilcox was drawn more to the artifact which fronted it—a stone carving of a nine-inch-long finger with a sharpened, deadly pointed end.

Agent Davis shrugged. "I was expecting someone taller."

Davis's sarcasm actually drew a smile from the Whitetrees. "Be careful, Agent Davis," Eddie said. "By the time I finish telling you about her, you'll pray she never gets out of this display."

5:21 PM

In the middle of Cherokee, the Oconaluftee River passed through the main section of town and split around several tiny islands of grass and hardy oaks. Known as Oconaluftee Islands Park, it became a place where any visitor could picnic, relax, fish or just splash around in the clear-flowing waters.

Simon Thompson, a real-estate developer from Georgia and an avid visitor of Cherokee, stood on the smooth-stone bank of the center-most grassy island, casting his favorite silver spinner, trying to entice his would-be catch of the day. The afternoon sun was providing just the right amount of shadowy light but there was little warmth in the air, and the angler found his enthusiasm for the whole process was beginning to fade.

He was about to pack it in when he saw someone crossing the river from one of the other islands to his right. The person was strangely dressed in some sort of black hooded clothing and was struggling to make it across the water in the afternoon's dying light. Intrigued, Simon put down his rod and walked to the far side of the bank to get a better look. The person continued a slow wade across as if elderly or perhaps injured.

"Hey, out there!" Simon called out. "Do you need any help?"

The hooded figure stopped and slowly turned back towards him. Almost immediately, Simon felt a sense of regret for wanting to help. There was something in the way the person was just standing there in the waters, faceless under the hood, pointed in his direction.

The figure then began to move... back towards him.

Simon began to slowly backtrack. He began to feel a sense of panic, his heart suddenly jumping in his throat. The mystery person was making a steady approach, getting closer.

Simon walked hurriedly back to his fishing spot. He gathered up his gear, fumbling and spilling his tackle all over the ground. Simon then made a snap-turn to look behind him. The mystery person had reached the bank of his island and was moving on a direct path toward him. His panic was full-blown now. Real or imagined, he felt death's icy grip closing in.

Simon threw his gear to the ground and began running in a full out sprint to the other side of the island. He didn't hesitate when he reached the river as he high stepped through the shallow waters, sloshing his way to the other side.

Simon then clawed at the bank that led to Tsali Boulevard, the town's main street. As he reached the top of the bank, he saw a couple nearby, walking down the sidewalk. "Help me! Please... help me!" He pointed behind him as he collapsed on the street's edge. The man and woman ran across the street, coming to his aid.

"Sir, are you okay?" the man asked.

"Behind me... someone is after me." Under desperate, heavy breaths, Simon turned to show them. But quickly, the reality of the situation set in. He was pointing only to the smooth-flowing river and the small grassy isles. There was nothing else. No black hooded figure. No dangerous assailant. Nothing.

5:52 PM

Captain Aaron Mitchell was leaning back in his seat of his squad car, his focus squarely on the Armstrong's house across the street. After delivering the upsetting news to the Rowland family, he had come back to this spot and set up camp. He waited for hours, but his patience paid off as his target finally pulled up.

Mitchell was quick out of his car and hustled over to the front door. "Marcos Armstrong?"

The young man fumbling a key in the front door lock turned upon being called. "Yes...?"

"Marcos, I'm Captain Mitchell of the Cherokee Police. I'm the one who called you yesterday. I'd like to talk to you if you have a few minutes."

"Uh, sure. Why not?" Marcos said as he finished opening up the door. He brushed his long hair out of his eyes and led the captain inside, flipping on the switch. They moved to the inside living room; their attention was immediately drawn to the blood stain on the floor. "So, this is where she got it, huh?"

Mitchell straightened at the callus comment and studied the young man before him. Marcos was thin like his grandparents but possessed little of the strength and charm that Mitchell had sensed in the elder Armstrongs. He bypassed his first impression and decided to be gracious. "I'm sorry for your loss, Marcos."

Marcos bobbed his head as he scanned the room. "Yeah. This really sucks." He wiped his hands down his face. "I've got so much to do at work. And now I've got to put on two funerals. It ain't like I got a ton of cash to begin with."

"We will help you, Marcos. Your people will help you?"

"My people?"

Mitchell furled his brow. "The Cherokee, Marcos. The tribe will be there for you."

He thought about it. "How much?"

"I'm sorry…?"

"How much do you think my people will give me? I've got some bills and things."

Mitchell gave a disappointed look. "I don't know a dollar amount, but there will be help. And I'm sure your grandparents have provided for you in their will."

"You think?" He then turned and looked at the furnishings. "They might have even left some of this stuff to me, huh?"

Mitchell had had enough. "Marcos, I don't mean to be blunt, but I need speak with you about your grandparents' deaths. And I would like for you to be direct with me. Your grandmother was brutally murdered as was your grandfather. These types of atrocities don't happen without reason. Do you have any idea as to who would want them dead? Did they mention anyone? Especially your grandfather. Did he say anything to you?"

Marcos gave it a moment's thought and then shook his head. "No. But I really haven't had much contact with them the past few years. I live over in Robbinsville now and they kept to themselves here in Birdtown. And they were just… older. More into the traditions of the people as you called them. We just never… talked, you know?"

Mitchell made a slow nod of acceptance as he looked about the tiny room. He then moved next to the couch and picked up a framed picture from the coffee table. He angled it toward Marcos. "There may have been a generational gap, but they apparently still cared for you. This is a picture of you, isn't it?" Marcos gave a sheepish nod as his eyes found the floor. "There are pictures of you and your mother throughout this room. Probably the whole house." Mitchell paused and then decided to change directions. "You say that you live in Robbinsville. What kind of work do you do over there?"

Marcos looked back up and sighed. "Look, Captain, is this really necessary? As I said, I'm kind of tired, and I've got a lot to do. Maybe we can continue this some other time?"

Mitchell watched the young man for a moment and then nodded. He placed the frame back on the coffee table. "Of course. Do what you have to do, Marcos. We'll be in touch."

Mitchell marched out of the house and back toward his patrol car. The captain knew to give the young man his space, give him his grieving time. But his lawman instincts were never wrong, and something was not sitting quite right about all this. There were several crucial elements missing in this case and he felt Marcos might hold the key to at least parts of it.

As he drove away, he thought about Attle and Lynette and their unsettled house. *Rest easy, my friends. I will keep an eye out until it is taken care of, until all of this madness finally makes sense.*

6:17 PM

Eddie sat on the edge of one of the museum's dioramic stages. The mannequin Cherokee figures behind him were frozen in time, crouched together on a rock ledge, spears in hand; ready to do battle with an approaching mountain cougar. Johnny and the two FBI agents were spread about the floor like school children attending a lecture, listening.

"In many of the variations, the arrow of the Cherokee warrior killed the witch, while in others, it merely wounded her and caused her to disappear, leaving our people alone forever," Eddie finished. He paused for a moment and then gave a wry grin. "And really, that's all there is."

Davis rubbed his eyes. "So then, all we need to do is find a suspect who has stone-like skin, can manipulate rocks, can leap from one mountain top to another and has a nine-inch finger that can magically suck out your liver without you ever knowing it." He shook his head. "I'll put out an APB right away."

Johnny hung his head for just a moment. Agent Davis's sarcasm notwithstanding, he was beginning to feel a bit foolish for even suggesting a connection to Utlunta. But then he looked back up. "Dad, is there anything in her legend about hanging her victims in a tree or in some high place after they died?"

Eddie cocked his head in thought for a moment. "Mmmm. No. Not that I am aware of. Once the liver was siphoned, the victim generally lived until he wasted away at his home. She never had anything to do with the bodies after."

"And where exactly is this mountain where the Cherokees supposedly finished her off?" Wilcox asked. Johnny looked over at her, appreciating that she was at least taking in what had been said.

"Whiteside Mountain in Jackson County. It's right on the Eastern Continental Divide," Eddie said. "Many believe she lived in a cave near the top of the mountain."

Davis stood and shot a look at his partner. "Are we about through here? I think we need to get on with the real investigation."

Wilcox rose as well. "Yes. We appreciate the information, but we need to head back…." Wilcox's mobile phone interrupted, and she pulled the attached unit from her belt. She and Davis walked away from the Whitetrees to a corner of the exhibit room.

Eddie took the opportunity and hopped off the stage, saddling in next to his son. "I don't think the FBI cares for our old legends too much."

"It was just a theory, Dad." He laughed. "Maybe I had one too many nightmares growing up."

Eddie smiled as well, but then spoke in a serious tone. "Don't discount your instincts, Johnny. Sometimes…." He paused and then looked directly into Johnny's eyes. "Sometimes there's more to a situation than when it first appears. Your great-grandmother, Unilisi, she had a special sense for such things. You may have inherited that trait as well."

Wilcox suddenly appeared in front of them, an excited look upon her face. "Lt. Whitetree, that was your station. A tourist just reported being chased by someone wearing a black hood and cloak."

"Chased? Where?"

"In the river park, downtown. C'mon, let's go." Wilcox turned and headed with Davis toward the door.

Johnny caught his father's eye. "Go, son. But be careful." Johnny gave a brief, affirmative nod and then followed out quickly.

Alone now, Eddie held his position for just a moment and then moved again toward the Utlunta exhibit. He ran his hand over the glass case. He bent down, looking directly into the slanted eyes of the witch's mask. He went to a whisper, "Stay away from us, you hear? Stay far away."

6:36 PM

Johnny whipped the Tribal Police patrol car along the side of Tsali Boulevard, joining several other police and ranger vehicles. He hopped out first, followed quickly by Wilcox and Davis. They ran to the edge and looked down onto the Oconaluftee. It was growing very dark, and the streams of flashlights were bouncing off the river and onto the grassy, oak-filled islands. Johnny could make out Sal's outline; he was standing knee-deep in the icy water, searching the center-most island. He left the two FBI agents and waded out to join his partner. "What happened here, Squirrel?"

Sal kept his eyes on the islands as he responded, "Guy came busting into the station a little while ago, scared shitless. Said he was out here fishing off this isle when he saw a person in a black hood cutting across the Luftee. He called out to him and then he said the guy in the hood turned and started chasing him like he was the Grim Reaper or something." Sal turned and pointed toward Tsali. "Chased him up to the boulevard."

"Where's the witness?"

"He's still at the station. We couldn't convince him to come back out here."

"What are his vitals?"

Sal shrugged. "A regular visitor from Georgia. Up here for another three-day weekend. He's staying over at Standingdeer Campground." Sal focused in on Johnny and his voice became a bit softer. "He didn't seem crazy, Johnny. And with what's been happening lately, I thought it was worth checking out. Called in Swain County and the guys at the ranger station to help us take a look."

Johnny nodded. "You made the right call, Squirrel. I just hope we can turn something up and soon."

Almost immediately Johnny's ill-fated wish was answered. "Over here!" a voice shouted out. It was coming from down the river, on one of the smaller grassy isles.

Johnny and Sal trudged down the shallow base of the river and then broke through a small team of law enforcement who had gathered about the isle. Ranger Tim Fitzgerald from the Oconaluftee Ranger Station was holding his powerful Q-beam light and pointing to the tall oak at the dead center of the island. Outlined by the purple dark sky, a body was hanging by a noose from a large center limb. The legs of the latest victim were rocking back and forth in the stiff evening breeze.

Captain Mitchell marched across the Cherokee Civic Center parking lot to where most of the law enforcement officials had now gathered. After leaving Birdtown, he had driven home, but made a speedy U-turn when he got the call. He took in the lawmen's despondent faces.

"Another victim, Lieutenant?"

Johnny blew out a breath and lowered his head. "Yes. Sherry Simpson." He bit down on his tongue to hold his emotions in check. "She's just a fifteen-year-old kid, Captain."

"She worked at the arcade in the plaza strip across the way," Sal added. "The other employees over there claimed she usually took a break around four every day—would go get some air. This time she didn't come back."

Mitchell caught Wilcox's eye. "And what does the FBI say? Still believe this is related to Ranshaw or to our casino?"

"Captain, I don't know what to believe at this point. But we've got to start taking better watch of your town. As of right now, I am officially ordering a curfew for Cherokee and the whole Boundary. I want you to put a temporary stoppage to traffic in and out of town—necessary personnel only. And please see to it that all guests in campgrounds and motels are given safe passage out of here."

"What about the inhabitants themselves?" Sal asked. "Most of the victims so far are Cherokee?"

"We can't force your people to leave if they wish to stay. We're just going to have to keep a sharp eye. I'll call North Carolina's State Bureau of Investigation; get some of their agents over here to help. They have a special task force for these kinds of emergencies."

Mitchell stepped closer to Wilcox. "It's not just this town, Agent Wilcox. The Cherokee are spread out all over Western North Carolina. I fear for their safety—all of them."

"I know, Captain. Me too. We'll just need to be quick about this."

Wilcox walked away from the others and was followed by Davis. Mitchell then took in Johnny and Sal. "The young girl... was she....?"

"The same as the others, Captain," Johnny replied. "Abdomen slashed; her liver was taken."

Mitchell stood for a moment squelching his own outrage. He then looked back to his men. "Get to work. Find this son of a bitch now!"

11:36 PM

Johnny walked back into the station and threw his coat on the rack. He bypassed the thin crowd in the squad room and headed for Mitchell's office in the back. He rapped on the door jamb. "Captain?" Mitchell looked up from his desk. "Highway 441 is secure. We've got posts on Soco Road and Big Cove. Fitzgerald has his rangers on the park entrance and the connector to the Blue Ridge Parkway."

"What about leads from the river park?"

Johnny shrugged. "So far everything is cold. Except for our guy from Georgia, nobody we interviewed reported seeing anything." He paused before adding, "Patrolman Grogan did get a call from a potential witness about an hour ago; said he would check it out tomorrow."

"Understood. Go home, Lieutenant. Get some rest. Be back here at five."

Johnny gave a weary salute and headed across the hall to his small office. He found it occupied. Wilcox was on the phone, sitting back in his chair. He hesitated, but she waved him in.

"Yes, sir," she said into the phone. "I'll let you know something tomorrow." She listened a moment more. "Will do." She hung up the phone and looked to Johnny. "My boss in Arlington.

He's not a patient man. Said we needed to get our asses in gear."

"I guess bosses are the same all over," Johnny offered.

"Yeah, I guess so." Wilcox began gathering her things. "Sorry about invading your space, but I couldn't get anything done in the squad room."

Johnny held up his hands. "It's okay. My space is yours."

She drew down the corners of her mouth, surprised by his concession. "Thanks. I'll try to tread lightly."

Johnny moved in and sat on the edge of his desk. "You have to admit now, Agent Wilcox. It's looking more and more like the perpetrator is a Spearfinger wannabe."

She nodded. "Black hood, black cloak, removing livers. And the victims seem to be a disjointed group. You may be right. Perhaps Ranshaw's men were just in the wrong place at the wrong time." She twirled a pen on his desk. "Still, I don't want to eliminate any possibility at this point."

"Johnny...?" Wilcox and Johnny turned to the office door. Sal leaned his rather large frame in the opening. "Just wanted you to know, I tracked down the Simpson girl's mother. She lives over in Suwanna near Asheville. Said she'd be here by tomorrow."

"The mother?" Wilcox asked.

"Sherry lived with her dad here in Cherokee. Her parents have been separated for years now. We thought she needed to be brought in," Johnny clarified. He then turned to his partner. "Thanks, Squirrel."

"You bet."

"Squirrel?" Wilcox inquired. She looked up and down at the big man. "Why do they call you Squirrel?"

"Big nuts," Sal said without hesitation. He gave an exaggerated wink to Wilcox and then disappeared down the hallway.

Wilcox smirked and then turned her piercing green eyes on Johnny. "I'm guessing that's not the real reason why, is it, Lieutenant?"

Johnny smiled. "No, it's actually his name, his Cherokee name, Sa-lo-li, which in my people's language means squirrel. Everyone has just shortened the Cherokee version to Sal at this point."

Wilcox nodded, appreciating the cultural lesson. "And what about you? Johnny doesn't sound like a Native American name or is it some kind of derivative too?"

"Many of us have an English name in addition to our Cherokee one. It makes it easier sometimes when you're taking out loans or applying for a job... you know, in the white man's world."

"So, what's your Cherokee name?"

"Ga-tu-gi yo-nv. It means bear that wanders in front."

Wilcox looked a bit confused.

"A better translation is Crossing Bear."

Wilcox nodded and then leaned forward. "And how did you get that name?"

"My dad, Eddie, he said that when he was taking my mother to the hospital on the day I was born, a black bear ran out from the woods and crossed right in front of their car; he had to slam on brakes to avoid it. Made quite the impression on him."

Wilcox smiled. "Your dad is an interesting man, very knowledgeable. What about your mother?"

Johnny cleared his throat. "She died about twelve years ago. Breast cancer."

"I'm sorry," she said softly.

"Yeah. It's just been me and the old man for a while. You can still tell how protective he is of me."

"He mentioned you were expecting a baby. I'm guessing you're married?"

"Going on three years now." He glanced down at his empty wedding band finger. He and Daya had promised gold bands for each other once enough money had come into the house. He looked back up. "How about you?"

Wilcox tilted her head. "Married to the job right now. But who knows? One day...." She looked at her watch. "You better head home, Lieutenant. See that wife of yours before you have to turn around and head back here."

Johnny nodded his agreement as he hopped off the desk. "Okay, you're right. Goodnight, Agent Wilcox." Johnny slipped out the door.

"Goodnight, Lieutenant," Wilcox called out. She developed a soft grin as she thought about Johnny. She then whispered to herself. "Goodnight, Crossing Bear."

OCTOBER 22, 1995

7:48 AM

Artie Gibson, a pathologist at the Harris Regional Hospital, hurried through the soft-lit corridors of the hospital's lowest level. The path team had had it rough over the past few days. Six bodies, all from Cherokee, had been dropped on their doorstep within the past four days—the latest, a fifteen-year-old girl with the same slashing injury and the same missing organ as the others. It was a bewildering case with frightening possibilities and little to no evidence to help break the case. But now, as the young doctor neared the office level, he felt they had found something to change all that.

Gibson walked into Dr. William's office unannounced. Etta was at her desk, sipping on a cup of coffee and processing forms. She raised her eyebrows at Gibson's entrance.

"Can I help you, Dr. Gibson?"

"The Cherokee case, Dr. Williams. They bought in another victim, 4:30 this morning."

"Yes. I am aware. Captain Mitchell called me late last night. Have you begun the procedure? I know the authorities are anxious for the results."

"Actually, we just finished closing."

"Good. And you have something to report?"

"Do you remember the piece of stone we extracted from the Rowland man's wound? We thought it might have been debris he picked up after he bled out from his injury and collapsed to the ground."

"Yes. I remember. Some bit form of flint, a type of river stone, correct?"

"That's right." He pulled a container from his lab coat and plopped it down on her desk. "We found the same looking stone in the young girl's wound as well. It's a smaller piece, but, as you can see, it has the same texture, even the same wave pattern within the rock piece."

Etta held up the container for a closer inspection. "The girl was found near the Oconaluftee River as was Mr. Rowland."

Gibson nodded. "Yes. But they found the girl hanging from a tree on one of the river islands, and she showed no other signs of being in the water or on the ground for any extended period."

"Still… the rock may be incidental."

"I don't think so. We extracted it from deep within her cavity. Near where her liver had once been."

Etta returned the container to her desk. "So, your theory then is that this was part of a stone used as the method of rupture?"

"It would make sense. The incision lines on the victims are fragmented at best. Those on the portal vein as well. There are no real smooth patterns you might get with a knife blade or some other metal instrument."

"In order to penetrate the skin, the stone would have to have a slicing edge, a razor-sharp point."

"We're talking Cherokee here, Doctor. Arrowheads, spear tips… I'm sure there is no shortage of possible rock-based sources."

Etta Williams leaned back in her chair. "Okay. Gather your evidence together. Get confirmation on the rock specificities and then send it to the FBI. I'll call Captain Mitchell and send your theory along." Gibson nodded and turned to leave. "Oh, and Dr. Gibson…" The young doctor turned back around. "…good work."

9:34 AM

Mary Ellen Runningdeer walked into the Cherokee Civic Center to the low murmurs of the gathered crowd. She was wearing her red and white chieftain frock with her ever-present spirit beads around her. Chief Runningdeer was followed by a trail of people including those on the Tribal Council, law enforcement officials, and several government-looking types. The somber mood was reflected in their faces as well as that of the crowd.

Runningdeer stepped bravely to the microphone. "Ladies and gentlemen, as the chief of the Tsalagi people, I have asked that we dispense with our regularly scheduled meeting of the Tribal Council and have this open forum today to discuss the ramifications of the past few days. I know you have many questions and concerns, as do I, and I wish to be as open with you as possible. First, I'd like to introduce you to the people behind me so that you may direct your questions to those concerned." Runningdeer looked to her right. "Representing our council will be Eddie Whitetree, the representative of Big Cove and Tow String and one of our local businessmen. To his left is Captain Aaron Mitchell of the Cherokee Police. Next, we have Special Agent Katherine Wilcox of the FBI. To her left is Deputy Regional Director Ken Wilkes of the Eastern Regional Office of Indian Affairs. And over here to my far left is Agent Sonny Walker of the State Bureau of Investigations. But before I open the floor for questions, I would like to make a brief statement." She cleared her throat. "The past several days have been the toughest of my life, having lost close friends and members of our community. But what we must do now in order to protect our citizens and business interests may be even more difficult. I ask only that you be patient and heed the words you will hear today."

A hand shot up from the crowd, but the person didn't wait to be recognized. "What about the casino? Today you were to vote on the final bid. We have waited for a long time."

Runningdeer nodded. She knew this would be a point of great concern. "Yes. And now I'm afraid you will have to wait a little longer. With what's been happening, we decided it best to table the final vote until we have cleared up this matter."

Angry buzzing began filtering throughout the wakening crowd. A man standing up front with his arms crossed called out, "Cherokee Police informed me this morning that all of the guests staying in my motel will have to leave. Is this true?"

"Temporarily, Mr. Nathaniel," Runningdeer said. "It's for the guests' own safety."

"How long is that?" another called out. "We have only a few more weeks until winter shuts us down for the year. We need that last of the tourist dollar to make it to spring."

"We are cutting our own throats," shouted yet another. "What if they don't come back? What if they decide not to return?"

The crowd's voices spoke loud and angry in unison again. Runningdeer shot a look to Eddie who approached the microphone. "My brothers and sisters, please listen to me. It is very inconvenient to lose our fall visitors, I know. But we must think of the larger issues here. We must let the police do their work and stay out of their way. Once this person is brought to justice, all will right itself."

"What if they don't catch him?" another called out.

"They will. That I promise." Eddie turned around to look at Wilcox who nodded appreciatively. "Listen to me… many years ago, Cherokee went through another difficult period like this. We were scared, confused, and we didn't know who to trust. But we survived. And we became a stronger people because of it. We are on the cusp of redefining who we are as a people again. Our best days lie ahead. Don't let fear of the unknown take away our future."

Two hours later and seemingly after hundreds of answered questions, the civic center had been emptied of everyone but the high-ranking officials. Chief Runningdeer and the Tribal Council were sitting at one table, facing the law enforcement and government officials at another.

"Are all of your districts represented here, Chief Runningdeer?" Ken Wilkes asked. The thin man with black rimmed glasses and jet-black hair sat with an open briefcase filled with papers.

"Yes, Deputy Director," Runningdeer began. "Yellowhill, Big Cove, Birdtown, Painttown, Wolftown, and the Snowbird Community are all represented on the council. Rest assured, what is decided upon in this meeting, will be communicated to all our Boundary and beyond."

Wilkes pushed the glasses up on his nose. "That's good to know, Chief. I could tell from the turnout this morning how concerned your citizens are. And rightly so I might add."

"Yes. And we made it clear that our plan today would be quick and effective. So, my question now is… what exactly is our plan?"

Wilcox leaned forward. "Despite a lack of connective evidence, no one in the FBI is convinced this is an isolated or random attack. There seems to be some premeditation to these killings, whether we're talking mob influence or some focused type of serial killing."

"Meaning what?" Councilmember Robert Driver asked.

"Meaning we believe these attacks will continue. They are

attacks with a message and specifically with the message to the Cherokee. The black cloak and hood—if that is indeed connected, the style of injury delivered upon the victims—it all seems to point directly to Cherokee culture."

"We've all heard the rumors," Councilmember Nancy Longfeather stated. "Someone is using Spearfinger as a way to scare us. So, how are we going to stop this witch? Or better yet, how are you going to stop this witch?"

Wilcox rubbed her hands together. "Well, we don't have any method for stopping witches, ma'am. Beyond Dorothy and her bucket of water, I don't think anybody in the practical world does."

Eddie registered a surprised look at Wilcox's choice of words. He then turned and caught Runningdeer's eye.

Wilcox continued, "But we do have a plan to prevent another attack in Cherokee. In addition to protection from the local police, the SBI will be providing a series of rotating squads to cover the districts in the Boundary."

Everyone turned their attention to Sonny Walker, the lead agent for the SBI. Walker was a tough-looking man in his early fifties who kept his head completely shaven. He leaned forward, trayed his stogie and rose to his feet. "Our agents are already in place. Some will carry their markers; others will be undercover. We ask only that the good people of Cherokee help keep an eye out for the next couple of days until we can bust this guy."

Agent Davis loosened his tie. "And tell your people to stay together. No one should go anywhere alone. Report anyone or anything that looks suspicious."

"That all sounds sensible. But what of the plan specifics? How exactly are the police going to trap this killer?" Longfeather asked.

Walker threw his short cigar back in his mouth and took in all the Cherokee with a forceful look. "Just take care of your end. We'll handle the specifics."

11:47 AM

Patrolman Allan Grogan pulled his squad car into the Cherokee Fairgrounds, located near the center of town, not too distant from the spot where the Simpson girl was found hanging in the Oconaluftee River. This was supposed to have been a huge weekend at the fairgrounds as Cherokee was to host the first Festival of Native Peoples, a gathering of several different tribal groups showcasing their various cultures.

Grogan parked and approached through the front gate. As he walked in, he saw a few people milling about the booths. Most were packing and following the FBI's order to shut down and vacate the premises.

As he continued in, however, there was a small crowd who had gathered near the center of the grounds. A hundred-foot-tall pole had been erected with a small platform on the top. As Grogan saddled in next to the crowd, he noticed there were five men who had ascended to the platform, and four were bound with rope around their feet. Each man was dressed in red pants, white shirts, and wildly decorated hats.

"What's this?" Grogan asked to those around him.

"The Totonac Pole Flyers," a young Hispanic woman responded. "From Mexico. Veracruz, actually. This is one of our people's dance rituals—to appease the gods of rain and sun. We were to perform this weekend, but now we've been told we must leave."

"Yeah, sorry about that, but it's for everyone's safety."

One of the five men on the platform suddenly yelled out and began beating a drum. The other four men nonchalantly rolled off the platform.

"Holy cow...." Grogan mumbled as he watched them fall.

The men began to descend, still attached to the rope at their feet. It was a beautiful, rhythmic performance as they moved like a flying pyramid, unwinding around the pole.

"Each represents a different element of our world—earth, air, fire, and water. We call them voladeres—those who can fly."

"Perfectly named," Grogan said. "Too bad we have to cancel this year. I think the people would have loved to have seen this."

As they continued to watch the performers, the woman turned to the patrolman. "My name is Marta. I'm the one who called your station."

"Right. You said you had something to report. Something you may have witnessed?"

"Yes, it was two nights ago. We had just arrived in Cherokee and were unpacking our equipment." She pointed to the north end of the grounds. "It was around dark when I saw someone jumping that back fence."

"Can you describe him?"

"Not too much. He was about six feet tall, wearing a black covering with a black hood. The head was completely covered. From the rumors I have heard, it sounds like the same person involved with the poor girl who was found hanging in the river."

Grogan merely nodded. "Anything else you can tell me?"

"No, except that whoever it was, also stole from our equipment truck."

"Oh, and what exactly did he steal?"

"Our performance ropes. And plenty of it."

12:43 PM

Johnny gripped the handles hard and bore into Toll Booth curve at lightning speed. He brought his Harley-Davidson XLH Sportster1200 to its lowest possible angle, the black road racing up to meet him. The centrifugal force in the back lash popped him back up, but within a matter of seconds he was leaning again into Gravity Cavity, another slick, dangerous turn. He was heading west to east in the last quarter of the Tail of the Dragon, an eleven-mile thrill road comprised of three hundred and eighteen curves that ran from Tennessee into North Carolina and skirted the Great Smoky Mountain National Park.

As the limitless skyline and deep valley drop-offs sped by, Johnny dared a peek in the rearview mirror. He saw that Sal was still hot on his heels. He stretched out his lead as he gunned it through Sunset Corner, but Sal made up his time in the topsy-turvy turns and dips of The Wall. Within another thirty seconds they were neck and neck as they tore down Cooper Straight. They both managed the insane turnaround of Crud Corner in record time and then ignited the afterburners to the state line. They passed the marked North Carolina line wheel to wheel and then throttled down to a normal speed.

Johnny signaled to pull over and they found a grassy patch. "Not bad, Squirrel. It must suck to come so close and come up short yet again."

Sal rolled his shoulders in laughter. "Whose wheels were you watching, Johnny? I had you by half a Harley."

"Maybe in your dreams."

"My dreams? No, in my dreams, a naked Pamela Anderson is strapped spread eagle to my handlebars, and I still end up whipping your ass."

Johnny smiled. Their races always seemed to come down to who had the better after speech and then later who had the most creative memory. "I ain't up for arguing with you today, Squirrel. We've got work to do."

Sal revved up his engine. "Lead on, Lieutenant."

Johnny and Sal traveled a half-mile more, past the tree of shame where wrecked motorcycle parts hung from the limbs, and then pulled into the lot at the Dragon's Breath Saloon. They were following Captain Mitchell's order to keep an eye on Marcos Armstrong. With the federal and state agents crawling over Cherokee, Mitchell felt now would be a good time for his men to do a little snooping on the Armstrong's grandson. It was just something in the way the kid reacted that bothered the captain to no end. He was suspicious; and in the climate of late, that was enough.

Johnny and Sal were happy to oblige, especially since it meant they could get a little time in taking on the dragon. After a few well-placed calls, they found out Marcos worked part-time at the Dragon's Breath. It was a saloon they knew well. It had been a place where, on a few occasions, they had decided the day's winner over a couple of cold ones.

And now as they entered the bar, they looked the part as well. Sal had on his old black leather vest and leather chaps. Johnny sported a ragged jean jacket and wrapped a red bandanna around his head. Both let their long, black hair fall freely about their shoulders.

"Two Budweiser's," Sal called out as they entered the dimly lit and near empty saloon.

Angelo folded his newspaper he was reading and reached into the bar's ice box. He plopped down the beers as Johnny and Sal slipped onto a couple of bar stools. "Boys hit the dragon?"

"Just whipped it," Johnny acknowledged. "Record time."

Angelo bumped his shoulders with a private, muffled laugh. He had heard that line on a daily basis. Sal turned up his bottle. "Thanks. Good stuff. Nice and cold."

"We aim to please," Angelo answered. He then eyeballed both Cherokees. "I've seen you boys in here before, right?"

Johnny gave a quick nod. "Yeah. We're from the Boundary. We come out here from time to time and give the dragon a spin."

Angelo retracted a bit, but the temptation for news was too great. "Hear some strange shit has been going down over there, that true?"

Sal and Johnny shared a quick look. "What did you hear?" Sal asked.

Angelo shrugged and turned up his hands in doubt. "Somebody said a couple of people bought it recently. Guy with a knife, maybe?"

Johnny took a swig and frowned. "Sorry, man, we don't know nothing 'bout that."

Angelo grabbed a rag and popped the bar and started to walk away. "Just what I heard." He turned to the back and went about his business. "Hey, Marcos! Get those kegs up here!"

Both Sal and Johnny turned and saw Marcos struggling to walk a keg from the back. He glanced up at the two customers at the bar but there was no recognition. Angelo walked past him. "Use the hand truck next time, numb nuts."

Marcos bumped a shoulder and continued working the keg behind the bar. He opened the cabinet and began attaching the draft hoses. With Angelo now in the back, Johnny saw his chance.

"Tough day?"

Marcos smirked. "Every day is a tough day."

"I hear you," Johnny said. "Nothing like working for the hard coin, am I right?" Marcos ignored the comment and continued his work. Johnny leaned forward. "You been working here long?"

Marcos popped up from behind the bar. "Couple of months now."

"You like it?"

"What's to like?" Marcos replied with little enthusiasm.

Sal quickly downed the rest of his beer. "How about another

one, barkeep?"

Marcos opened the cooler and pulled out another two Budweisers. He slid one down to Johnny and then Sal. He wrote the purchase down on a tab and then headed from behind the bar to the back room again.

"Not much of a talker, is he?" Johnny asked.

"No, but he said plenty."

"He did?"

Sal gave Johnny a serious look. "He's on the wrong way train to hell, Johnny."

"What do you mean?"

Sal did a quick brush up his sleeve and indicated the inside of his forearm. "He's on the wrong way train, and he's got the tracks to prove it."

3:34 PM

Chief Runningdeer stood at her office window, looking out at the leaves constantly falling like a hard snow behind the civic center. She was deep in thought. The past few days had been overwhelming, almost to the breaking point. Her people were strung out, distraught, confused, and rightfully so. This serial attacker, whoever he was, had caused much pain and suffering. The people's collective psyche was in danger of imploding, and Runningdeer felt powerless to stop it.

The chief was reluctant to turn over the issuing of commands—especially the running of the Boundary's day-to-day operations—to the FBI, the SBI, and other government agencies. It just felt wrong. This was supposed to be their land, their problems. And any solution to these problems should also be coming from them. Cherokee should have autonomy over it all, but it was seemingly about to fall out of their hands. To Runningdeer, the sentiment she got from the FBI was that playtime was over—the adults wanted to be back in charge.

What brought this upon us? Where did I go wrong?

Runningdeer turned to the wall behind her desk and looked at the pictures of the previous leaders of the Eastern Band of the Cherokee. They were aligned according to date from 1824, the year of the first chief, Yonaguska, to the present. She sought out the sixth one from the end, a grey haired, one-armed Cherokee, pictured next to the Oconaluftee River. The old man in the photo stared back at her.

What am I supposed to do, Grandpa? Things are getting worse. Please help me…

"Can he hear you?" a gentle voice asked from the doorway. Startled, Runningdeer turned quickly, but then smiled at her visitor. Eddie Whitetree stood in the entrance.

"Oh, yes, he can hear me. It's just… right now, I can't hear him."

Eddie nodded and came on into the office. "Hope you don't mind me intruding?"

Runningdeer slid into her comfortable desk chair. "No, of course not. I'm always glad to speak with you."

Eddie sat in one of the red leather wing-back chairs that were reserved for the chief's visitors. "Being chief is a pain in the ass, ain't it?" Eddie said good-naturedly.

Runningdeer laughed. "You don't know the half of it." She leaned forward and became a bit more serious. "Thank you for today. The people really listened to you. You are a well-respected man."

Eddie shrugged. "I've been around for a while, Chief. I know them well. But to be honest, I was just trying to be a good citizen."

The chief nodded, accepting his response. "So, what can I do for Cherokee's good citizen?"

Eddie folded his hands in his lap. "This situation… it's beyond what we can control."

"I know. The FBI and SBI want to take matters out of our hands. If we're not careful, everything could become their call. Mitchell warned me. These government types are always itching to get control of our Boundary for some reason. I guess meddling in the affairs of the rest of their country just isn't enough for them."

"But perhaps there is something we still can do."

Runningdeer sat up with interest. "I'm all ears, Councilman."

Now Eddie leaned forward. "This is not easy to say. There must be a degree of faith involved."

"Faith?"

"Yes. It may stretch your ideas of acceptance."

"Ideas of acceptance? You're not making any sense, Eddie."

Eddie scooted his chair even closer. "Tell me, Chief. What do you know of ka-i-e-le u-de-li-da?"

She gave him a blank stare. "Ancient secrets? I have no idea what you're talking about."

Eddie's expression turned cold, and he took on a sterner tone. "Yes, yes you do."

Runningdeer shook her head. "No, I'm afraid I don't…"

"Don't deny it, Chief. The book of ancient secrets. You have it in your possession."

"Eddie, you're mistaken." She turned her head briefly. "I have no book…"

He held up his hand. "Chief… Mary Ellen, I know the book exists. I once held it in my hands. It is the secrets of our people, hand-written by Sequoyah himself nearly two hundred years ago. Its powerful knowledge goes back to the ancient times—before the white man, before history. Only a handful of our people have ever known of its existence. It is for our chiefs' eyes only. To be used only in grave emergencies. Two decades ago, during one of those emergencies, and at the behest of your grandfather, important information was …" He searched for the right words. "… extracted from the book."

Runningdeer held comment for a moment, instinctively running her hands across her spirit beads. "Okay, Eddie. Let's say for the sake of argument the book does exist. Why do you want it?"

"Are you kidding?" Eddie threw out quickly. "I would say what's been happening these past few days also fits the definition of a grave emergency, wouldn't you?"

"But for what specifically? Why would we need to consult it?"

Eddie rubbed at his chin. "I don't know everything that is involved in the book. I have no idea what our ancient leaders wanted to warn us about. But if there is any truth to Spearfinger…"

"Oh, for God's sake, Eddie. Spearfinger? That's what this is all about?"

Eddie blew out a hard breath of frustration. "I know... I know... that's what I meant about faith. I just think there may be more to this than some random serial killer." He paused. "You won't have to be responsible for any of this, Chief. I'll read the passages and then give the book right back."

Runningdeer put her hand to her head and made a little laugh. "This is so insane, Eddie. All the problems we have going on right now, and you want to play tribal medicine man?"

Eddie smiled at her words. "Mary Ellen, in the Cherokee's world, what we see, hear and feel is not necessarily all that we believe, is it? I mean we, the Tsalagi, are a spiritual people. There is much more to us than meets the eye. These mountains and rivers are more to us than simple rock and water, yes? I mean, most people see the smoke of a fire as just that; we see it as a message from the on-going spirits of life, something to be interpreted. What is the wind to us? What is the sun?" He made a momentary pause to let his point sink in. "Cherokees are unique. And our problems are unique. I will never be able to convince someone from outside our Boundary that there may be more to this than some random killer. But as Cherokees we have the right...the responsibility to see and hear those things that exist on different planes, different worlds. That's who we are." Eddie paused again and leaned back, looking above Runningdeer's shoulder. "Edami Sanooke taught me that." The chief took another brief look back at the picture of her grandfather. She then refocused on Eddie who smiled and continued, "So... what's he telling you now?"

Runnningdeer returned his smile. She hesitated briefly, then got up from her desk and walked over to a bookshelf that fronted her office. She pulled out a well-worn Bible and flipped to the back. A hidden key was taped between the last pages of the book of Revelations. She then went back behind her desk and removed the picture of her grandfather, revealing a wall safe. She spun the combination and then pulled out a dusty box from inside. With the key she managed the lock. Runningdeer pulled the sealed leather tome from the box. She walked it carefully around her desk and placed it in Eddie's hands. "To be honest, I've never even glanced at this. As the last chief warned me, 'drink deeply from the well or not at all.'" She then said with conviction, "I do so hope this serves some purpose, Eddie."

Eddie stood. "Thank you, Chief. I promise to take great care of it." He moved to the door and then turned back around. "And when this is over, and we have found closure with all this, I'd like to get together again and talk with you about your grandfather. Some stories you may want to hear."

Runningdeer beamed. "I'd like that. I understand he was a very brave man."

"It runs in the family, apparently." Eddie then disappeared through the door.

4:22 PM

Johnny and Sal brought their bikes to a stop at the SBI's checkpoint on Highway 19 on the west side of town. The agent dressed in tan fatigues and wrapped in a bullet proof vest held out his hand and began an arrogant walk toward them.

"What business do you have here?" the agent asked.

Sal lifted one finger from his handle and pointed ahead. "We live here."

"Cherokee is on lockdown. So are the park and the southern half of the parkway."

Johnny reached into his shirt and pulled out his badge he had attached to a thin chain he wore around his neck. "Yeah, we know."

The agent studied the badge for a moment and then took a hard look at Johnny and Sal. He made a dismissive laugh through his nose and started walking back to his post, waving them through.

In no time, Johnny and Sal were back at the station and headed into Captain Mitchell's office. Mitchell was standing next to his desk studying a roll-out map. Seated in the captain's chair and also reading the map was Special Agent Sonny Walker.

"Gentlemen, you're back," Mitchell stated upon their entrance.

"Yes, sir," Johnny confirmed. His voice then went soft, directed only at his captain. "We can talk later at your discretion."

Mitchell nodded and then looked back at his desk. "Oh, this is Special Agent Walker of the State Bureau of Investigations." He pointed at his two men. "And this is Lieutenant Johnny

Whitetree and Corporal Sal Beck of our police force."

Walker eyeballed the strangely dressed lawmen. "Must be casual Friday around here."

Sal ran his thumb down the crease in his leather vest. "Casual? This is formalwear in Cherokee."

"We've been on assignment, Agent Walker," Johnny quickly followed. "But I'd also be extremely interested in what you two have come up with for the overall plan. From the greeting we got out on the road, it looks like you've got our little town securely handcuffed."

"Precautions, Lieutenant," Walker said. "It is the state's belief, as well as the FBI's, that a controlled environment is a protected one."

Johnny shot a look at his captain. "Well, provided you don't knock over any of our teepees while you're here, I guess we can live with that." Mitchell raised his chin and returned the glare at the not-so-subtle jab. "But what about the perpetrator? How do we plan on nabbing this guy? We have few leads, almost zero crime scene evidence and no witnesses."

Walker pointed at the map on the desk. "From the indicated areas of attack, I'd say our man has an intimate knowledge of the Qualla Boundary and the park. He knows how to move around the area without being noticed, knows when to strike, knows the timing of the town...."

"So, you're saying he's a local person," Sal jumped in. "A Cherokee maybe."

Walker stood and straightened his shirt. "More than likely. After all, except for the two hoods from Maryland, the victims have all been Cherokee. What interest would someone from outside your reservation have in killing your people?"

"Remind me to give you a little history lesson on Anglo-

"Funny," Walker said without a hint of a smile. "But the fact remains, this person of interest has only struck locally and has possibly been using Cherokee folklore as a method of attack and to strike fear in the local inhabitants." Walker once again pointed to the map. "But now, we've got him isolated and on the defensive. If he makes any kind of move, any whatsoever... we'll have him."

SPEARFINGER

6:28 PM

Kate Wilcox sat across from her partner at the Soco Diner near Cherokee's Wolftown district. Unbeknown to the FBI agents, Soco was the old Cherokee word for ambush place and covered a large swatch of the Boundary from the northern most part to nearby Maggie Valley. Had they any inclination as to the meaning of the word, they may have chosen another place to grab a bite. But the history and irony of the original name went straight over their heads. Besides, with the area on lockdown, the diner was one of the few remaining places to still receive customers.

Davis was digging into his fresh trout and coleslaw and slurping down his iced tea. Wilcox spooned her greens and bits of turkey around her plate, her interest in food trumped by the ongoing concerns of the case.

"I think we need to begin our follow-up on the coroner's report, Frank. There may be something to these rock fragments that were found in the two victims."

Davis gave an affirmative nod as he took another swallow. "Sure. But I wouldn't get your hopes up. With the wounds as savage as they were, all kinds of debris were likely to find their way inside."

"The examiner report said the fragments were deep inside, not likely picked up from any fall. And the same kind of rock in two separate wounds? I'd say that's worth a follow-up."

Davis held his pose for a moment, a piece of the smoky grilled trout hanging off of his fork. "But the method of rupture? That would have to be one hell of a sharp rock to do that."

"Lithic reduction, Frank. Many rocks can easily be filed down to a point. Remember that witch's finger in the museum? It was carved from some kind of crystal, and it looked like it could cut right through you."

Davis chewed a bite in thought and then gave in. "I reckon. And following the weapon is standard procedure." He drank his tea. "So, what do you suggest?"

"It stands to reason that just about anyone could come up with a sharp rock of some kind. But this one was different—the report called it a durable form of quartz, essentially a type of flint rock—the kind used in making spearheads, arrowheads, et cetera. So, I think we need to check out the local artisans, those skilled in the making of these kinds of weapons, with this type of rock."

"Sure, but there has to be a ton of those guys here in Cherokee."

"True. We could ask Whitetree and the others in the department. They would certainly know where to start."

Davis threw his shoulders up with indifference and went back to digging in his plate. "I guess. Although having another powwow with the lost boys is hardly something I'm looking forward to."

Wilcox grinned at her partner. "I'll talk to Whitetree. I'll handle it."

"Good." Davis grabbed at a toothpick and then stood next to the table. "I'll check with the boys in D.C. see if there has been any movement from Ranshaw. I doubt our Baltimore bootlegger has totally given up on the easy pickings of this place. And then I'll have another talk with our witness at the river. Maybe there was something more he can remember now that he's had a chance to settle down." Wilcox gave a confirming nod. Davis then threw some bills on the table. "You about done?"

Wilcox stood and tossed her napkin over her plate. "Yeah. Let's get back to work. We've got a lot to do."

They moved toward the door. As Wilcox wrapped up in her heavy pea coat, she turned and scanned the inside of the little diner. It was nearly empty, only two tables occupied, the waitresses hanging out by the kitchen door. It seemed so surreal, all that had happened to this point. She had come to this little town in the Smokies hot on the trail of Ranshaw and his men. She was so sure of her purpose, so determined in her intentions; nothing was going to slow her down—not the reservation's idiosyncrasies, not the Appalachian climate, not the narrow twisting roads, and certainly not the headstrong local cops. But now with all that had happened, Wilcox began to feel a little differently. These were real people hurting, struggling with a problem that seemingly magnified every new day. She had gotten a sense of the Cherokees and their feeling of community. And their worried faces were beginning to work on her.

SPEARFINGER

Kate Wilcox tightened the belt on her overcoat and headed out into the cool, thin air. She was going to help these people, help this town. She would heal their open wound. She would do whatever it took to stop this killer—no matter the consequences.

7:47 PM

Daya opened the pantry cabinet in her kitchen and grabbed at the bottle of aspirin which she kept with the cold medicines and other first aid remedies on the bottom shelf. She rubbed at her belly and reminded herself that she would have to rearrange the pantry as well as a hundred other things in order to get their cabin crawl-proof ready.

She grabbed a glass of water and headed for her bathroom. Johnny was sprawled out in the tub, his feet propped up on the sides. Daya knelt down next to him on the bathtub rug.

"Here you go," she said as she handed him the aspirin.

Johnny popped the two pills with a quick swallow. "Thanks." Daya picked up the washcloth and started rubbing his arm and chest. "You don't have to baby me, Daya. I just want to relax for a few minutes."

"I don't mind," she said as she moved to his shoulders. "I know you've had it rough lately. I just want to help."

Johnny grabbed at her arm and leaned over the side of the tub. He drew a solitary finger gently down her cheek. "You help plenty. You do a lot around here, getting everything ready. Besides, you give me something to look forward to at the end of the day. Someone to talk to... to come home to." He paused, finding the right words. He looked deep into her brown eyes. "You're my whole world, Daya." He leaned in and kissed his wife. He held the kiss for a few moments, the intimacy speaking volumes. He pulled back and smiled.

She leaned back into a sitting position, her legs under her, and returned the smile. "Okay. But you don't know what you're missing with the washcloth. I was just about to get the more interesting areas."

Johnny laughed. "Well now wait a minute. Maybe I was wrong...."

Daya tossed the cloth in the tub and held up her hands. "No, no, sorry. You had your chance, buddy."

"But..."

Daya stood, laughing. "No. Sorry. Too late." A sudden knock on the back door interrupted their playful banter.

"Who is that?" Johnny wondered.

"I'll get it."

Johnny relaxed his body, sinking further down into the tub. He heard the voices at the door but couldn't make out the words. After a few minutes, Daya reappeared in the doorway.

"Johnny, there's an Agent Wilcox here to see you. She's with the FBI."

Johnny made a quick change, throwing on a pair of grey sweats and an old black Harley-Davidson tee-shirt. He moved into the den. Wilcox was sitting on the couch and Daya was across from her in the recliner. Johnny looked at the agent and then to his wife. "Give us a few minutes, Daya." She nodded and immediately went to the back. "Agent Wilcox, can I help you with something?"

Wilcox stood to face him. "Sorry to bother you at home, Lieutenant. Your corporal, the one you call Squirrel, told me I could find you here—gave me directions."

Johnny nodded. "Of course."

"We've got the coroner's report from Sylva on the Simpson girl."

"Anything interesting?"

"Yes. Well... possibly. They found fragments of rock in the girl's wound, embedded at a deep angle. It is the same type of rock that was found in the Rowland man from the other day."

Johnny processed the information. "So, we're thinking these fragments are from the murder weapon."

"It may be a long shot, but it's our only possible evidence so far."

"Do you have the piece?"

Wilcox reached into her coat pocket and pulled out the small container. She handed it over to Johnny who held it up to the light. "The one from the male victim was a bit larger, but with the same type of swirling pattern of rust within the grey."

"It's definitely flint," Johnny said as he continued to look from different angles. "It could be a shaving from a sharp weapon." He looked at Wilcox. "I'm guessing the FBI now wants to look for those who are skilled at the knapping process and work with this type of rock."

Wilcox grabbed the evidence again and slid it into her coat pocket. "Yes. That seems to be a logical move at this point. If this was used as the weapon, finding the artisan behind it would get us one step closer."

"Yes. And I have a pretty good idea where to start. Meet me at the station tomorrow around eight. We can begin our search then."

"Good. I'll see you around eight." Wilcox made a move towards the door. "Oh, one other thing, Lieutenant." She turned back around. "In the Spearfinger legend, the witch's finger...."

Johnny picked up on her question before she asked it. "Just like her skin—solid rock."

10:28 PM

Sonny Walker threw his half-cigar into the side of his mouth. He chewed it around to find just the right gnashing spot and then held it there, sucking out the juice. He dared not light it as it would give his position away. He picked up his Aviator Night Vision goggles from around his neck and brought them to his eyes. From his position on the centermost isle of the river park, he scanned Tsali Boulevard and saw only the refracted lights of streetlamps and a few businesses through the grainy green image. It was quiet as it had been for the past few hours. For the most part, the Cherokees were obeying the curfew, and any visitors to the town and the nearby Great Smoky Mountain National Park had long since evacuated.

The idea was simple: set up a wide band around the town, get the perpetrator to feel the squeeze and force him out of hiding and into a mistake. Walker didn't understand the reason why the killer had to dress up as this so-called witch, but that didn't make a wits difference to him anyway. *Dress like Bozo the Clown for all I care.*

He checked his watch and went to the call-mike he had pinned to his down vest. "10:30. Report."

In his earplug, he picked up on rapid series of call backs:

"Santa Land, clear."
"Seven Clans Road, clear."
"Whitewater, clear."
"Tsali south, clear."
"Big Cove, clear."
"Tsalagi Road, clear."

Walker held for a moment, waiting. After a few moments he went to his mike again. "Acquoni? Report…" He waited a few more seconds. "Acquoni? Agent Strickland, report…. Agent Strickland, come in please."

A few more agonizing moments of silence followed.

"Dwyer here, sir," a voice cut in. "I'm only ten minutes away. I can check…"

"No, hold your position. I'm actually closer. I'll check it out." Walker took a final look around, cursed under his breath and then trudged across the north riverbed and to his waiting squad car parked up on the street.

Across the way, hidden in the deep bear grass of the embankment someone was watching as Walker made it to his car and drove off. The person then looked to the Cherokee Museum of Natural History and saw a glimmer of light coming from within the lobby's office.

The plan had worked perfectly.

10:47 PM

Eddie sat in his small office in the museum—a desk lamp the only light in the room. He wore thin cotton gloves, which he often used to handle ancient artifacts. He carefully unsealed the ka-i-e-le u-de-li-da, the dusty, leather-bond tome on his desk, excited to think that only the great chiefs of his people knew of the information contained within. The temptation of reading through all of the secretive Cherokee knowledge was great for Eddie, but he knew the material on Spearfinger was of paramount importance right now, and he would spend all of his limited time with the book searching only for that.

Over twenty years ago, he had held this same book of knowledge in his hands when another bizarre crisis had arisen in the Boundary.

At the time, he was a bigger disbeliever in the book's power than Chief Runningdeer. He had to be convinced by Runningdeer's grandfather and his own grandmother that there was more to the crisis than human intervention. He became a changed man as a result of what became known as the Devil's Courthouse incident with a greater appreciation for the spiritual side of all things Tsalagi. He argued with himself that perhaps it was just a sign of his age—the need to believe in a force that worked beyond everyday life, beyond the sciences and the practical. But either way, even if the events of twenty years ago had been just a series of coincidences, he figured there was nothing wrong with covering all the possibilities.

Eddie took note of the early spellings and word formations that Sequoyah used for their language when the leaders had the Cherokee icon write the information down over two hundred years before. He created drawings of strange animals and mythical monsters along with the printed words in a beautifully scripted calligraphy.

Eddie continued to carefully turn the brittle parchments until he came to an odd drawing of a cloud-covered mountain top. It was crude and not to scale, but Eddie recognized the flattened ridge top, immense sheer-rock faces, and wide, sloping valley: Whiteside Mountain. From the crest of the middle ridge there were several squiggly lines leading in different directions which Eddie interpreted as the old mountain trails. Sequoyah had drawn lightning streaks across these trails at certain points and each was inscribed with ganiyegi—the Cherokee word for danger. There was little doubt; he had recreated Spearfinger's mountain home and gave stern warning at which points in the trails the Cherokee were to dare not cross.

Eddie began reading the next page—it was written as an eye-witness account to Utlunta's treachery. What had been told in the oral tradition for centuries had finally been written down. And for the first time in Eddie's life, her story seemed more historical, more factually based, than some ghost-story or far-flung legend.

Since the time before the great storm, she has hunted our people. She lives as rock until hunger awakes her. She comes as the old one and calls to the children. She sings the song of sleep and rakes her fingers through their hair. She steals inside with her spear finger....

Eddie knew of the story basics and moved ahead, scanning the seemingly endless incidents in which Spearfinger dispatched his people—stories of mostly children, the elderly or the defenseless falling to her prey. The individual stories were told in a precise manner with dread as a common denominator.

He continued scanning until he came to her first confrontation with the Tsalagi warriors:

And the great chief Owl Claw called the men to the high ridge of the devil. They waited with their bows and arrows and long knives. They sent up a great smoke from the valley and waited on her. But the bat had betrayed its people and gave warning to Utlunta. She threw the great rocks from her mountain top and killed the brave warriors.

Eddie looked up from the parchment. The bat?

He continued reading—more stories followed of how the Cherokees tried to ensnare the witch, but each time she saw through their clever traps and ended up killing them all. And each time the Tlameha, the bat, was responsible for letting her know of their plan. Eddie had heard the tale thousands of times and in many different ways but never once with the flying night creature.

He then came to another significant passage:

And it was in the time of the great rain, the wolf drove the bat far from the blue smoke mountains to the caves of the hilltop fire, banished forever.

Eddie let his index finger rest on the word for fire and then whispered it to himself, "A-tsi-lv." Did he translate that right? *Where is the hilltop fire?*

Eddie suddenly looked up from the book, startled. A noise had come from the back of the museum that sounded like the backdoor rattling shut. But he knew that was impossible as he was the only one in the building, and he had locked the back door behind him when he first arrived. He surmised that the museum's heaters must have kicked in and made the odd noise.

Eddie regained his focus and was but a minute back into his reading when another noise, a thumping sound, came from within the museum. That is definitely not the heaters.

Eddie moved from behind his desk and looked out into the

lobby. "Hello…?" he called out. The interior lights were out and there was only the glow of the exit sign above the front entrance and the filtered light coming from his office. Eddie moved out into the darkness. It was quiet, but Eddie paused and strained to hear—something did not seem quite right.

He tracked softly through the lobby to the exhibit room. Only the recessed lights in the base of the walls gave any definition to the room—the dioramic scenes of Cherokee history on the stages above the lights seemed to hover in the air—the mannequins appeared as ghostly, shadowed visages.

Eddie scanned the room as his eyes adjusted to the low-light and that was when he saw it. One of the smaller exhibits had been tipped over—broken glass lay strewn about the floor.

He moved closer, kneeling next to the upturned pedestal. He reached out and picked through the glass and lifted the object, a ceremonial mask. He felt the tuft of deer hair at the top. It was her mask, her exhibit.

Eddie then felt a presence behind him. He grew rigid—his breathing quick and shallow. He stood and turned to look. Cold-blooded and quick as lightning, the witch's dreaded spear-finger flashed before him.

It was the last thing Eddie Whitetree saw.

OCTOBER 23, 1995

12:33 AM

Johnny rode down Acquoni Road on his Harley and pulled off behind the FBI agents' Crown Victoria at Cherokee Central High School. Other vehicles from the various agencies and ranger units were also there.

Johnny hopped off the bike and made a quick step to a tightened circle of cops who included Captain Mitchell, Sal, Wilcox, Davis, Walker and several other SBI agents. Their breath frosted in the chilly air.

Mitchell caught his lieutenant's approach. "Good. Lieutenant Whitetree, you're here now. I want you in on this as well."

"What's going on, Captain?"

Walker took the lead and said, "One of my men, Agent Strickland, was on stakeout on the corner of the Children's Home Road and Acquoni. He was surprised approximately an hour and a half ago by an unknown assailant—clubbed over the head. His skull might be fractured."

"He's been sent to the Medical Center," Mitchell added. "It was a severe injury, but they think he'll pull through."

Johnny looked briefly at Sal then to Agent Wilcox. "Is this the work of Spearfinger?"

"Certainly doesn't follow the m.o. of our killer, but with all that has happened to this point..." Wilcox said. She looked at Johnny a bit bewildered and finally shrugged.

"A brazen son of a bitch, whoever it is," Walker said—his jaw muscles tight with anger. "Anybody that would go after one of my men is either mental or has a goddamn death wish."

"Have we scanned the area? Checked homes?" Johnny said.

Mitchell nodded. "All the businesses are closed. Officer Tobias is continuing a house by house, but nothing has been reported by residents at this point."

Johnny gave it a few seconds of thought. "And where was Agent Strickland found?" He waited and then asked to clarify, "Where was his body positioned?"

Sal picked up on his partner's thoughts. "They found him flattened in the grass behind his car—no tree or building or high place of any kind."

"Perhaps Agent Walker got to him before he could enact the Spearfinger routine," Wilcox said.

"Or there might not be a connection to this witch-thing at all," Davis added with exasperation.

Everyone was quiet for a moment until Sal broke the silence, "Well, there's no reason for us to stand around here with our thumbs up our asses. We need to do something."

Everyone looked to Wilcox. She turned to address Walker. "Get back in position and continue to monitor the streets. There's a distinct possibility we may have been duped into coming to this spot. There may be action elsewhere."

Walker agreed with a slight nod—his frustration still evident in his face.

"I'll have the rangers beef up patrols of the park and parkway," Wilcox continued. "Captain Mitchell, I want Cherokee Police to continue searching this road. Make sure all of your citizens are safe."

"Yes, Agent Wilcox," Mitchell said as he broke from the ring. Sal and Johnny followed their captain.

"Lieutenant Whitetree...?" Wilcox called out. Johnny turned. "I'd still like to pursue the weapon angle tomorrow, if that works for you."

"I'll be at the station at eight," Johnny confirmed with a slight smile.

Johnny headed toward his bike and Sal fell in beside him—a growing grin on the big man's face.

Johnny noticed. "What?"

"Getting a little chummy with the female fed, are we, Johnny boy?" Sal said.

"No, Squirrel, I'm not."

"It's okay. I don't blame you. That's one hot looking lady under that badge and trench coat."

"You're so full of it sometimes, Squirrel."

"C'mon, Johnny, I saw how she cut her eyes at you. You can tell your ol' buddy, Sal."

"There's nothing to tell."

"C'mon, partner. You know what I mean. Is she, or isn't she?"

"Is she or isn't she what?"

"You know— interested in checking out whether you're a real redskin?"

Johnny stopped and conceded a laugh. "As you know, ass-wipe, I'm a happily married man."

Sal whispered as he noted Mitchell make an about-face return. "So, was I once, Johnny boy. So was I."

Mitchell stopped in front of both men and had their attention. "Corporal Beck, please join Lieutenant Tobias in the house search. Make sure all of our people can be accounted for. Report any discrepancy immediately."

"Yes, sir," Sal said. He quickly headed for the squad car.

"And what do you want me to do, Captain?" Johnny asked.

Mitchell paused for a moment and then said, "Follow me back to the station, Lieutenant. We need to talk."

1:12 AM

"Coffee, Lieutenant?" Mitchell asked.

Johnny plopped down in the chair in front of the captain's desk and unzipped his jacket. "No, thank you, Captain. I'm okay." The thought of coffee at this hour did not exactly appeal to Johnny who would gladly trade a good night's sleep for just about anything at this point.

Mitchell sat in his chair and leaned into his desk. He appeared calm but alert—much more so than Johnny. Mitchell decided to get right to the point. "The covert operation yesterday. You have not told me how things went with young Marcos."

Johnny stifled a desire to yawn. "Not much to tell, Captain. He was working at the Dragon's Breath, but he didn't seem to care to be there that much. He was depressed, lethargic. He seemed an unhappy young man."

Mitchell nodded but remained quiet, wanting more.

"Corporal Beck noticed needle tracks in his arm. I'm afraid Attle's grandson is a user—a junkie, Captain. Probably heroin."

"I thought as much," Mitchell said lowly. "That would hurt his grandparents to know such a thing."

Johnny agreed.

"Anything else?" Mitchell asked.

"No, that was the extent of it. He's a lost kid with little going for him. We didn't have a chance to interview him further." He paused and then, "So, what are you thinking, Captain? Because he's a junkie, owes money or perhaps more, he's easily coerced? That he gave up information on his grandfather to Ranshaw's men?"

Mitchell stood without answering and poured himself a cup of coffee from a serving table behind his desk. He took small sips. He turned back to Johnny.

"It would make sense, wouldn't it? Ranshaw wants in on our town—needs influence on the council. He has possible ties to the Dragon's Breath Saloon. Marcos would be the logical next step."

"Then another organization gets wind of Ranshaw trying to muscle in and goes after all of them. As Spearfinger perhaps." Johnny theorized.

Mitchell frowned. "But then why go after Mrs. Armstrong? Or Dan Rowland? Or the Simpson girl?"

Johnny furled his brow. "Good questions. They would have little to no influence on the casino. Their deaths can't be related to the council elder." He laughed at the irony. "It's the same argument I've been making to the feds since the beginning."

"What are we missing here?" Mitchell wondered. "And why were the Cherokee victims placed in some high location? What could that possibly mean?"

Johnny rubbed at his tired eyes. "That may be the key, Captain. My father said he did not know of any ceremonial reason, or anything related to the legend as to why, but I'll get him to continue to look into it—he has vast resources at the museum."

"Yes, yes. If any man can figure out that angle to the mystery, it's your father."

4:22 AM

The low light flickered in and out of Eddie's vision as he came around. His head throbbed, and he could taste his own blood—salty, metallic-like. He tried to focus, but the extreme pain and his restricted breathing kept his mind in shut-down mode.

More in-and-out, agonizing minutes followed—periodic bursts of pain, surfacing memories, pangs of fear, feelings of entrapment. Finally, he broke through the confusion and managed to raise his head. He opened his eyes fully now and scanned around him. He was in a small, unfamiliar room. He was surrounded by cardboard cases stacked ten high and metal shelves filled with liquor bottles and other storage items. Ten feet beyond was a solid metal door. The low light was coming from a singular bulb that hung from a cord in the ceiling.

Eddie tried to shift in his chair but realized that he was restricted—a nylon rope had him strapped to the chair, his arms pinned to his side. As he bent over to look at his bindings, fresh blood poured from the gash in his head and dripped onto the thigh-area of his pants leg.

A jangling of keys outside the door drew his attention. He heard the locks disengage and then the door opened. A large man in an ill-fitting suit with a huge, round head came into the room. He had the nine-inch finger from Utlunta's exhibit in his hand—he was popping the heavy end of the quartz sculpture into the palm of his other hand. He dragged a metal folding chair from the wall, flipped it open and sat in it reverse-style, his arms leaning on the back. He took the carved spear-finger and pressed the pointed end into Eddie's neck.

Eddie blew a hard breath upward to blow back his fallen hair and to flick off a drop of blood which hung on his nose. "Are you planning on jamming me in the neck with that or are you just happy to see me," Eddie said calmly.

The big man roared with laughter, showcasing a mouth of canine-like teeth. He then lost the mirth of the moment and pressed the pointed object further into Eddie's neck. "As you can tell, Councilman Whitetree, I'm very happy to see you."

"You have me at a disadvantage. I don't even know who it is I have the pleasure of speaking to," Eddie fired back.

"Let's not worry about that right now. Let's just say I represent someone with a great interest in your town—specifically the casino you're thinking about bringing to these smoky mountains."

"You and your interest will be welcome to visit anytime. Come during the late spring—the rhododendron will be in bloom."

The man pressed the spear-finger deeper to an uncomfortable level. "Not exactly what we had in mind, Whitetree."

Eddie tried to recoil the best he could—the skin on his neck was giving way. "What do you want?" he managed through gritted teeth.

"As I said, we have interest in your casino. To put it simply, we'd like to run your little operation."

"Too late. The Tribal Council has already narrowed it down to the final bid—a reputable operator."

"Are you saying we're not reputable, Whitetree?" He leaned in more. "Perhaps you don't think we can handle the operation, but I assure you we can." He paused and then, "The fact is we want the business, and we want you to get it for us."

Eddie felt the burn, his neck was compromised, but he did not give in. Instead, he did the only thing that came to mind—he spit into the thug's face. "To hell with you!"

The big man hopped up, wiped the phlegm away and used the spear-finger to smack Eddie hard against the side of his head. Eddie shook off the blow—his right ear ringing.

"Don't mess with us, red man, or you'll pay for it."

"There's nothing I can do for you. There's nothing I will do for you. And there's nothing you can do to me to change that."

Jess Cooper paused; he tapped the spear-finger against his palm again and then smiled wickedly, baring his teeth. He leaned to within an inch of Eddie and force-lifted Eddie's chin up with the tip of the carved finger. "I guess we'll just see about that, won't we?" He eyeballed Eddie closely. "Don't go anywhere, okay?"

Cooper pulled at a string attached to the light, throwing the room into darkness. Eddie watched as the man's hulking frame exited through the open door and pulled it shut. He then heard the dead-bolt lock slot in.

Marcos waited in the annex room of the Dragon's Breath Saloon basement where the beer kegs were stored. Jess Cooper entered; the spear-finger still clutched in his hand.

"How'd it go?" Marcos asked, trying to suppress his anxiety—but failing. "We did good, huh?"

"The target will do, but he's a tough ol' bird. He ain't cooperating. I need more leverage."

"Leverage?"

"Yeah," Cooper said. "You know, stuff I can use against him—his wife, family—his weaknesses. Kinda like we did with your grandpop."

Marcos's mouth felt dry; he tried to swallow. "But I don't know much about him. Only that he's on the council."

"You're a rat, kid—scurry around—find out for me." He poked Marcos in the chest with the spear-finger. "It will be well-worth your effort."

7:56 AM

Johnny came out of his office, threw on his tribal police jacket, and headed for the station door. Patrolman Allan Grogan, who was seated at his desk with the phone cradled between his ear and shoulder, flagged him down with a wave of his hand.

"Headed out now, Lieutenant?" Grogan asked.

"Yeah, Agent Wilcox will be waiting. Might be gone for a couple of hours."

"Okay. By the way, I got word they matched up the noose used to hang the Simpson girl with the missing rope from the Mexican pole flyers. I thought you should know."

"Hmmm. I guess we better keep a watch on our friends from south of the border then."

"They're staying at the fairgrounds; they know not to leave until this is over. But they have strong alibis in the other killings; I'm confident it's not any of them."

"So then, our murderer is also a thief, huh? Not surprising, I guess."

"And since the rope was stolen, there goes another lead we can't trace," Grogan added.

"Right. Whoever is doing this has been very careful not to leave anything for us to follow." Johnny paused and then, "How about my father? Any luck getting through to him?"

Grogan shook his head as he replaced the receiver. "No. But

he may be out, you know. Could be checking the museum or running errands."

Johnny checked the station's wall clock. He would have agreed with the patrolman's theory if he didn't know his father so well. Rarely in all the time he lived with the man did he know him to leave the house at such an early hour.

"Keep trying for me, will you, Allan? And give me a holler on the radio when you get through."

"Gotcha, Lieutenant," Grogan said with a smile.

In a flash Johnny was out of the station and bounding down the stairs to the lot. He saw Wilcox in her Crown Vic, waiting at the wheel. She was dressed for the bite in the air with her long navy pea coat and red scarf over jeans and boots. Johnny slid in on the passenger's side.

"Morning, Agent Wilcox."

"Lieutenant, hope you got some sleep since the last time we spoke."

Johnny laughed. "Not much, but I'm getting used to walking around bleary-eyed." He looked over at her. "Any word on Agent Strickland?"

"Walker called an hour ago. He said he's in stable condition. It was strictly blunt trauma to the head. No serrated objects used—no broom sticks or cackling laughter heard."

Johnny nodded, fully comprehending. "Cherokee checked out as well. No new incidents were called in."

"Good," Wilcox said as she threw the car into gear. "I think having the new sets of eyes have helped out. Hopefully, next time, we'll catch the bastard before he gets away."

She came to a stop at the station's lot entrance. "Which way?"

"Hang a right," Johnny said. "We'll take the main drag out to Wolftown Road. There's a place out there on the way out of town—should be a good place to start."

As the Ford rolled through the quiet streets, Johnny noticed a heavy morning fog had settled into the mountain town. He looked out the window at the darkened shops and abandoned motels—the frozen pumpkins and scarecrows standing guard. He mused how the fog was indicative of how he had felt over the past few days—clouded, unsure—with possible dangers lurking at every turn.

8:08 AM

Ranger Tim Fitzgerald left the Oconaluftee station and drove his way down fog-covered Highway 441 toward Cherokee. He knew everything was shut down—that the gates were secured—but he still felt uneasy, and this brief patrol at least gave him something constructive to do. The past few days had been excruciatingly hard for everyone connected to the area, and the rangers of the Great Smoky Mountain National Park were no different. The park, like neighboring Cherokee and the Blue Ridge Parkway, had seen a steady increase in visitors over the past several years—it had become one of America's favorite playgrounds. The thought of shutting everything down because of some psychopath bothered Fitzgerald to no end.

As he rounded a curve, he slammed on brakes as a new rockslide left the right-side of the road impassable. Fitzgerald groaned. It was not an uncommon occurrence in the Smokies to have rockslides or fallen timbers across the road—unfortunately, they injured or killed a number of drivers in Western North Carolina each year. Sudden changes in temperature or after rain or snow seemed to be the most prevalent times for the slides.

The ranger got out of his patrol car and surveyed the slide. It was not one of the bad ones with heavy, enormous boulders, so he took it upon himself to clean it up. He reached into his glove box and retrieved his White Mule work gloves. With the low beams of the patrol car's headlights directed in front of him, he picked up the oddly shaped rocks, some weighing thirty to forty pounds, and tossed them to the side of the road. He then used his boot to sweep the smaller chards away.

Within twenty minutes he had the road cleared and he hopped back into his cruiser. He headed south again, focused on making his way through the heavy fog. He leaned over the steering wheel as if it gave him a more penetrating view into the soupy mess.

As he drove down the road, Ranger Tim Fitzgerald was completely unaware of the black cowl that popped up in his back seat, its reflection looming in the rearview mirror.

8:29 AM

Wilcox made the sharp turns around Wolftown road with care, happy there was no need to go at a break-neck, emergency pace.

"You get used to it," Johnny said. "You train yourself to anticipate the turns. Of course, with all the traffic that runs through here, the locals have learned it's best to leave the lead foot at home."

They rounded yet another curve when Johnny pointed to the right.

"There it is, pull off over there."

She parked right up against the wooden rail fence that fronted the green-roofed trading post. Wilcox got out and scanned the establishment.

"Bearmeat's Indian Den," she read on the sign. "This is the place?"

"Yeah," Johnny said as he rounded in front of the vehicle. "C'mon."

He led her up a short stair to the porch. Wilcox was immediately taken in by the charm of the place. Potted plants, hanging baskets, wood carvings and baskets filled with a variety of apples were all about the western-style porch which angled across the entire store. Wilcox stopped and picked one of the apples from the closest basket.

"Now this is what I call an apple. What kind is it?"

Johnny took it from her hand. "That, Agent Wilcox, is a Rome Beauty—good for baking or…" He took a quick bite. "…eating straight out of the basket, if you can't wait."

A young woman, dressed in jeans and a yellow pullover, came out on the porch with a broom in her hand. "I thought I heard varmints out here trying to steal our apples," she said with a laugh.

Johnny turned to her. "Hey, Anita, how're things?"

She smiled but then raised her shoulders with a bit of exasperation. "Kind of slow lately. A complete stop to be honest."

Johnny nodded his understanding. "Where's David?"

She pointed to the open door. "Around back. Working on the addition."

Johnny led Agent Wilcox through the store—a maze of vibrant colors, salacious aromas, and glittering trinkets. Wilcox noted hand-made items of all types: smoking pipes, baskets, pottery, beadwork, silver and turquoise jewelry, scented candles, carvings, clothing, knives, and constantly twirling dream catchers. A huge sign in the store indicated all the commodities were authentic—locally crafted.

Newly installed French doors in the back of the store were opened to a new covered wooden deck which sat on twenty-foot beam poles and overlooked the steep mountain side drop-off behind the store. Johnny and Wilcox stepped onto the wooden deck—the sound of a hammer on nails drawing their attention.

"David...!" Johnny called out.

The hammering stopped, and they soon saw arms and hands appear around the railing of the far-end of the deck. The man hoisted himself up and over the railing and landed on his feet. He was a Cherokee about the same age as Johnny, and also, like Johnny, had his long, black hair in a ponytail hanging behind his back He had on just a white tee shirt despite the cool temperature—the hammer was now hanging from a loop in his jeans. He smiled at his visitors—a ten-penny nail stuck between his teeth.

"Well, if it ain't, Johnny Law. Whatcha say there, Lieutenant?" He pocketed the nail and reached out and shook Johnny's hand. "Excuse the mess." He stepped over a small pile of 2x4 boards. "Just trying to make good use of all this down time."

"David, I'd like you to meet Special Agent Wilcox of the FBI." Johnny then turned to Wilcox. "Agent Wilcox, this is David Smith, the owner."

"Mr. Smith, it's nice to meet you. Interesting name for your business: Bearmeat's Indian Den."

"Yeah, Kmart was already taken, so we went in a different direction," he said with an amiable grin. He paused, taking them in with a look and then, "We don't get the FBI in here too often, and I doubt this is a social call. What's this all about, Johnny?"

"Lieutenant Whitetree tells me that you have the most extensive collection of locally carved weaponry in Cherokee," Wilcox said.

SPEARFINGER

"Uh-huh. Arrowheads, spearheads, axes, blades—you name it." David moved inside the store—Johnny and Wilcox followed.

"When we started out a few years ago, we only had a lean-to on the side of the road. We wanted to showcase the talent here in Cherokee: the artisans, sculptors, weavers, carvers of the Boundary—no plastic tomahawks from China, if you know what I mean. The local-only idea caught fire pretty quickly and we soon ended up having to expand the store." He indicated the deck with a tilt of his head. "Still at it, as you can see."

"It's very impressive," Wilcox said, running her fingers under a strand of turquoise beads. She turned her attention directly to Smith. "We're most interested in the local carvers, Mr. Smith—those who excel in the knapping process."

David shrugged. "I know most all of 'em. What do you need to know?"

Wilcox pulled out the sample evidence container from her coat pocket and handed it to Smith. "Have you seen this type of rock come through here?"

Smith held it up to the light then lightly rattled the container. "It's flint of some kind—quite common. Most of the carvers use flint, although some use chert or obsidian."

"The rust swirl pattern," Johnny followed. "Do you recognize it?"

Smith took another look and furled his brow. He gave the container to Wilcox and began walking the aisles of the store—again Johnny and the FBI agent followed.

Smith knelt in front of a glass case of hand-carved knives, opened a cabinet and searched inside. After a few minutes, he pulled out a small carrying case and flipped it open—inside was a beautifully crafted knife with a shaved deer-antler handle. He held the knife up for Johnny and Wilcox—it had the same rust swirl pattern running throughout the gray-cast blade.

"It's a long shot, but what do you think?" Smith said.

Wilcox took it in her hands. She slid her finger down its knapped surface. "Almost identical. Do you know who the artist is?"

Smith turned the box over, frowned and then read the name, "Amadahy."

Johnny read his disappointment. "What's up?"

"Nothing. It's just he's a bit bull-headed—hard to deal with sometimes."

"Is that a first name or last name?" Wilcox asked.

Smith shrugged. "That's all he goes by. You know these artist types."

"Do you have an address on him?" Wilcox continued.

"Nope. But I hear he lives out in the woods over near the Nantahala River somewhere—a bit of a hermit. He brings in his work to the store from time to time."

"Phone number?"

Smith shook his head. "Never had a need to call him." He then added, "I doubt he has a phone anyway."

"What about his payment? Is there a file on him for where you send his payment? Records for Social Security?" she followed.

Smith smiled. "I pay him a percentage on what's been sold. Cash only."

"David," Johnny said. "It's crucial we get a hold of this guy. There must be something."

Smith mulled it over and then led them to the back of the store where an impressive, life-size wood carving of a Cherokee chief stood with a long, flowing feathered headdress that reached well beyond the feet of the chief. Smith reached behind the statue and removed a painting from the wall.

"Amadahy painted this several years ago. I remember him saying that it was close to where he lived."

Smith turned the oil painting so that Johnny could see it. It was a rendition of a large waterfall as it flowed over a massive black rock face. Johnny took the painting and studied it.

"Bird Falls?" Johnny finally asked.

"That would be my guess," Smith said. He turned to Wilcox. "It's on the Nantahala River so that would make sense. You must take a boat from Almond to get to it. Might be a good starting place for y'all."

Wilcox shared a brief look with Johnny then turned back to Smith. "Okay. Thank you, Mr. Smith. You've been a big help."

"Yeah, David, we appreciate it," Johnny confirmed as he hung the painting back on the wall.

Smith shrugged. "The way I see it, the sooner you guys catch this idiot messing up our town, the sooner the tourists will return." He pulled the hammer back out of his belt loop. "Then maybe I'll finally get some rest around here."

9:44 AM

Chief Runningdeer stood in front of her chair scanning the fiscal reports spread out on her desktop. The Deputy Director of Indian Affairs, Ken Wilkes, stood on the other side, leaning against the edge of the desk, a cup of coffee in his hand.

"We can set-up a temporary loan from the government," Wilkes said. "That way we won't have to shut down the basic operations when the coffers run dry."

Runningdeer rubbed her hands. "I'm not ready to do that just yet. I hope we are long done with this before we have to resort to a handout from the government."

"But you are already dangerously close to shutting down now. There's no revenue being generated whatsoever. What will your people do?"

"They'll survive, Deputy Director. We've come under hard times before. Besides, soon we will have the casino up and running and then…"

"Are you sure that's wise?"

"What?"

"Pursuing the casino? It seems your problems began when the council voted to go in that direction."

Runningdeer blew out a held breath. "We've been through all this. We carefully weighed all the pros and cons. It is what's best for Cherokee."

"All evidence to the contrary."

"That's easy to say now, Deputy Director, but when this is over…"

Wilkes put his cup on the desk and leaned forward. "And how many Cherokees will suffer in the meantime? Their blood will be on your hands, Chief."

"Mr. Wilkes, what do you suggest? That I end our chance for economic independence? That I tell all the Cherokee that we just forget about expansion? About growing as a nation?"

"Look around, Chief. You call this expansion? You call this growth?" Wilkes held his position for a moment and then, "This is a dangerous game you're playing."

"Three years ago, I sat in your office, and you welcomed the idea, remember? We looked at this from every angle. You helped us set up the agreement with the governor's office. You fought for us in our discrepancy with the Catawba tribe. And now we are to throw in the towel because of some... psychopath?"

"That was a different time."

"But our nation needs this," Runningdeer said. "Besides if we pass on the casino now, our other loans will be retracted. It could be very crippling to us."

Wilkes straightened and crossed his arms. "Really, Chief Runningdeer, you would risk the lives of your people over a gaming operation?" He looked over the black rims of his glasses to make his point clear. "So, when is the next election for chief scheduled anyway?"

Runningdeer frowned. "Not a very subtle way of putting it, Deputy Director."

"But a very real probability, Chief. The people will blame you for their misfortune. It's the price you will pay unless you change direction now."

"Yes, but, we don't even know if the Spearfinger murders are tied into the casino in the first place. They may be totally unrelated."

"Are you willing to take that chance?"

Runningdeer eased into her chair as she contemplated Wilkes's words. She looked back up at him with conviction. "Make no mistake; I don't give a damn about losing my office if the interest of my people is upheld—even in the slightest. But if halting the casino saves one life..." She paused. "I shall consider our options carefully, Director."

Ken Wilkes picked up his cup and tapped it on her desk. "That's all I think anyone would ask, Chief. I'll be in touch." He turned and walked out the door.

Runningdeer ran her fingers over her spirit beads. She looked at the Bible in her bookcase across the room and prayed that Eddie Whitetree was having better luck than she.

10:10 AM

Johnny held his flip phone to his right ear and leaned a bit toward the passenger side window, keeping his conversation guarded. "Nothing yet, huh?" He listened and then, "Okay. Do me a favor, Allan. Go over to his place for me and check things out." He listened some more. "Yeah, he still lives over in Big Cove—near the KOA Campground Road—right, the green one with the covered porch." He paused and then, "Yeah, I'm sure he is... thanks."

Johnny pocketed the flip phone and noticed Wilcox. "My dad. I haven't been able to get in touch with him."

"Do you need to swing by his place? Check it out?"

"No. One of our patrolmen is doing just that. Besides, I'm sure he's fine. Probably just out for a walk or something."

Wilcox smiled slightly, accepting the explanation even though she could tell Johnny didn't believe it himself.

She soon slowed the car as they approached the checkpoint on Highway 19. She rolled the window down and flashed her badge to the approaching SBI agent.

"Headed out for long?" the agent asked.

"Might be a while," Wilcox replied. She looked ahead to the empty highway. "Much traffic this morning?"

The agent shook his head. "No. Had a park ranger come through here a little while ago, but that's been it. I guess the word is getting out."

Wilcox acknowledged the man with a brief nod and pulled out onto the highway. She turned to Johnny. "So, where is this Bird Falls?"

"Stay on 19 until you hit the Smoky Mountain Expressway then head north on 28. Shouldn't take too long to get to Almond."

"You've been to these falls before?"

"Yeah. My dad and I often fished the Nantahala when I was growing up. Nantahala is Cherokee for land of the noonday sun—covers a large swatch of area south of here. There are some beautiful stretches of the river that way—heading away from Fontana Lake." He paused, looking out of his window, and then, "After mom died, we went fishing practically every weekend. It became our way of holding on—of pushing through the tough times. Sometimes we'd come home without a single bite, but it didn't matter. It was good therapy, you know?"

Wilcox grinned at his honesty. She glanced over at Lieutenant Whitetree, a bit remorseful for having come down so hard on him when they first met. She was beginning to appreciate the man behind the badge. And for the first time, she allowed herself to appreciate him physically as well. The ponytail, which she at first thought so off-putting for a lawman, now seemed oddly attractive to her. And she could tell he was well-cut under his uniform; he possessed a certain youthful strength and vitality.

"My dad never had time to go fishing," Wilcox said without his prompting. "He was always busy at work."

"In what line?"

"Law enforcement. He was the chief of police in my hometown. He didn't have time for much else. There was always something going on."

"You're both in the same profession. I guess there's a connection there."

"No other choice really. In my house you were either one of the good guys or else. My two brothers ended up as cops as well."

"And your mother?"

"A cop's widow—staying up nights, worrying all the time." She allowed a sparked memory to sink in and then, "Unfortunately that became an all-too-real description for her eight years ago. Dad was out patrolling a pretty rough neighborhood one night—saw two kids breaking and entering, climbing through a window. He pulled in and caught them ripping the house of all things electronic." She paused and pursed her lips. "Didn't know there was a third in the yard acting as lookout. Kid, about seventeen, snuck in behind him, put a .38 to the back of my dad's head... took his life."

Johnny wasn't sure what to say to that. He looked to Wilcox who remained unemotional—just staring out at the passing black top.

"I'm sorry," Johnny finally said.

"We all have our crosses to bear, Lieutenant. Your mother, my father... And you know as well as I, our professions don't exactly lend themselves to an easy life, do they? Hectic schedules, eating when you can, sleeping when you can..."

"No, you're right about that."

"Sometimes," she summarized thoughtfully, "we cops must grab our moments when we can, or we may never get them."

They looked over at one another at the same time—both acknowledging the truism with a shared smile.

11:26 AM

Jess Cooper unlocked the door and proceeded into the dark storage room in the basement of the Dragon's Breath. He came to the center of the room and pulled at the string to the overhead bulb. The light came to life with enough wattage to cause Eddie to squint. He looked up at his keeper.

"Back again so soon?" Eddie asked with bravado. "I was only beginning to catch up on my sleep."

Cooper showed his fang smile as he sat in the folding chair in front of Eddie. "I thought you might like some company, Whitetree."

Eddie glanced around the room. "Nah. Me and the storage rats are doing just fine."

Cooper smiled again. "How about some water then? Got to be getting a little thirsty." He pulled a plastic bottle from his coat pocket and dangled it invitingly in front of Eddie's face.

Eddie eyed the bottle and rubbed his dry lips together. "I don't think I'd care who I had to thank."

Cooper shrugged, then took a swig from the bottle himself. He fastened the top back on the bottle and set it next to his feet. "So, I've given you a little time to consider our offer."

Eddie made a tsk sound of disgust as he looked away. "You can keep me in here until kingdom come and the answer would still be the same."

"All we need is your persuasion, Whitetree—your voice on the council to get us the bid."

Like I told you earlier: it ain't gonna happen. I will not help you secure anything. And I really don't give a damn what you do to me."

Cooper nodded and then leaned back, eyeing Eddie closely. "And what about your progeny?"

Eddie stiffened. "My what?"

"You a grandpa yet, Whitetree?"

Eddie seethed in silence before uttering, "You sorry bastard, don't you dare…"

Cooper snorted a laugh. "Didn't take us too long to find out, Councilman. That pretty, little daughter-in-law of yours—all alone up in that cabin in the woods. It'd be a shame if something was to happen to her—so close to the child being born and all."

"You listen to me, and you listen to me good. If anything happens to her or any other member of my family, I'll personally rip out your goddamn lungs!"

Cooper smiled again. "Now you're getting it, grandpa. That burn, that hatred, that helplessness—that's exactly how you should feel." He leaned in closer. "Of course, it doesn't have to come to that. You can end this right now." He moved even closer—nose to nose. "Get us on the table. Get us the operation. If you do, you and the rest of the Whitetrees have nothing to worry about."

"You're a heartless son of a bitch."

"True. But the person I work for is far worse. I can promise you; you do not want to cross him."

Eddie held his defiant look for a moment and then hung his head—his shoulders sank like flattened tires. "You will leave Daya alone? You will not harm her?"

"That's the deal, red man."

"How do I know you will keep your word?"

Jess Cooper stood tall and looked down on the beaten man. "You make it happen; no harm will come to her. We'll disappear into the shadows."

"But always lurking. Always there," Eddie said looking up.

"Always," Jess Cooper hissed.

11:43 AM

Johnny and Wilcox walked up to the Riverrun Stationhouse near Almond where whitewater enthusiasts and nature lovers alike could rent an array of kayaks, canoes, and jon boats for trips up and down the Nantahala. The building itself wasn't much to look at—a gray, wooden structure whose warped frame and decking had seen a better day.

Just beyond the structure, however, was the flowing Nantahala—a pristine river dotted with mossy-covered, slab rocks and lined by hardy trees dressed in an explosion of fall colors.

As Johnny continued inside, Wilcox walked around the building to take a closer look. Orange, yellow, and blue canoes and kayaks were stacked six high in the back; the storing slips were completely full. Wilcox figured the chilly autumn air and recent events near Cherokee kept most of the would-be boaters at bay.

She continued out onto the dock area. The low spots in the river near the dock ran across beds of smaller rock formations and reminded her of the Oconaluftee. But this river was much wider, and it deepened quicker on a more angled slope.

Wilcox stuffed her scarf down into her coat as a mountain wind swooped down the river basin—just being around the water made the temperature seem a few degrees cooler. She turned as she heard Johnny approach.

"Any luck?"

"Yeah. The manager knows Amadahy, said he lives about two miles south of here on the Nantahala. He said there's an old logging road that leads to his place, but it would be much quicker and safer if we went by boat." Johnny took a look back at the building. "Said he wouldn't mind renting us one of his for the day."

Wilcox laughed. "I'm sure. So, what did you tell him?"

Johnny simply held up a small key—tagged with the number 15.

Ten minutes later, Johnny and Wilcox were in boat 15 heading out into the river. It was a green jon boat—a three-seater with an Evinrude nine horsepower engine. Wilcox sat up front as Johnny navigated from the back.

They left the tributary offshoot of the Riverrun Station and turned south picking up on the swiftly flowing current of the Nantahala. Wilcox sat in a semi-crouched position as the breezes, spray and stirred air from the boat's movement seemed to cut right through her.

As they motored passed a particularly high bank, an eighteen-car train rolled by, sounding its deep horn twice.

"The Great Smoky Mountain Railroad," Johnny announced.

"Probably its last run through the Nantahala Gorge this year." He then added, "It's a great way to see the Smokies—the lakes and mountains and forests."

"How many times have you ridden it?"

"Oh, I, uh, actually have never ridden on it," he said sheepishly. "But that's what I hear anyway."

Wilcox turned and laughed at Johnny's confession, tossing her head back in delight. Johnny's eyes found the bottom of the boat but then quickly returned to Wilcox. With her blond hair back, he could see her face with its strong yet elegant features. He also noted more of a spark to the green hue of her eyes—much more so than at any time to this point. He enjoyed seeing her this way—even if the moment had to come at his expense.

Fifteen more minutes passed, and the river opened up by twenty yards. The current slowed and things became quiet—gone was the rush of water and passing motorists—even the sweeping mountain wind had died down.

"Beautiful," Wilcox said looking around. "I feel like we've reached some special place, you know? Some magical, enchanted part of the river."

It was strange for Johnny to hear Wilcox say that as he was thinking the same thing.

"Ataga-hi."

Wilcox waited for the translation.

"The Lake of the Wounded, a place of healing and magic."

"Hmmm," she said with interest. "Another story you heard... on one of your father-son fishing trips, perhaps?"

Johnny nodded as he continued to guide the boat into the deeper reaches of the river. "Somewhere in our Smoky Mountains, the lake exists. It is known to the birds and animals but not to man. Some say we see it as purple fog or a rolling cloud, but only temporarily—it escapes us—it is not meant for us."

Wilcox smiled, looking to the river's shoreline. "So then, no one has truly been there?"

"As the legend goes, one brave hunter, who was tracking a wounded bear, was led to its mystic shores. He had been injured himself and after fasting and offering high praise to the bear's spirit, he was allowed to bathe in its healing waters."

"And he had to keep the place secret as part of the trade-off?" she asked looking back at Johnny.

"Yes. The story speaks to our symbiotic relationship with nature—our give and take. The Cherokee believe everything is connected."

Wilcox turned her attention to the front of the boat. She leaned slightly and reached with her right hand into the bitterly cold waters of the Nantahala. She retrieved a floating golden oak leaf and held it up for Johnny to see. "Everything?"

Johnny nodded. "Everything."

She paused, smiled, and then dropped the leaf back in the water, sending it on its way.

2:34 PM

Corporal Sal Beck pulled into the vacant parking lot of The Cherokee Museum of Natural History. He was coming from his lunch hour when he received a call from Patrolman Allan Grogan about Johnny's missing father. A search of the elder Whitetree's home had come up empty so Grogan asked Sal if he would check the museum. Sal agreed and made the quick journey over.

The big Cherokee got out of the squad car and checked the front glass door. The lobby was dark, but he did notice a light on in the central office. He rapped on the glass with his forefinger but to no avail.

Sal traveled around to the back of the building. He came to a halt as he noted the back door was slightly ajar. Sal went to one knee and inspected the lock. It had been worn through the years, but he noted several harsh scratch marks along the plug in the frame.

Sal stole a look behind him and then entered. The alarm system had been deactivated. After he depressed several wall switches, the overhead can-lights in the exhibit room came on. Immediately, he was drawn to the upturned pedestal and broken glass on the museum floor.

Sal went to his sidearm. He tip-toed around the glass, keeping his weapon in front of him and his eyes scanning.

After a careful search of the other exhibit rooms, he made it into the atrium-style lobby and then ventured into Eddie's office. At this point, he felt the building was secured and holstered his weapon. He searched the office and saw the odd-looking collection of parchments on Eddie's desk.

Sal pulled on a pair of latex gloves and sat in the curator's chair. He looked at the strange calligraphy, recognizing that it was Cherokee but unable to understand its apocryphal intent. It was obviously historical, obviously important, but...

What the hell is this?

He carefully turned the book page by page, stopping to study the intricate renditions and detailed maps. He flipped through a few more pages and then stood, figuring he shouldn't waste any more time. But as he moved from behind the desk, one particular etching drew him back in.

Sal pressed his hands on either side of the ancient manuscript and leaned over to get a closer look. It was a picture of an enormous cliff with fourteen Native Americans warriors, hanging by their legs over the precipice. Their bodies were limp, lifeless, punctured by several gaping wounds. Above the cliff circling the dead bodies was a flying creature. Sal wasn't positive, but it looked like a...

"Tlameha...."

3:43 PM

Johnny slowed the boat and they drifted past the immense Birds Falls. The thunderous sound of the cascading waters was deafening and neither Johnny nor Wilcox tried to speak over it. They both studied its massive rockslide from crown to pedestal. The black rock, hidden just out of reach of the river, was slick and smooth from the constant flow and sprouted green foliage at various juts around the perimeter.

"That was impressive," Wilcox said as they finally steered clear. "The waters around here are so beautiful."

"It is earth's eye; looking into which the beholder measures the depth of his own nature," Johnny said from memory.

"Interesting," Wilcox said. "Is that a Cherokee saying?"

"Henry David Thoreau," Johnny answered. He paused, shrugging off her look of surprise. "C'mon, we Cherokee can't come up with everything."

Wilcox laughed and then said, "You're quite the source of information, Lieutenant—keeper of old legends, knowledgeable tour guide and now quipster of Thoreau."

"Blame my father. He double-majored in history and English in college—never missed an opportunity to impart wisdom on his juvenile delinquent son." He thought about it as she laughed. "And you can call me Johnny, by the way. Lieutenant is a bit formal for two people sharing a jon boat."

"All right. But only if you call me Kate in return."

Three minutes past the falls and Johnny angled the boat clear of a small rock island and headed for a soft, clinking sound coming from a grouping of spruce-firs on the right bank.

"Is this the place?" Kate asked.

Johnny pointed to the metal wind chimes hanging from the arms of the sturdy trees. "Looks like the doorbell of a hermit artist to me."

He managed the boat down the narrow stream with only inches to spare on either side. He raised the prop of the engine as the depth thinned out as well. They rounded under more ancient oaks and maples until the boat could travel no more. Ahead, a one-man canoe was beached atop a bank of wavy green bear-grass—lush and inviting.

They hopped out and Johnny pulled the bow of the boat onto the bank. Kate looked around, taking in the scenery.

"There seems to be no shortage of stunning sights on this river. It's like some enchanted forest out of a storybook. I can see why Amadahy would want to live here."

"Yeah. Let's see if the artist is in," Johnny said and led her up the bank.

They marched down a well-worn path, the hardened woods giving way to stretches of rhododendron, rocky monoliths, and open grassy patches. It looked like scenery out of a fairytale.

Kate kept expecting to see a buzzing sprite or a dancing elf along the way. But instead, as they emerged into an open pasture, they were greeted by a five-foot tall frog tipping his bowler hat and bending at the waist in a welcoming gesture. It was an artwork design sculpted out of scrap metal. The green paint on the design was faded and rust shown on the edges, but it still made for a whimsical piece of lawn art.

"I'd say we are definitely heading in the right direction," Johnny said as they passed.

They continued down the trail, bypassing several more metal art sculptures of animated animals, including an over-sized squirrel chomping on an acorn—stealthily positioned under an oak tree.

"Well, I know what to get Sal for Christmas this year," Johnny said, invoking yet another laugh out of the trailing FBI agent.

After hiking one more tree-filled knoll, the two emerged onto a plateau which housed a small log cabin. A thin line of smoke streamed out of the stone chimney on the side of the cabin—it was quaint, aesthetic—much in a way they both expected. They walked up stone steps to a deck overlooking the plateau. Tiny wooden sculptures of walking bears and howling wolves aligned the railing of the cabin's back porch.

A simple screen door was the only barrier to the inside of the cabin and Johnny gave it a solid rap as he peered through the screen. "Hello? Anybody home?"

He could see a messy kitchen table and the smoldering fire, but there was no movement inside. He knocked again.

Kate didn't wait for a response. She reached for the handle, pulled it open and stepped inside. The cabin interior was small, smoky, and unkempt.

"Maid's day off," she said, looking around.

Johnny stepped around her. "Amadahy," he called out.

He moved toward the fireplace and gazed out of a small window. "Looks like there's a barn of sort in the back—maybe his workshop."

Within minutes they were back outside walking toward the gray-board, Dutch-style barn with its high-sloping snow roof. They both slowed and then came to a stop as they recognized the vehicle parked out front.

"That's a ranger unit, right? From the park?"

Johnny slowly nodded as he processed what he was seeing. "Yeah. Looks like one from the Oconaluftee Station—maybe Tim's."

They began again towards the patrol car; their pace increasing. "The SBI agent at the blockade said a park ranger had been the only one to come through the checkpoint this morning," she said.

"Right. But why the hell...?" Johnny abandoned the question as he noted Kate shared his confusion.

Kate stood beside the driver's side window, bent down, and peered inside. "Oh, shit!"

"What?!"

Kate slung open the door. She stood back and allowed Johnny to witness her discovery. The driver's side seat was darkly stained. Splattered blood covered the steering wheel, dashboard, and instrument panel.

"Jesus..."

Johnny took a quick glance into the empty back seat before focusing on the door frame. He traced a heavy blood trail which led from where they were standing to the back of the patrol car. Johnny then used his glove and flipped open the trunk latch next to the driver's seat.

Kate, with weapon drawn, made a guarded approach. She saw another smear on the back bumper. She took a quick look at Johnny. He slid to the back and lifted the trunk while she directed her weapon with both hands.

Silently, they both stared at the crumpled mass that was once Ranger Tim Fitzgerald. His body was twisted into a semi-fetal position—his neck savagely ripped to the point of near decapitation. Another gash crossed his mid-section—the trunk carpet soaked in his blood.

Johnny glanced at Kate who tilted her head toward the barn. She really didn't have to think about it. There would be no calls for back-up. This was their one shot.

Johnny pulled his weapon and reached the heavy door first. He opened the right side and covered for Kate as she stepped through.

The barn was dark with little filtered light, but Kate saw that the dirt floor was covered in piles of rock and stacks of stone and wood, trade work of the artist. She made her way past the objects and headed for the back of the barn—Johnny followed closely.

They passed a long, wooden table that was covered with egg-sized hammerstones, deer antler tines, leather straps, copper ishi sticks and an odd-looking notching tool made from a cow rib bone. Beyond the table was a wire wastebasket filled with broken attempts at flint arrowheads and spearheads.

They continued past a silent table saw and more oddly shaped tools until they came to the very back of the old barn. Kate slowed and held up her hand.

"About ten feet ahead of me, Johnny," she whispered. "Someone is there—appears to be sitting."

Johnny moved in beside her. He could barely make out the person's outline.

"FBI," Kate announced. "Mr. Amadahy?"

There was no movement.

Johnny scanned the wall next to them and saw a two-foot ribbon of light near a section of the base. He groped along the side like a blind man until he found the access. He took hold of the handle and slid the door all the way open, allowing the sunlight to pour in.

Now in full view, Kate moved in an arc pattern around the man—her weapon squarely pointed at his head. As she rounded to the front, she let her arms drop a little and shook her head in disappointment. She cut her eyes over to Johnny who also moved in front of the latest victim.

The Cherokee man, whom they both assumed was Amadahy, was tied to the chair with a heavy rope. He was slumped over, his chin pointing at his chest. He sat in a puddle of blood that had only recently been pumping inside his body. Another rope was tied to the back of the chair. Johnny followed the rope upward and saw that it wrapped around a pulley which hung from a large crossbeam.

"Still on the ground," Johnny said.

"Yeah. Wounds look fresh too. We may have interrupted," Kate said, her eyes scanning the old barn.

At that moment, they heard the patrol car engine crank. They both took off, running full steam towards the front. As they came to the opening, the patrol car was kicking up dust and gravel, reversing at top speed.

Kate and Johnny both leveled their weapons and fired. The windshield crumbled but the ranger's patrol car continued to accelerate away. The driver whipped the steering wheel, throwing the car into a 180-degree spin and then speeding towards the logging road.

Kate took a half-second look to the right of the cabin and then headed across the grass field of the plateau.

"Kate…!" Johnny yelled out before following.

Kate was at a full out-and-out sprint. She saw a curve ahead in the road and realized the driver would have to make a turn back towards them on the other side of the field. She systematically adjusted for the speed and distance and angled her approach.

The car was maxed out at top speed as it ate up the distance on the logging road. Kate was now only 100 yards away but judged she would not be able to cut it off in time. Instead, she dropped to one knee, cupped her .40 Smith & Wesson, waited for the target to pass, and then squeezed off a round. The bullet ripped through the back tire sending the car careening into the bank on the right side of the road. It spun out, flipped, and landed on the driver's side, continuing to slide until it came to a halt against a tree 30 yards within the reaching forest.

Kate rose to her feet as she felt Johnny rush past her. He leapt the brush lining the field and continued his sprint to the wrecked patrol car. The back wheel was still spinning as he reached the automobile. He slowed—his weapon trained on the front of the vehicle. He circled around and leveled his weapon where the windshield had once been.

"Not here," Johnny yelled to Kate.

She came to his side, out of breath, scanning the woods beyond. "Gotta be."

Johnny turned and searched the woods as well.

That's when they both saw it. Through the tree line, a black-cowled mass was moving quickly. Kate yelled, "There!"

Johnny and Kate took off again, running full speed, following the elusive witch, both determined to end the nightmare once and for all.

4:34 PM

Sonny Walker entered the Cherokee Café and shook the cold from about him. He ignored the "please wait to be seated" sign and headed straight to a booth in the back. He slid into the seat across from FBI Agent Frank Davis. Davis was tearing open a Sweet-N-Low packet with his teeth—his cup of coffee steaming in front of him.

"You wanted to see me?" asked Walker.

Davis stirred his brew. "Need an update, Agent Walker. I need to know what's happening."

"As I told your partner this morning, we are still in position—watching—waiting, but nothing new."

"No leads?"

"That's what I'm telling you. FBI getting a little antsy?"

Davis took a sip, careful not to scald his tongue. "Not antsy, just don't want to waste my time."

"I take it you don't believe in witches, Agent Davis."

"No, I don't. This is all bull as far as I can tell. How about you?"

"Many of the Native Americans have interesting malevolent characters in their backstories: the Shoshone in Wyoming, for example, told of the Nimerigar, a tribe of little people that would attack them with poison arrows. In the Uinta Basin, the Navajo and the Ute had a terrible shape shifting creature called the Skinwalker. This Spearfinger of the Cherokee is no different."

Davis dismissed Walker's surprising knowledge of Native American lore with a quick suck of his teeth. "I think it's time we put an ear to the wall, Agent Walker. Or an ear to the teepee if you will."

Walker shifted in his seat and smiled without enthusiasm. "Wire taps? Bug the whole local system?"

Davis leaned forward. "You know, as well as I, this is just some crazed Indian, some head case, looking to put his face atop the local totem pole. He's gotta be a local."

Walker nodded.

"He's probably bragging about his antics to all of his loony friends—probably a whole tribe of loonies stuck up in these mountains."

"We can monitor the whole band without much difficulty, but the go-ahead is going to take a whole lot of authority. More than what we have on the streets now."

"Let me worry about that. I'll get it approved."

"What about your casino angle? How does that fit in?"

Davis smirked. "Listen, with all that's going on with this Spearfinger witch, I think the mob's influence is the last thing we have to worry about."

4:44 PM

Kate was completely winded as she ended her stretch into the forest having hurdled rock formations and fallen trees like an Olympic track star. As she leaned over to catch her breath, she saw Johnny a hundred yards to her right. He too had slowed in the chase, looking to the forest floor for clues of Spearfinger's path.

"Anything?" Kate yelled.

Johnny shook his head 'no.' He then raised his right hand with the weapon and signaled to the deeper forest in front of them.

She caught his message and advanced into the darkening woods. Within a matter of yards, the forest blocked her view of Johnny. She moved cautiously—her eyes scanning for any movement, anything out of the ordinary.

All manner of tree and shrubbery surrounded her, birds called out from the treetops and chipmunks scurried from dark corners—it was a world of flora and fauna, a botanist's dream. But as the thick brush grew denser around her, so did possible hiding places. Like Johnny, her eyes went to the ground. She scanned for any disturbances in the compacted leaves and needles.

And then… a possibility.

To the right of an ancient stump, Kate saw a torn piece of black cloth. She examined it up close. It had been caught on a twisty off-shoot of a fallen beech timber. Kate crossed the log and squeezed between two small spruce firs. There was a small deer path beyond which led down an embankment and into a ravine.

Fairly confident the witch was not close by; she grabbed at

her walkie-talkie and turned the dial. "Lieutenant," she whispered. "I have a marker. Following it into a ravine."

"Careful," Johnny called back. "I'll circle back to your position. Be there in a sec."

Kate did not wait. She hooked the walkie-talkie back to her belt and proceeded down the bank. Once at the bottom she made out a fresh footprint in the mud.

Now I've got you.

She leveled her weapon in front of her and followed the bottom of the ravine until the mud and leaves gave way to solid rock. In the distance she heard the constant pounding of a waterfall. She cautiously walked past more rock and trees until she emerged at the precipice of the falls. This one was not as impressive as Bird Falls—only thirty feet from top to bottom. The tributary feeding the falls snaked to her left and disappeared under a huge rock formation several yards wide.

Kate found several dry stones within the stream and continued out to the top of the falls' crest. About midway of the rushing water, she stopped and scanned below her. The water crashed onto the large rocks below. It was so peaceful and mesmerizing. She imagined very few people even knew this waterfall existed.

The FBI agent felt a sudden chill at having let her guard down. She swung back around to her right, and there, no more than two feet from her, stood the witch, the spear-finger lashing towards her. Instinctively, Kate drew her weapon and fired. The shot rang out echoing in the ravine. It was direct hit to the chest of the witch who momentarily froze. But instead of clutching at the wound and crumbling to its knees, the witch took a step forward and lashed out again at Kate. This time the razor-sharp finger nicked Kate's throat as she pulled away from the attack. She lost her balance and fell over the side of the falls.

5:07 PM

"I know of no Cherokee legend concerning a bat, Corporal," Captain Mitchell stated. "But I would certainly not claim to be an expert on such matters."

Sal leaned over the captain's desk. "Neither would I, Cap.

But I think the elder Whitetree may have been on to something with that book. The drawing clearly showed several of our ancestors, dead, placed on a high point somehow—and there was definitely a bat-like creature circling the bodies."

"Did you bring the drawing with you?"

Sal shook his head. "No, it was extremely old, in a delicate condition. I didn't want to move it in fear of it falling apart."

"And what of Eddie Whitetree?"

Sal shrugged. "We've checked all over and so far, nothing."

Mitchell rubbed at his chin. "That is disturbing. I hope no harm has come to him. Lt. Whitetree told me he was going to ask his father to further investigate that angle."

Mitchell rose from behind his desk and went out into the squad room—Sal followed.

"Patrolman Grogan, any word on Lt. Whitetree's father?"

At his desk, Allan Grogan looked to the captain. "No, sir. And I can't seem to get a hold of the Lieutenant or Agent Wilcox either. They left the Boundary earlier, but every time I try to raise them now, I get static—cell phones too. And get this: Oconaluftee Station just called—one of their rangers has gone missing. It's getting a little crazy around here. I don't know what's going on."

Mitchell turned back to Sal. "Do you know where Wilcox and the Lieutenant were headed?"

"They were following the weapon, Captain. I think Johnny said they were going to try Bearmeat's this morning and go from there. Should I follow?"

"No. We'll give them a little more time. Hopefully, it is all just a case of miscommunication. But I do want you back in the streets. I need to know what's happening in our town."

"Yes, sir," Sal said. He gave a weary salute and headed out of the station.

Mitchell paused for a moment. As carefully as law enforcement had tried to entrap the perpetrator, nothing had seemingly gone as planned—and now possibly more damage had been done. It was becoming all-too crazy like Grogan said. He looked briefly around the room and then started back toward his office.

"Fix another pot of coffee, Patrolman," he said to Grogan. "I've got a feeling we're headed for another long evening."

5:12 PM

Although it took only seconds, to Kate, it felt like forever as she completed her free-fall into the icy waters. She became immediately conscious of three things: she had lost hold of her weapon; her knee had taken a tremendous jolt against one of the bottom rocks; and more to the point: the frigid temperatures had sucked the breath right out of her. She clung to her instinct to survive and broke on top of the swiftly flowing water. She managed to squeeze in a few precious bouts of air among what felt like gallons of water. She placed one foot down on the stream's bottom and then pushed off, lunging forward in a disoriented manner. She slipped again and submerged under water that was so cold, she felt her skin was on fire. She grabbed for an exposed river rock but missed and tumbled again under the current.

It was then that she sensed a hand grabbing the back collar of her coat and lifting her up. She broke from the water and inhaled deeply, coughing and spitting. Johnny was laying on a rock over-hang next to her—his fingers gripped strongly on her coat.

He managed to pull her to the shallows and then jumped in up to his knees to carry her to the bank. He held her there for a moment. She was conscious, breathing, but she was still in bad shape, coughing up water and wincing in pain. A trickle of blood ran from her scalp and her throat. He managed to get her to her feet and helped walk her out to the wood-lined edge of the river. As she oriented herself, she felt her right knee throb with torrential pain. She leaned onto her left side and stood on her own power, but she was shivering, freezing, already suffering from an early stage of hypothermia. Johnny reached in and unbuttoned her soaking coat and carefully managed it around her shoulders and off her bruised arms. He let it fall to the ground.

She looked up at him, pleading without saying the words. Her teeth were chattering; her lips were blue; goose bumps were forming on her pallor skin.

Johnny knew what he had to do, but as he leaned in, he hesitated. He looked into her eyes. "I'm sorry, but I've got to get this off of you."

She nodded, shaking.

He took off her empty holster strap and tossed it. He then snapped her flannel shirt apart. Some of the buttons broke off and scattered to the ground. He gently peeled the rest of the shirt away and pulled her soaked t-shirt over her head. Her sports bra, which covered down to her midriff, clung to her wet skin. He hesitated for a moment but then pulled it up and over her head as well. She grimaced each time she had to raise her arms, but she did not protest.

Kate instinctively wrapped her arms around her chest as soon as Johnny freed her from the garment. He stood close and vigorously rubbed her arms. He then hand-dried her as best as possible, flicking away the moisture from her back and stomach.

With her top as dry as possible, Johnny took off his own coat and carefully slipped it on her arms. In doing so, she had to temporarily expose herself to him. Their eyes met again but nothing was said.

Johnny zipped up the jacket, which hung loosely to the top of her thighs. She was still shivering so he knelt down and removed her boots and wool socks. He reached up under the jacket and unsnapped the button on her jeans. He unzipped the fly and worked her pants down to her ankles. He could see that her right knee was severely bruised and was continuing to swell. One by one, he managed each pants leg around her feet until they were completely free. And then without hesitation, Johnny reached both hands up to the sides of her underwear and quickly rolled the briefs from around her waist to her knees and then to the ground.

She was freezing, still wet, still pleading. Johnny ran his hands quickly up and down her legs, careful not to press too hard around her knee. It was clinical, fast-paced, done with intentions of saving her, yet there she was—shaking and vulnerable—her naked body barely covered by his jacket.

After doing his best to brush her dry, Johnny stood. "Kate? I need to get you back. Can you move?"

Kate moved one exhausted step and winced in pain. Her right knee buckled a bit under the pressure. "I don't know. I don't think so. Not yet anyway." Her voice sounded weak, raspy.

Johnny looked deep into her eyes again. "I'll carry you, Kate. Okay?" She gave a brief nod, signaling need over pride.

"I know your arms are hurting but try to hold them round my neck if you can." Once again, she agreed with a simple nod. Johnny swung his arms up under her and grabbed her from the back. He picked her up and brought her close to his chest. He held her there for a moment, feeling the tremors in her body. He rationalized that he was allowing his body heat to warm her; but deep-down, he knew there was more to it than that.

Johnny carefully maneuvered her around to his back. Kate wrapped her arms and legs around him. He ran his hands down behind him and adjusted the jacket to cover her. After bending to pick up her wet clothes and then positioning her legs in his forearms, he began hiking back toward Amadahy's.

Chasing after Spearfinger, he did not realize how far they had traveled into the forest. As he continued blazing a trail, Johnny figured it must have been well over two miles. He kept a steady pace as he held her close. He knew the longer she was exposed to the elements the worse it would be for her.

He was surprised at how light she felt. She was close to five-eight, but her body was strong and taut, and he could sense her keeping herself from being dead weight. He also felt her breath periodically on his neck—it was warm and soft. Certain thoughts began to creep in and cloud Johnny's mind. He tried to displace them, tried to deny them, but he could not. It took every ounce of control to keep from wanting to stop and lay down with her somewhere in the secluded forest.

They finally reached Amadahy's cabin and found dry clothes and blankets inside. After a brief rest and finding no other mode of transportation, they made their way down the trail to the boat. He had Kate lie down on the bottom and elevate her knee on the front seat as they headed home. Every so often, he would peek down at her in the bottom of the boat. She was quiet for most of the ride in and seemed to be resting comfortably.

At Riverrun they made the change to the Crown Vic and headed back to the Boundary. With Kate propped up in the backseat, Johnny drove and used the car's radio to signal the station and explain their situation. Captain Mitchell informed the SBI who sent a team to swarm the area.

As they neared the town of Cherokee, Kate began to stir.

"Are you okay?" Johnny asked.

She nodded but remained quiet.

"Should we have a doctor look at your knee?"

"No, just take me back to the motel. I think I'll be all right."

Johnny nodded and continued to drive.

"Johnny?" Kate said from the back. Johnny looked into the rearview mirror and caught her stare. "I shot that bastard at point blank range. Right in the chest. Didn't slow him down at all."

Johnny considered her words but said nothing.

Once they arrived at the motor lodge, Johnny helped to usher her inside. He then ran her shower water for her until it reached a luke-warm temperature. Johnny led Kate into the bathroom. He stood behind her as she slipped off his jacket and stripped out of the borrowed clothes. He helped navigate her into the shower. He heard her moan a bit as the water stung and then caressed her skin.

"Kate…?"

"I'm okay," she answered. "I think I can manage from this point."

Johnny walked back into the main room. He sat down at the desk chair next to the bed.

As the water in the shower continued to run, Johnny sensed a deluge of his own chaotic thoughts. Spearfinger continued to be a deep thorn in his side. Five Cherokees and three Caucasians were dead, and he had no answers; he was not even close. And now the witch had gotten away—again. It was his number one priority but there were other problems as well. His people were scared and confused, the town was in disarray, his father was still missing, and Daya was home in a delicate condition—pregnant with his child. And yet despite all of this, he could not get the woman in the next room out of his mind.

There was no doubt that Kate Wilcox was a highly dedicated cop. But she was so much more than that. She was smart, savvy, tough, as well as being a remarkably beautiful woman. And now after seeing her so vulnerable, so much in need of him at that moment, his attraction had grown even stronger.

He knew these thoughts were wrong. He knew he should not act on his desires, his impulses. He knew he should not, but....

The bathroom door opened, and Kate hobbled out, wearing a soft, white robe. Her blond hair was pulled back wet on her head, accenting her beautiful high cheek bones and her stunning emerald-green eyes. Despite her exhaustion, she flashed Johnny a brief smile.

"How are you feeling?" Johnny asked.

"Better." She laughed. "After that shower, much better." She walked gingerly toward him, and he got up out of his chair.

"Do you want me to get you some ice for your knee?"

"No... no, I can get that later. I just wanted to thank you, Johnny. It's not easy for someone like me to admit, but I appreciate what you did for me out there."

"You don't have to thank me," he said softly.

She reached out and grabbed his hand. Johnny felt the warmth of her touch and he rubbed his hand in hers. She leaned in and pulled Johnny a little closer. She pressed her body against his and ran her free hand behind Johnny's neck. Her fingers lingered there, and their eyes locked. Johnny could now feel the heat of her body through the opening in her robe. His heart began pounding. It was now or never—the moment of truth. She pressed her lips against his and he closed his eyes. At that moment, he could not think straight; he felt like he was in a dream world. He held her even tighter, clenching his hands into the folds of her robe. He wanted her badly and was only a moment from tearing the robe from her body.

But then, as he swung her around toward the foot of the bed, Johnny caught a quick glimpse of himself in the mirror. He held his position for a moment and then broke from the kiss. He pulled back and slid his hands onto her shoulders. He gently brushed strands of her hair back over her ears. "I'm glad you're okay. I guess I should be getting back, make our report."

Kate withdrew her hand and forced a smile. "Of course. Go do what you have to do."

Johnny gave a brief nod and then turned for the door. As he reached for the doorknob, Kate called out, "Johnny...." He turned back to face her. She let out a deep breath. "You're a much stronger person than I am."

Johnny shook his head. "No, Kate, I'm not strong at all."

Kate could only nod her understanding. Johnny pulled at the door and then headed out into the cold, Smoky Mountain air.

10:00 PM

The station was a madhouse of activity as the Cherokee police force, National Park rangers and SBI agents had congregated for the latest updates following the most recent witch sighting. The room was abuzz with talk of Johnny and Kate's contact and subsequent pursuit of the suspect in the Nantahala Forest. Spearfinger had taken the life of yet another Cherokee and managed to disappear despite being shot at point blank range. It was a bit much for all to comprehend. And now some of the SBI agents, who had been sent to scout the area, filed back in with little to report.

"Vanished like smoke in the wind," Walker announced for his scout teams. "Whoever it was is nowhere to be found. We left a command team at the last known point. They'll resume search in the morning along with the National Guard's air support."

Captain Mitchell, Johnny, and Sal walked from the far side of the room where they had been studying the wall map of the Nantahala Forest. Mitchell broke away from Johnny and Sal and talked quietly with Walker.

Sal looked to his partner. "You okay? You haven't said much since you've been back."

Johnny shrugged. "Exhausted, man. Been a helluva day."

"Right," Sal agreed but squinted his eyes with doubt.

"Any word on my dad?"

Sal shook his head. "Sorry, man. I checked everywhere."

"What about the fragment of cloth that the Fed found in the woods? Where is it?" Walker asked, engaging the two policemen from across the room.

Johnny looked at the SBI officer. "She lost it when she fell. Lost her gun too."

"And she fired her weapon at him directly?" Walker continued, gesturing with his fingers as if firing a pistol.

"Dead on, she told me. Stunned him for a moment but then he kept coming."

Walker turned back to Mitchell. "Must have body armor of some kind. Something under that cloak. Your mountain witch has thought of everything."

"Yes, well-planned, well-trained, and well-equipped. A protective vest is not something your run-of-the-mill criminal is going to have laying around. Military perhaps? Law enforcement?"

"Perhaps," Walker said indifferently. "But I think we should focus more on motive now." He went over to Sal and hovered over him. "Tell us again about those drawings you found in the museum."

Johnny looked at his friend. "What drawings?"

"I went there looking for your dad," Sal said. "No one was there, but there was a light on in his office. On his desk he had some ancient-looking manuscript—drawings and symbols."

"Of what?" Johnny asked.

"It looked to be several Cherokee warriors, gutted, and hanging from a cliff. Above them was a flying bat."

"A bat?" Johnny sat up in his chair.

Walker focused on the Lieutenant. "Does that mean anything to you—a flying bat?"

"No, but... maybe if I could see this manuscript."

"Right," said Walker. "Why don't we three take a quick trip back over there?"

11:03 PM

"What the hell happened here?" Johnny asked as he stood in the exhibit room of the museum. The overturned pedestal and shattered glass were at his feet.

"It was like this when I first got here," Sal said.

Johnny went to a knee and picked up the broken mask. "It's the Spearfinger exhibit."

"The witch didn't care for her cage, huh?" Walker said.

Johnny searched the floor. "The carving of the finger seems to be missing."

"Is it valuable?" asked Walker.

Johnny stood and grimaced as he thought about the time and effort the artist would have needed to create it. "It's irreplaceable. Like everything else in here."

"If it turns out to be a robbery, we'll help investigate, but we can't worry about that now," Walker said. He turned to Sal. "C'mon, show us these drawings you were talking about."

They entered the lobby but stopped when Sal threw up his hand in alarm.

"What?" Johnny asked.

"The light in your dad's office. I know I left it on earlier."

The three lawmen drew their weapons and cautiously approached the darkened office. Sal stood on the left side of the wall and Agent Walker on the right. Johnny went low, entered the room, and then flipped on the light. Sal and Walker swung in from the outside and covered him.

"Clear," Walker said. He and Sal holstered their weapons and followed Johnny to the desk.

"Where is it, Sal?" Johnny inquired.

Sal ran his hands along the empty top and then went behind the desk. He looked up at Johnny. "It was right here."

11:33 PM

Mary Runningdeer stared up at the ceiling from her bed. She had tried sleeping, but there was too much going on to let her mind rest. She had spent most of her evening preparing a brief to present to the tribal court to have the gaming operations dismissed. She knew the ramifications, the public outcry, but she felt there was no other choice.

She got up as she heard a knock on her front door. She threw on her housecoat and opened the door.

"Eddie Whitetree? What in the world are you doing here so late?"

Eddie slid past the chief without invitation. "Sorry, Mary Ellen, this could not wait."

"You've found something in the book?" she asked as she closed the door behind them.

"No, I...." He hesitated. "It's just... we need to talk."

The chief nodded and led him to her kitchen and a small dining table.

"Would you like some coffee? I could...." Eddie waved off the thought. "What's the matter, Eddie? I've never seen you like this. You're so jumpy—like the rabbit avoiding a fox."

Eddie blew out a breath as he sank into his chair. "That's a good way of putting it."

"Well, what is it?

Eddie looked directly into her eyes. "It's about the casino."

OCTOBER 24, 1995

7:17 AM

"Where the hell have you been?" Johnny demanded of his father. He did not wait for the response and barged into his father's small house.

Eddie closed the door and followed his son into the living room. "I had business in Sylva. Ended up staying the night. Why?"

"Business? What kind of business?"

"I had an accident at the museum—tipped over the Spearfinger display, of all things. I went to Sylva to see if I could get the finger repaired; it has a major crack along the side."

"And you didn't bother to tell anyone where you were going?"

"Sorry, Son, I didn't know I had to."

"Dad, with all the bullshit going on in town, a little consideration would go a long way. I had Sal and the whole force out looking for your ass."

Eddie threw up his hands as if surrendering. "Sorry, Lieutenant. I didn't mean to cause you and Cherokee's finest any worry. I promise I won't do it again."

Johnny frowned but made a conciliatory nod. "Good," he said with a final huff, and then, "At least you're okay."

"I'm fine."

Johnny frowned again, leaned forward, and touched his father's forehead. "What happened here?"

Eddie turned away slightly. "I cut it when I knocked over the display. It's still a little sore."

"Jesus, Dad, you've got to be more careful. My whole life I've never known you to be careless about anything—especially in your museum."

Eddie grinned. "Getting old, I guess. Comes with the territory."

"Yeah, well, keep it up and Daya and I will be sticking you in an old folks' home."

"Dribbling pudding down my chin? Wearing adult-diapers? No way. I'd rather you just stuff me and stick me in the museum somewhere."

They both laughed, easing any remaining tension between father and son.

"So, what did you find out about Spearfinger? When Sal went looking for you yesterday, he said he saw ancient-looking scrolls or something on your desk. We went back for them last night, but they were gone. I assume, now, you were the one who came by and got them. Do they have anything to do with our witch?"

Eddie's smile disappeared, and he rubbed his hand across his brow. "Sa-lo-li saw these papers?"

"Yes. He described a drawing of several Cherokee warriors who had been ripped apart and were hanging from a cliff—a bat circling above them." Johnny paused and then, "What are these ancient papers and drawings? I know you have certain historical accounts tucked away in the museum, but nothing like that."

Eddie turned from his son and paced, rubbing his hands together. "I'm not at liberty to discuss the source, Johnny."

"What…?"

"You must trust me on this, Son. I can't talk about it. And you can't ask me about it. Sorry."

Johnny mused on his father's words and then, "Can you at least tell me about what Sal saw? Is there any significance to the drawings and what's been happening?"

Eddie hesitated in answering. He moved to a little table on the far side of the living room where he picked up a decanter and poured into a glass some homemade scuppernong wine from his own backyard vineyard. He then drained the glass.

"Dad, its 7:30 in the morning."

"Good a time as any," Eddie said without humor.

"Okay, so what is it? What did you discover? What does this have to do with a bat?"

Eddie was deliberate with his words. "It has to do with our tribal system, our clans."

"What about the clans?"

"You, of course, know that the Cherokee have survived into this century with seven clans of which we are all represented, the Ugaya." Johnny nodded, anxiously waiting. "And you also know that these clans have absorbed other clans, from the early times."

"Yes, you told me that there were once fourteen clans in Cherokee history. But they eventually merged to become the seven that represent us now."

"Correct. But what I did not tell you, because I didn't know myself until recently, was that there were actually fifteen clans."

"Fifteen? Another clan from the early times."

"Yes. And this clan was represented by the Tlameha, the bat."

"Okay, an old clan. So, what does that have to do with the Spearfinger witch?"

"According to this source, this ancient clan betrayed their fellow Cherokee in their war with the Spearfinger witch."

"In what way?"

"Again, according to my source, they secretly met with the witch and offered their help in destroying the rest of the Cherokee tribe in return for her sparing of their clan."

"A deal with the devil."

"Yes. So, they helped trap the children of the other clans and offered them up as sacrifices."

"Okay, okay, I get it. But what does it have to do with putting the victims in high places? The sycamore? The top of the house? Sequoyah's Nose?"

"It is the nature of the bat to hang upon the tops of things, so there is that. But more to the point, this was the Tlameha's way of taunting the other clans. The victims were probably placed on high so that the entire Cherokee world would know of their impending doom. And we would know who we had to thank for it."

Johnny's eyes found the floor as he thought about it. "This is an old story, another one of our legends, albeit a hidden one. How could someone from today's world even know about all this?"

Eddie shook his head. "I don't know, Son. Very few eyes have ever looked upon the source of which I speak."

Johnny rubbed at his chin. "Well, what happened to this Bat clan?"

"Again, according to this same source, they were defeated by the Wolf—which no doubt refers to your mother's clan, the

Wolf clan."

"So, the entire Bat clan was destroyed?"

"Most, I believe. However, there is mention of some being chased far away to the caves of the hilltop fire."

"The hilltop fire? Where is that?"

Eddie shrugged. "Don't know. Could be anywhere, really. Remember, this was an ancient tale, an ancient description."

Johnny put his hands on his hips and sighed in frustration. "Okay, so what are we saying here? Based on an ancient legend from a source we can't discuss, there's some serial killer out there, who is possibly a descendant of this Bat clan, who's appearing as the Spearfinger Witch and who's trying to gain vengeance against the remaining clans of the Cherokee Nation? Jesus, we'll really have the FBI laughing at us now."

"Yes, it will take a lot to convince the non-believers."

Johnny laughed. "Hell, Dad, it will take a lot to convince me. None of this makes sense. Let's say for the sake of argument that all of what you told me is true, why would someone affiliated with the Bat clan want to do this now? What possible reason would cause them to commit murder in this century?"

"It's been calculated. A lot of thought and planning has gone into these murders. This isn't just some random nut job out running around."

Johnny shook his head. "It's a lot to process." He paused for moment. "At least we've had the good sense to put a halt on the casino operation for now. No need to pursue that while all of this is going on."

"It's back on, Johnny."

"What is? The casino?"

"Yes, Runningdeer is convinced we should resume the process."

"But, Dad, that seems very callous—all things considered. Besides, Harrah's may not want to even set up shop in Cherokee with all this madness going on."

"We're not going with Harrah's."

"What do you mean? I thought they had been vetted—thought they had the best bid out of the three."

Eddie paused, turning his back on his son. "No, we are going with Pub and Casino America."

"Pub and Casino…? They weren't on the original list, were they?"

"No. They're small, but they can do the job. I think we'll be... very satisfied," Eddie forced out.

"The Council voted for this?"

Eddie turned back around and shrugged. "There won't be a vote on the casino. Chief Runningdeer is enacting special privilege. She's taking it out of the Council's hands."

"Whoa, wait a minute. She can't do that. Can she?"

"Yes. It's in our bylaws. During times of great duress, the Chief can bypass council and enact special laws or, as in this case, go into contract with some entity to benefit the tribe. With the closing of our community and these awful killings, it was determined these conditions met the emergency criteria."

"But that's just wrong, Dad. We've got this unknown out there killing our people—the whole goddamn town is shut down—and our chief wants to shove her casino preferences down our throats now? What the hell?"

"It's the right move, Johnny. It's what must happen."

"And you're on board with this, too?" Johnny asked with disgust. "I can't believe what I'm hearing."

Eddie grabbed Johnny by the shoulder. "Listen to me, Johnny. This need not concern you. You and the police need to focus on stopping this Spearfinger wannabe. Let those in government handle the casino."

Johnny studied his father for a moment and then broke free from his grasp. "You're right about one thing: I do have work to do." He turned to go but stopped at the door. "By the way, you may want to have somebody look at that head wound of yours. Obviously, it's affecting the way you think."

Johnny stomped out and slammed the door behind him. Eddie held still for a moment and then turned back to the table and poured himself another cup of wine.

9:12 AM

Captain Mitchell, cradling a stack of folders, walked from his office into the squad room. He dumped the foot-thick files on Allan Grogan's desk. The young policeman looked up at his boss with wide eyes. "This all for me, Cap?"

"Routine reports, Patrolman. I hate to burden you, but we have everyone else working the Spearfinger case, and someone has to shoulder the load."

"Lucky me," Grogan said with little enthusiasm.

Mitchell nodded his understanding. "Soon, Patrolman. Soon this will be over, and this office can get back to standard operations."

Grogan began sorting through the files. "Yes sir, Captain. Looking forward to that day."

At the same moment, Johnny and Sal walked through the front entrance and Mitchell signaled over to them. "My office, gentlemen."

Johnny entered the office ahead of Sal but stopped momentarily as he saw Agents Davis and Wilcox seated in chairs to the left of the captain's desk. He locked eyes with Kate but neither uttered a word.

Mitchell closed the door to his office as Sal and Johnny took the chairs to the right of his desk. "Glad to hear your father has been found and is well, Lieutenant."

"Thank you, Captain."

"And what is this he has told you which concerns our case?" Mitchell asked as he took his seat behind the desk.

"It's about our clans, Captain. Apparently, our witch is also invoking an ancient killing method of a forgotten clan."

"A forgotten clan?" Mitchell asked.

"Yes, sir. The Tlameha. The clan of the Bat. It was an ancient clan that was terminated before the history of our known clans—before any of our history was recorded."

Davis bumped in his chair with a single belly-laugh. "Okay, I'll ask. If it was before recorded history, how would someone know about it now?"

"My father..." Johnny started. "He has a... different source."

Davis shook his head at the foolishness of it all and leaned back in his chair.

"What was the ancient clan's method, Lieutenant Whitetree?" Kate asked with formality.

Johnny got everyone up to speed with the history of the clan's betrayal and their method of depositing dead bodies. As he gave the details, he kept sneaking a look at Kate who returned his subtle gaze.

"I'm still confused," Mitchell offered. "What's the point here? Why would someone affiliated with this ancient clan want to do this now? Even if all of what the Lieutenant says is true, what could possibly be the motive?"

"That's the million-dollar question, Captain," Johnny said. "No one alive today has any reason to hold such a grudge."

"Unless he's just a whack-job like I've been saying. Dressing up like a witch. Hanging dead bodies from trees," Davis said. "In my opinion, somebody's just taking a deep dive off the reservation." His implied racist remarks drew long stares out of the Cherokee policemen.

"The clans," Kate said, quickly covering. "Which one did the Armstrongs belong to?"

"They were a traditional couple, Agent Wilcox," Mitchell said. "Our clans are matriarchal, and it was once considered bad form to marry into one's own clan. Attle Armstrong descended from the Wild Potato clan and his wife was of the Deer clan."

Johnny picked up on the line of the thinking. "Dan Rowland was from the Bird clan and the young girl, Sherry Simpson, was from Long Hair. The man, who was killed yesterday, Amadahy, was a Paint. I saw the traditional Paint mask in his cabin."

"You think he's targeting specific people based on clan membership?" Sal asked.

"If that's his game, perhaps," Kate said. "He's acting out this Spearfinger angle and is looking to make a statement. He chooses his victims from each clan to gain some kind of misguided justice for what happened to the bat clan." She thought about it and then, "Which clans have not been affected?"

"There's Blue clan—sometimes known as Panther or Wild Cat," Johnny answered. "And then there's my clan, the Wolf."

"This is bullshit," Davis said. "Wolf clan, Blue Paint, Mr. Potato Head clan—who cares? It's just some guy off his rocker—probably toked too long on one of those funky peace pipes you people are always smoking."

Sal jumped to his feet. "What did you say?"

"Sit down, Corporal," Mitchell instructed.

"Mr. FBI son-of-a-bitch here needs to shut his mouth, Cap.

Or maybe he'd like someone to do it for him."

"I said sit down," Mitchell said more firmly. Sal kept his eye on Davis but did as he was ordered.

"Relax, pal. It was just a joke," Davis said with a cross between a smile and a sneer.

Mitchell calmed himself and looked at the FBI man. "Agent Davis, perhaps less jokes and a little more insight from the FBI would be prudent."

"My apologies, Captain," Kate jumped in. "You're right. We need to focus on the case. All of us." She cut her eyes at Davis, who simply shrugged.

"Sir," Johnny said, garnering everyone's attention. "If I may, we should follow Agent Wilcox's suggestion and keep an eye on members of the remaining clans."

"The targeting of certain clans may be coincidental, Lieutenant," Mitchell said.

"Yes, sir, but it's the only angle we have right now. The Armstrongs were an older couple, and our assailant might have known that they were from different clans. The hitmen from Baltimore made the attack on Attle Armstrong easier by dragging him off into those woods—making him vulnerable. Afterwards, Mrs. Armstrong was by herself, grieving—again an easy kill for the assailant. He obviously studied the habits of Dan Rowland and the Simpson girl, knowing when and where they would be before attacking. Getting rid of Amadahy was probably always a part of his plan, using him to forge his weapons, then killing him to keep him silent as well as to knock off another clan."

"The old two birds, one stone saying," Sal threw in.

"Exactly," Johnny said.

"So, he has a manifest of Cherokee names and clan affiliations," Kate said. "A hitlist if you will. He scopes out the clan member most susceptible and then attacks." She paused and then looked to Johnny. "How many Cherokees are in the Blue and Wolf clans?"

"Too many to keep a permanent eye on. That much is certain."

"We could get the official roll from the Tribal Council's office," Captain Mitchell stated. "Review the names, the families. See who is still here in the Boundary; narrow down who might be the most vulnerable of those two remaining clans."

"And in the meantime, this witch of yours continues to run around the Smokies without anyone witnessing a goddamn thing," Davis said.

"Meaning what?" Sal asked with bitterness.

"You need it spelled out for you? Okay. It means that this person goes around committing crimes completely unnoticed by anyone. Which could only mean one thing: this person is like everyone else around here, a Cherokee."

"Perhaps, Frank," Kate said. "Or perhaps we have allowed our prejudices to blind us to what's really going on." She stood and gathered everyone's attention. "When we first got word that Ranshaw's men had been killed in Cherokee, we were sure we knew the assailant's motive. And then as other victims fell, we assumed a crazed serial killer was at work. But the longer I've been here, the less assured I've become." She took a quick glance at Johnny. "Something about these Smoky Mountains, gentlemen. Nothing is as it appears to be."

With the meeting over, Johnny returned to his small office. He sat at his desk, rubbing his hands together, waiting. A few minutes passed, there was a brief knock on the door and Kate entered.

"We're getting ready to head out," Kate said, hobbling toward him. "You said you needed to see me?"

Johnny stood an offered a seat with a wave of his hand. "Yes, thank you."

As Kate sat, Johnny moved to the front of his desk and leaned against the edge. "How's the knee?"

"Hurts like hell. Still swollen, but I'll manage."

"Kate, I'm sorry about last…"

"You don't need to apologize, Johnny. We both got caught up in the moment. We shared a life and death experience yesterday. We were in the trenches together. It happens."

"Yes, but I…"

"Listen, Johnny, you did nothing wrong. And you have nothing to feel guilty about."

Johnny grinned. "So, why do I feel guilty then?"

"Because you're a good person. And that's what good people do, apparently." She stood, reached out, and grabbed Johnny's hand. "Like I told you in the car yesterday, as cops we have to take our moments when we can. Sometimes it works out, but far more frequently it doesn't. You're a good cop, Johnny. And from what I can tell, you're a good husband and father to be. But you're human too. Don't beat yourself up over what happened."

"Still. I feel like you're letting me off the hook."

"There was no hook given." She dropped his hand and took a step back. "We have a case to solve, Lieutenant. That's where your head needs to be right now."

Johnny paused and then nodded his agreement. "Yes, of course. You're right."

Kate made a move towards the door. "We'll reconfigure our surveillance areas once your captain gets us the information on the Blue and Wolf clans. I'll radio Walker and have his men keep their eyes open."

She headed out leaving Johnny still leaning against his desk. He smelled a trace of her perfume and still felt the warmth of her touch in his hand.

Kate limped out to her Crown Vic, slid in, and started the car. She hesitated, glanced at the station, and momentarily closed her eyes. She then banged her fists on the steering wheel before pulling out of the lot.

2:06 PM

Johnny sat in the driver's seat of the patrol car, parked just beyond the Oconaluftee Bridge on Tsalagi Boulevard, looking back towards town. It appeared empty, deserted, a ghost town— he half-expected tumbleweeds to come spinning down the asphalt.

Sal sat on the passenger side keeping the same watch while also digging through a bag of peanuts. He grabbed a handful from the bag and casually tossed them one by one into his mouth.

They watched judiciously; the silence broken only by the occasional munching coming from the big man.

"Stakeouts," Johnny finally said, shifting in his seat to find a comfortable position. "Never liked them. They're so boring, and after a while, my butt goes numb."

"I always liked 'em," Sal said. "Peace and quiet suits me—lets me get in touch with my spiritual side. I'm one mellow dude, Johnny."

"Bullshit," Johnny laughed. "There's not a mellow bone in your body, Squirrel. You're one-part Cherokee and three-parts jet engine."

"May be. But even jet engines have to idle occasionally."

Johnny shook his head. Typical Sal.

Sal yawned and stretched. "What are we waiting for anyway?"

"Movement. Of any kind."

Sal frowned. "The tourists are gone. The shops are closed. The only movement we're gonna see is the river sneaking below us. The town is dead, Johnny. We should at least be sitting in a residential area somewhere watching houses."

"The FBI and SBI have those areas covered according to Kate," Johnny said. He then corrected himself, "Agent Wilcox."

Sal caught his friend's eye. "Uh, huh. So, tell me about this Kate. Agent Wilcox, I mean."

"What about her?"

"What happened out there, Johnny?" He paused and then added, "I'm not the most observant person around, but I saw the way she was looking at you in Cap's office. And the way you were looking back."

"It's nothing. We just shared a tough situation together yesterday. That's all."

"You and I have shared tough situations too, Johnny. I don't remember you looking all googly-eyed at me after."

"Just drop it, Sal."

"As I told you before, she's an attractive woman, Johnny. You wouldn't be the first…"

"I said, drop it!"

For the next minute, both men stared out the patrol car's windshield in icy silence—the trickling of the Oconaluftee below making the only notable sound.

Johnny sighed and then spoke, "Look, man. I'm sorry. It's just... I don't know how to handle this, okay?"

Sal nodded. "How far did it go?"

"Far enough."

"Do you care for this white woman?"

"She's special, Sal, but no, not like that. We had a moment together, and I just hate that I let it get to that point, you know? I mean I'm in love with Daya—she's having my child. Why in God's name would I want to screw that up?"

Sal turned and leaned up on the middle console. "Listen to me, Johnny. You're a smart man, perhaps the smartest I've ever known. And you've always had the instinct to gravitate toward what's most important in life. That's a good thing—a real good thing. I've known Daya since we were kids. She's a great person too—smart, funny, kind-hearted, and, if you don't mind me saying, one hot little lady. And I've seen you two together. How you do things for one another. It's a relationship anyone, including an asshole like me, would die for. Your life with Daya, in my humble opinion, is pretty sweet. I think that this thing with the FBI woman was just a bump in the road, a temporary moment of insanity, a slip. It doesn't define you or your relationship with your wife. So, let it go and move on." He waited and then added, "Besides, if I thought you ever did do anything to hurt Daya, I would kick your stupid ass from one end of the Boundary to the other."

Johnny stared at him for a moment—finally a slight grin waxed across his face. "You always know what to say, don't you, partner?"

"Yes. Yes, I do," Sal said.

Johnny nodded a wordless bid of thanks.

Itching to move on, Sal leaned over, offered the bag, and had Johnny fish out a couple of peanuts. "So, is that the area there?" Sal asked. He pointed out his window at a cleared lot down the road.

"For the casino?" Johnny asked. "Yeah, that was the intended spot, originally. But with this new vendor now, who knows."

"What new vendor?"

"Dad told me this morning that Chief Runningdeer is going with a new outfit for the casino operations... uh, Pub and Casino America."

"Pub and Casino? Can't be, Johnny. That's Ranshaw's operation."

"What!?"

"Yeah, it was in the report the feds gave us on the two vics killed with Councilman Armstrong. Ranshaw is listed as their CEO. I'm sure of it."

5:17 PM

In his spacious office filled with colorful and museum-worthy Native American artwork, Vernon Early stepped out from behind his handsome oak desk and moved to a plate glass window, overlooking the Toe River. There, an antique serving table held an array of fine liquors. He poured a half glass of twelve-year-old scotch and downed it.

Early was a beefy man of 50 with a dark complexion and grey-streaked spikey hair. His matching peppered beard stubble was but one indicator of another long day of waiting. He put down his glass, clasped his big hands behind his back and rocked on his heels as he watched the flow of the river below in the dying light of the late afternoon.

A knock on his office door interrupted his thoughts.

"Come."

The door swung open. Andrew Connors, Early's assistant, a much younger, thinner man, entered. He stood at attention, waiting for his boss.

Early held his position at the window. "You have some news?"

"SBI completed their search of the Nantahala Forest. They found nothing," Connors said.

"Have you heard from him?"

"He's back at the safe point, waiting for instructions."

"The Boundary will be crawling with cops and agents now. Tell him to be patient. Tell him to wait a few days."

Connors frowned. "We may not have that much time. Runningdeer appears to be moving ahead with her plans. They're looking to schedule a meeting in a few days with a casino operator."

"A few days? Damn this insufferable woman! What's it going to take to stop her!?"

Connors thought momentarily and then cleared his throat.

"Perhaps, Mr. Early, it's time to up the ante and provide a more powerful consequence to their unwarranted actions."

7:32 PM

Eddie answered the door on the first knock. He took one look at Johnny and Sal standing on his front porch and smiled. "What took you so long?"

"You were gonna take on the Ranshaw mob all by yourself?" Johnny asked.

"They threatened the entire family, Johnny. I didn't want to risk telling you until I had a plan figured out."

"So, do you have a plan?" Sal asked.

"I think so," Eddie said. "But it's going to be risky. And we're going to need a lot of help."

OCTOBER 28, 1995

10:11 AM

Four tension-filled days later, and everything was set. Mary Ellen Runningdeer looked every bit the tribal chief as she sat behind her desk. She wore a black and red traditional Cherokee Tear Dress, black and red headband, and was draped with her thirteen turquoise and gold beaded spirit necklaces. She rested her arms on the desk with her hands out flat trying to get her breathing under control. Next to her stood Eddie Whitetree who was wearing a suit and tie for the first time in years. He lightly drummed his fingertips on the desktop.

"I don't think I can do this," Runningdeer said.

"Yes, you can. It will all be over in a few minutes."

The chief closed her eyes and offered a silent prayer.

Without any warning, the door to her office opened and Ranshaw's meaty front man, Jess Cooper, walked in. He leered in the Cherokees' direction, then moved off to the side and stood. Joe Ranshaw followed. He was dressed plainly, white shirt and brown slacks—a heavy winter coat hid his smallish frame. Without being offered, Ranshaw took the chair closest to the desk. He sat there smugly like a king awaiting his coronation. His eyes settled on the chief.

Another older man, also white-haired, but dressed smartly and carrying a briefcase, was the last to enter. He approached Runningdeer and stood momentarily with his arms at his side. "Chief Runningdeer, I'm Gerald Koch of the Furlong and Koch Law Firm in Baltimore. We represent Pub and Casino America and Mr. Ranshaw's interests in this matter."

Runningdeer rose and offered her hand which the man shook. "Welcome to Cherokee, Mr. Koch..." She looked to the man in the chair. "...Mr. Ranshaw. May your visit here today prove enlightening."

"Thank you, Chief," Koch said as she returned to her chair. The man laid his briefcase on the desk, unfastened it, and flipped it open. He pulled papers from the case. "As I understand it, you have bypassed the Tribal Council and are acting as sole authority here today—a capital idea in my opinion—much more expedient that way. So, in light of this, we have prepared a standard transitions and percentages contract for today's signing, giving Pub and Casino America the rights to operate in Cherokee." He looked to Eddie. "Your lawyer and I can hammer out the boring details of the actual running of the casino, the physical properties construction, management, and all gaming operations after this brief formality."

"But I'm not a lawyer," Eddie said. "I'm Eddie Whitetree, a local businessman. I am here solely to support our chief."

"Oh? I'm sorry. I thought we made it clear you should have the tribe's lawyer present for this meeting, Chief Runningdeer. We have an enormous amount of contract lines to cover."

"It won't be necessary, Mr. Koch," Runningdeer said. "We will not be signing a contract with Pub and Casino America or any of Mr. Ranshaw's enterprises."

Koch made a face of disgust. "I'm sorry… what?"

"You heard our chief," Eddie said, sneaking a glance at Jess Cooper. "We will not sign a contract with you—today or ever."

"What is this?" Ranshaw hissed from his chair. "What the hell do you mean, you will not sign?"

"Chief Runningdeer, this is highly unusual," Koch interjected. "Did we not get a verbal commitment from your office as of yesterday? Is that not why we are all here?"

"Yes, but to put it succinctly, sir, I've changed my mind," Runningdeer said with bravado.

Koch turned, looked at Ranshaw in disbelief, and threw up his hands.

Ranshaw stood and glared at the chief—fire in his eyes. He leaned over and pressed his hands on the desktop. "You're making a huge mistake."

"I can live with that," Runningdeer said.

"Are you sure? I'd hate for anything to happen to you or this fine, little Indian town."

"Are you threatening us, Mr. Ranshaw?" she asked, fighting a slight quiver on her lip.

"Take it as you will, Chief. Bows and arrows are no match for what I can bring to the table."

"Bows and arrows? You underestimate the modern Cherokee,

Mr. Ranshaw."

"No, woman, you underestimate me," Ranshaw said, thumping his chest with his fist.

"Well, then, it sounds like we have nothing further to discuss."

Ranshaw turned, caught Cooper's eye, and then looked back at Eddie. "And what about you, Whitetree? Do you have anything to say?"

"Yeah," Eddie said. "Go fuck yourself."

Ranshaw flashed his teeth in contempt and then stormed out.

Koch gathered his things and followed Ranshaw. Cooper hesitated, taking a long look at Eddie, and then slithered out the door as well.

After the door to her office closed, Runningdeer made an exasperated sigh and sank into her chair. She looked to Eddie. "You better be right about this."

Outside the chief's office, a grey and black Stretch Limo awaited. The attentive driver opened the back door for Koch and Ranshaw and both slid in. The door was shut but Ranshaw lowered the window as Cooper approached.

"Goddamnit, Jess," Ranshaw said through clenched teeth, "you gotta right this ship and quick, you hear? I want that redskin on his knees begging us to come back."

"Our man is in position," Cooper said, leaning into the open window. "All we need is your go-ahead."

"Do it. Kill that pregnant bitch."

10:42 AM

Hiram Espinoza lowered the binoculars after seeing movement again behind the curtain of the kitchen window. He had been in position since 4 A.M. and had seen her shadow through that window curtain several times over the past hour. And now that his contact had given the go-ahead, he readied himself for the perfect kill shot.

Espinoza was an accomplished killer having performed plenty of assassinations for mob reprisals and for helping, as he put it, "... rich people get rid of their problems." Although he had never met the man, he had been hired by Ranshaw for two other hits in previous years. Espinoza was not cheap, but he was efficient. And Ranshaw preferred efficiency.

He moved his German-made Blaser 93 Tactical sniper rifle into position. The hill behind the woman's cabin was steep, but there was enough of a ridge for him to lay flat and make the 200-yard shot with ease.

His right eye went to the rifle's sight, and he leveled the weapon to take in a small section of the kitchen window. His right finger tapped lightly on the trigger. He slowed his breathing. He was ready.

Only ten minutes had gone by when her shadow appeared again. She seemed to be standing right in front of the little window, perhaps washing dishes.

Cleanest shot I've had in a long time.

Espinoza zeroed in on the top of the shadow, came down just a hair, and then without any further hesitation, he pulled the trigger.

The shot rang out, echoing throughout Deer Gap Hill. Through his sight, Espinoza saw the broken windowpane, the hole in the curtain, but no more of the woman's shadow. The deed was done.

He needed to confirm the kill, but he waited twenty minutes before moving. No one came to investigate the shot, so he finally rose. He grabbed his pistol from his equipment bag, attached a silencer, and made his way down the leafy slope. Save one motorcycle chained to a post, the driveway next to the isolated cabin was empty of vehicles. He had seen the husband leave in his patrol car at 6 AM, and no one else had come by.

Espinoza made it to the cabin porch. He then eased the door open and looked inside. He saw no movement and continued into the cabin. He bypassed the den area and made his way into the kitchen. There he saw the result of his shot spread out all over the floor.

But there was no blood, no bone, no tissue, no woman. In their stead was an orange, pulpy mess—a mix of a shattered rind, a wig, and the straw body of one of the town's Halloween scarecrow props.

"You owe me one jack-o-lantern, you son of a bitch."

Espinoza turned to the voice behind him but only in time to

feel Johnny's knuckles smash into his cheek and right eye. The assassin was knocked out immediately and crumbled to the floor.

Johnny stood over the unconscious man and kicked him in the ribs until he heard a crack. Resisting the urge to beat him further, he forced handcuffs on the man then retreated to the den and collapsed into a chair.

From a side table, he picked up a framed photograph—he and Daya on a day hike at Clingman's Dome in the park, taken the day he proposed—and traced her outline with his finger. He felt a rush of emotions overcome him. Pent up feelings of guilt, anger and now overwhelming relief came pouring out.

Daya and his soon-to-be-born child were safe with friends just over the mountain in Maggie Valley. Part one of his father's plan was complete.

12:05 PM

Jess Cooper sat at the bar in the mostly empty Dragon's Breath Saloon and ran his thumb up and down the cold bottle of beer as he waited. Once word reached Whitetree about the death of his daughter-in-law, the old man would run back to him, begging to spare the rest of his family, and pleading for Ranshaw to return. Today was just a hiccup. They would get that contract soon enough.

Just as that thought crossed his mind, Eddie Whitetree appeared at the door. "We need to talk," Eddie stated weakly.

Cooper smiled, took his time to down the remainder of his beer, and then headed for the Cherokee. "Sorry about your loss, grandpa, but you can't say I didn't warn you."

"Let's do this outside, please," Eddie said with a long face.

Cooper shrugged and followed Eddie through the saloon door.

"What's this?" a startled Cooper asked. In the parking lot before him, Little Elk and ten members of the Nunnehi awaited—all were wearing the red and white warrior face paint, and all were holding either chains or tribal war clubs.

"It's your day of reckoning," Eddie said as he turned, drew a .38 from his waistband and pointed it at Cooper's head. "But you can't say I didn't warn you." Eddie leaned in, fished

Cooper's pistol out of a holster inside his coat, and then backed away.

Cooper dropped to his knees as the Nunnehi began to encircle him. They made the high-pitched war cries of their ancestors as they tightened the circle. "No, wait, you can't do this," he pleaded. "Ranshaw made me do it; I swear. It was on his orders. It was all Ranshaw!"

A push in the back sent Cooper face-first into the gravel of the parking lot. A kick from a boot drew blood from his mouth.

He managed to get to his knees again, wiping away the blood. "Please, stop, I'll do anything."

And then a moment of relief as he saw Sal in his police uniform breaking through the throng of Cherokees and approaching. "Thank God. Officer, sir, please help me…"

"Sorry, pal. I'm off duty now. Just here to get a cold one," Sal said as he continued into the Dragon's Breath.

1:02 PM

Ranshaw sat in the limo and stared out the window. They were heading up squiggly Soco Road, looking to connect with the interstate and the road back to Maryland. It had taken nearly ten hours to get to Cherokee from Baltimore, and the prospect of driving another ten long hours without the Cherokee's casino contract in his pocket would have been enough to leave Ranshaw pissed as an angry hornet. But the old man knew Espinoza was his ace up his sleeve, and he would soon have what he wanted.

His lawyer, not knowing of Ranshaw's backup plan, wasn't as calm about the day's events. "I'll file for breach of contract," Koch said, sitting next to Ranshaw. "We had a verbal agreement with these people. They won't get away with it."

"Don't worry about it. Them red bastards will be singing a different tune by the time we roll into Fredericksburg. I suspect we'll be heading back down here tomorrow."

"I have court tomorrow so I may not be able to do such a quick turn-around. We may have to wait on the contract until next week."

Ranshaw cut his eyes at his lawyer. "You'll go whenever the hell I say we go. Got me?"

Koch smiled contritely, gave a slight nod of understanding, then eased back into his seat.

"Mr. Ranshaw," the driver called out, "blockade ahead."

As the limo came to a halt, Ranshaw leaned up and looked through the windshield. A line of flashing blue lights emanated from several Cherokee police cruisers and SBI vehicles, which had cut off all access to and from the mountainous road.

FBI Agents Wilcox and Davis led a group of well-armed lawmen in surrounding Ranshaw's limo. They had their weapons brandished and aimed at all vulnerable points. The driver hopped out with his hands held high and was taken away by two SBI agents.

Kate opened Ranshaw's door and then held out her badge. "FBI. On the pavement, Ranshaw. Let's go."

The old man eased out the limo and took an up-and-down look at Kate. "Well, lookie what passes for FBI these days. Hell, sweetheart, I would stop for you any time."

"Flattered," Kate deadpanned as she put handcuffs on him. "You're under arrest, Ranshaw—for extortion, racketeering, attempted murder and a helluva lot more. You have the right to remain…"

Ranshaw's eyes went dark as he jumped her words. "You got nothing on me, missy. I'm just out here on business—we're cooking up a deal down here."

"There's no deal, Ranshaw. You're finished. We've got your hitman and your other goon, Cooper; both are primed to give you up real fast. The only deal you'll be cooking will be in a prison kitchen. Now, do you want to hear your Miranda rights, or not?"

Ranshaw held still for a moment and then yelled back into the limo. "Get out here, Koch!"

The lawyer slid out, nervously straightened his tie, and cleared his throat, "I would strongly encourage you to stop and desist with this illegal action against my client at once."

Davis stepped in and pushed Koch back toward the limo. "Back up, asshole—unless you want to join him in the lockup. I suggest you head to the FBI offices over in Asheville; that's where your client is headed."

As Wilcox ushered Ranshaw toward her waiting Crown Victoria, Chief Runnindeer, escorted by Captain Mitchell, broke through the police line, and approached the Baltimore crime lord. Ranshaw forced Wilcox to a stop so he could confront the chief.

"Come here to gloat, squaw bitch?" Ranshaw asked.

"No. But I do appreciate the irony," Runningdeer replied.

"Irony? What are you talking about?"

"For centuries many have come down this road thinking they could waltz into Cherokee lands and take whatever they wanted. But they were often stopped here on Soco—never to be heard from again. And now you, Mr. Ranshaw, will share that same fate."

"Think you're clever, Chief? Well, let me tell you savages something: this ain't over. This ain't the last you'll see of me; I promise. You're in the casino business now. Your problems are just beginning." Wilcox began dragging Ranshaw to her car. "Just beginning… do you hear?"

"And so are yours, Ranshaw," Runningdeer said. "You may have avoided a scalping from us savages today, but what awaits you in prison will be far worse."

5:42 PM

In the dying light of the late afternoon, Wilcox and Davis drove back to Cherokee and parked on Seven Clans Road in front of the police station. As they got out of the car, they noticed Johnny and Captain Mitchell standing nearby.

"Ranshaw squared away?" Mitchell asked the approaching agents.

"Being processed now. Hopefully, this will put him away for a long time," Kate said. "What are you two up to?"

"Waiting on Corporal Beck to return from the Dragon's Breath Saloon," Mitchell answered. "Tying up some loose ends."

Kate nodded and then looked to Johnny. "Your wife okay?"

"Yes. Sal and I were able to sneak her to a friend's house late last night. She's going to stay there until things calm down a bit."

She hinted a smile. "Well, we appreciate your efforts in this case. The FBI owes the Cherokee Police, as well as your father, a huge debt of gratitude."

"Yeah, you boys did pretty good," Davis added.

Johnny almost laughed at Davis's concession. "Glad to help." He then searched Kate's eyes for any lingering emotions, but she remained unwaveringly stoical.

Almost immediately, everyone became focused on Sal as he pulled up in Johnny's patrol car. He hopped out, opened the back door, and pulled out Angelo Moore and Marcos Armstrong—both were handcuffed.

Captain Mitchell approached them and forced Marcos to stop and look him in the eye. The young man's face was wet with tears. "I didn't mean to get anyone hurt, Captain, especially my grandparents. But it's my fault. I couldn't help myself." He gasped at the realization of his actions. "Please, forgive me."

"You have gone down a path from which you cannot return, Marcos, and I am sorry for the choices you have made. I only hope that you will get the help you so desperately need in the years to come. But I cannot forgive you—only God can do that." Mitchell turned to Sal and said vehemently, "Get him out of my sight."

Sal grabbed both men and hauled them inside the station. Mitchell went back and stood with the others.

"Sorry, Captain," Johnny said. "I know you were close to the Armstrongs."

"Yes, it's another sad chapter in this unfortunate case. But there are still too many unanswered questions. Too many loose components. I can't help but still feel unsettled."

10:38 PM

Agent Davis walked the brief corridor from his room to that of his partner and gave the door a series of knocks. Kate answered quickly. With the day done, she was dressed for the night in shorts and an oversized grey t-shirt emblazoned with the FBI Academy insignia. Davis stood momentarily, taking an uncomfortable linger at his partner's legs.

"What's up, Frank?" Kate hurried out.

"Oh, well, I thought you should know Jess Cooper has given up everything on Ranshaw. He's looking to make a deal."

"Is he still in the hospital?"

Davis laughed. "Yeah, he'll be taking his dinners through a straw for some time now. Those Indian boys did a helluva job on the guy."

Kate only nodded at the good news.

"Between him and the punks at the bar," Davis continued, "Ranshaw's got no place to hide. We've got the subpoenas to search his home, his lawyer's office, the liquor store, everywhere. It's over."

"Good."

"Yeah, which also means our time here is nearly done. We can probably be outta here in a day or two."

"What are you talking about, Frank? Ranshaw might be out of the picture, but that killer is still out there running around. Until these murders in the Boundary stop, we're not going anywhere."

"I just got off the phone with Quantico. There will still be an FBI presence here, but our team is being recalled. Besides, it's a local problem now. A Cherokee problem. And they've got the state police. Walker can handle it."

"Bullshit. These people need our help. They helped us with Ranshaw, remember? Now it's our time to do the same."

Davis diverted his eyes from her gaze. "Are you sure about that? Are you sure there's not another reason why you want to stay?"

"What are you implying, Frank?"

"Nothing. It's just… I know you've gotten close to these people, the cops, Whitetree in particular. Sometimes we lose a little perspective…."

"Listen to me," she said, cutting him off. "I don't know what you think is going on, and quite frankly, I don't care. But this case is not over, and I plan on seeing it through. If you want to take off, then go. I don't really give a damn."

She slammed the door shut.

11:09 PM

SBI Agent Sonny Walker hiked up a turn on Yellow Hill Road near Spray Ridge to better observe the three houses across the gorge in this residential area of the Boundary. With his night vision goggles, he could continue to keep a close watch on the homes of the Williams, Baker and Crowe families—all three members of the Blue clan. Their houses were a stone's throw from one another and shared a single road access. Walker was informed of their unwillingness to leave the Boundary and figured them to be an appropriate target.

He left the safety of the road and chose a spot on a rock ledge that jutted from the hill. He climbed to the edge and sat with his legs hanging over the side. He pulled his stogie from a jacket pocket, popped it in his mouth, grabbed his goggles, and, as he had done for the past two nights, he began his watch.

He scanned around the houses, the yards, down forest paths and the along the twisting road. Everything seemed settled, deserted, empty. Prior to taking his position, he had run through his call-in rotations with his field agents and found the rest of the neighborhoods to be quiet on all fronts as well. With Ranshaw's influence now muted, he wondered if this witch business might be over too. He hoped so. This had been a strange and difficult case, dealing with the different personalities of the law enforcement agencies, the bravado of the mafia wannabes and all of the tribe's idiosyncrasies. And despite all the clan history surrounding the case, he agreed with FBI Agent Davis that this was probably the work of some psychopath who had no larger purpose than just being a pain in the ass.

Walker tilted his head slightly when he heard a rustling noise to his right. It sounded heavy coming through the brush—perhaps a deer or even a black bear walking through the fAllan leaves. As Walker craned to hear more, the noise stopped. He hesitated for a moment, but his curiosity got the best of him and drew him off the rock ledge. He ditched his cigar and made his way past a gnarly cluster of yellow poplar trees and held for a minute, straining to hear. The noise came again, but more to his left and deeper in the brush. Walker pulled his .357 Magnum and penlight from his belt and scanned the dark avenues before him. He traveled just a few feet more before the bush became impenetrable. He perused the purple darkness of the night, listening.

The noise came again—heavy-footed, close. Walker turned all about, unable to pinpoint the source's exact location. He cocked his weapon and held it and his flashlight straight in front of him. He then turned to look behind him.

The strike was lightening quick. By the time Agent Sonny Walker realized what had happened, his life was at an end. He dropped his weapon and collapsed onto the ground—blood seeping from the massive wound to his abdomen. He took a final breath and was gone.

Leaving the SBI agent dead on the ground, Spearfinger completed the night's objective by going back into the brush and returning moments later with a long rectangular box. Using the same rock ledge that Walker had used, the witch crawled out to the end, dragging the army-green rectangular box.

The box was opened, and a Mk Shoulder-Launched Multi-purpose Assault Weapon was quickly assembled. The witch then sighted the target across the gorge—not at one of the houses grouped together but at the large, massive rock face in the hill above them.

OCTOBER 29, 1995

2:15 AM

Johnny stepped out of the patrol car and stared in amazement at the destruction before him. All three houses in the Yellow Hill Subdivision had been crushed by the landslide. The roofs were pocketed and caved, splintered lumber was scattered about, and glass from broken windows lay on every inch of the ground. It was near impossible for Johnny to tell foundation rubble from the rockslide which had crushed it.

Emergency vehicles and concerned neighbors jammed the cordoned off area. Johnny squeezed his way past the crowd and made his way under the yellow tape.

A frantic neighbor was describing the events to Captain Mitchell. "I heard the whistling noise and then the explosion," the old man described. "Sounded like the loudest clap of thunder you ever heard in your life and then the rumbling—as if hell had opened up and was swallowing the earth whole."

Mitchell nodded as his eyes searched the hill face from where the giant rock once stood. He then turned and searched the darkened hillside across the gorge. "And this took place around midnight?"

"A little before," the old man confirmed. He shook his head. "Ain't never heard nothing like it."

Mitchell thanked the man and then escorted him back behind the tape. The captain then saddled in next to Johnny and lowered his voice. "This is insane, Lieutenant. A forced rockslide to kill our people?"

Johnny pointed to a sizeable rock slab. "Part of her legend, Captain. Spearfinger was known for moving large boulders through her magic and tossing them at her enemy."

"Some type of launcher was used—military grade," Mitchell said. "This has gone way beyond a serial killer. We are at war."

"But with who?" Johnny asked. "And why?"

"I have no idea. But we must protect our town—the Boundary. We should have the governor send in the National Guard."

As Johnny mused on the logic of such a move, Kate Wilcox

arrived; her somber expression was very telling.

"They found Walker," she said. "He's dead. He's got a fist-sized hole in his midsection. Mitchell briefly closed his eyes at the tragic news, but Johnny kept his focus squarely on Kate.

"Agent Davis and a couple of the SBI guys are still up there looking for evidence, but so far, it's clean. How about down here?"

"We are in the process of searching the rubble. But no signs of life yet," Mitchell said.

"What about the taunt? Is there an indicator of the bat somewhere?" Kate asked.

Johnny indicated the wreckage. "Massive deaths on the hillside. I'd say this time no taunt was necessary."

"These families were all the same clan?"

"Yes, they were all A-ni-sa-ho-ni, Blue Holly. Which leaves only one clan left untouched: my clan, the Wolf."

9:12 AM

Chief Runningdeer grabbed at the bottom folds of her dress and hiked them enough so that she could clear a line of the rubble and still maintain a hold on the jug of water which she held in her left hand. She made her way to each of the emergency personnel and volunteers, who were helping to clear the night's destruction, and offered a quick drink from the jug. Their faces told the story: anger, exhaustion, depression. It was all too distressing for the chief, but she felt it was the least she could do for her people.

"Chief Runningdeer!" a voice called out from beyond the police line.

Runningdeer passed off the jug and made her way over to Ken Wilkes, who stood with his arms crossed. "Mr. Wilkes, from the look on your face I'd say you have more bad news. And to be honest, I don't know if I want to hear it."

"You don't," Wilkes agreed. "And I don't want to give it to you. But you will find out soon enough."

"Out with it then."

"The Bureau has been in touch with the national office in DC. Concerns for the safety of the Eastern Band have grown exponentially the last few days. Changes are being mandated."

"Changes? What kind of changes?"

"Leadership. Direction. All protocols."

Runningdeer searched the thin man's eyes. "What are you saying, Deputy Director?"

"You're out, Chief. You and the entire Council."

"Out? On whose authority?"

Wilkes took a breath and then tried to placate Runningdeer by using a poised tone. "The National Director, Andre Hampton, has been following things here closely. It's just gotten to be too much. These awful murders, the destruction, the criminal element. Things are wildly out of hand." Wilkes briefly lifted his glasses to rub his eyes in melodramatic fashion. "I'm afraid he's decided to terminate the Boundary's autonomy until at such time that it can be returned to the Cherokee people."

"We're guaranteed our authority. The seal from the United States government is in my office. You can't do this," Runningdeer said sternly.

"It's just temporary, Chief. Your autonomy will return when things calm down—a few months to a year at the most."

"A year? And who the hell is to govern during the interim?"

"The Bureau will step in – our regional agency. Me, specifically."

Runningdeer stood slack jawed for a moment as Wilkes's words hung in the air. She glanced behind her at the work crews as they continued their search. Then, with heavy resignation, she turned to face him again. "These are good people, Mr. Wilkes. They don't deserve this. As I told you before, my administrative position means nothing to me if my people are being harmed in any way. I will do what's best for the Tsalagi."

12:44 PM

Kate cinched her raincoat tighter as she emerged from her motel room. The grey, misty morning had turned darker, and the cold rain was falling with greater frequency. In the motel's breezeway, she noted Agent Davis standing there with his luggage at his feet.

"Heading out?" she asked.

"Cab's on the way. Got a flight in three hours. There's some follow up the head office wants me to do on the Ranshaw case. How about you? Where are you headed?"

"Station house. Picking up Whitetree. We're going back to Yellow Hill—see if anything else has been found." She paused and then, "I asked McQuillen if I could stay on for a few more days. He agreed."

Davis nodded as he watched the rain pour off the roof. "FBI should be sending another investigative team over from our satellite office in Asheville in a day or two. Hopefully, they'll be able to help you out—find this wacky Indian killer."

Kate looked at her partner of three years with a mix of disappointment and disdain but held her words in check. "I'm sure the people of the Boundary will be thankful for any help we can give them."

Davis agreed but thought about it for a moment more. "Be careful with this one, Kate. It's really not our fight."

"Only if we run from it," Kate said before heading out into the rain.

2:23 PM

Despite an important client still on the line, Vernon Early hung up on him as his assistant Andrew Connors entered the office and moved before Early's desk.

"Well?" Early asked.

"It's done, sir. Cherokee is out of the equation. Wilkes will be running things for now."

Early grinned and leaned back in his chair. "And the proposal?"

"We may still need more time. The Bureau has all the necessary papers and now it will come to a vote. You know, without the Baker Roll, it's going to be an uphill battle."

"We've got thirteen blood samples verifying our status, and I've put plenty of grease into the right pockets to get past that. Those sons-a-bitches at the Bureau better not disappoint me." Early leaned forward again, elbows on his desk. "I'm already in talks with several casino venders who are itching to get the bid."

"I should warn you about putting that cart before the horse," Connors said diplomatically.

Early frowned and slapped his hand down hard on the desktop. "To hell with that! This needs to happen before Cherokee gets back on its feet!"

"Of course, sir. I'll see what I can do to expedite the process."

"Good. You do that."

Connors turned to go but pivoted back again. "And what about our man in Cherokee? Should we call him off?"

Early hesitated to answer. He stood and looked directly behind him. On the wall was an oversized and ornate clan mask of the Tlameha. Like the ceremonial masks of the seven clans of the Cherokee, this red and black mask had its own distinction: bat wings extending from beneath the eye holes and off the sides. Early ran his hand down the mask in a reverent manner. "No. He has one more job to do."

4:45 PM

Johnny stood at the pay phone outside a dark and closed Bearmeat's Indian Den. The cold wind and heavy rain had intensified out of the Smokies, and he pulled his jacket tight around the collar.

"Hey," he said into the phone, "I just wanted to check on everything. You okay?"

"I'm fine," Daya said. "I don't like being away from you, though. Can I come home now?"

"Uh, not yet. It may be a few more days."

"A few more days? I thought this was over, Johnny. Sa-lo-li told me they have Ranshaw and all his men. Why can't I come home?"

"It's not safe, Daya. We still have someone running around, acting like Spearfinger, committing these awful crimes." He thought better of giving any of last night's tragic details. "And I can't do my job and worry about you home alone with this going on. You do understand, right?"

Daya sighed and then, "Yes, of course. But just hurry up, will you? Get this guy as soon as possible." She then added with mock authority, "You read me, Lieutenant?"

Johnny smiled as the rain came down a little harder. "I will. I promise. Gotta go, okay?"

"Yes, okay. Love you."

Johnny looked up at the Crown Vic parked on the side of Soco Road and then back to the pay phone. "Love you, too." After hanging up, he made a mad dash to the passenger side and slid in.

"How is she?" Kate asked.

"Good. Anxious, but good."

Kate only nodded as she pulled onto the road. "So, where to now?"

"Back to town. The Cherokee Inn."

"What's there?"

"Our tipping point hopefully," Johnny said.

Kate turned to him and merely raised an eyebrow.

Johnny continued, "My dad and Chief Runningdeer were sure that whoever was behind Spearfinger would make their purpose known. And they believe they have this morning."

"How so?"

"Power, Kate. It's always about who's in control."

"I don't follow."

"Ken Wilkes, the Deputy Director of the Eastern Region of the Bureau of Indian Affairs, just relieved Runningdeer and her Council of their authority here in the Boundary."

"He can do that?"

"Apparently so. Said it came as a mandate from the National Office. Because of all the recent events."

Kate shook her head. "Leave it to us feds."

"But it wasn't the feds—at least it wasn't their idea initially. It came from our regional office, from Wilkes himself. My dad has friends in the national office who let him know."

"So, why the power grab? What's in it for this Wilkes guy?"

"Don't know, but that's why we're headed to the Inn—he's staying there."

"You going to beat it out of him?" Kate joked.

Johnny maintained his focus on the road ahead, "Whatever it takes."

5:12 PM

Sal's poncho served two purposes: protection from the rain but also from the forest's prickly briars and thorns. He made his way to the open area that he and Johnny had come to before. Little Elk was already there, huddled around a smoky, rain-pocked fire. The old man wore no raincoat and was dressed in buckskins with ceremonial paint on his face.

Sal took a seat opposite the elderly Cherokee and pulled the poncho from about his head. "I received word you wished to see me again, Little Elk."

"Yes, Sa-lo-li. Thank you for coming. I hope it was not too much trouble."

"No trouble at all. What is it I can do for you?"

"I understand we have lost more of our brothers last night. In Yellow Hill?"

"Yes. Three families. All A-ni-sa-ho-ni. All Blue."

The old man sadly nodded at the news. He poked at the fire with a stick. "It is as I have feared. The killings have continued. And it is the work of Utlunta, yes?"

"Yes, we believe so," Sal paused to correct himself. "Well, someone who is pretending to be the witch at least."

Little Elk shook his head. "No, this is what you and the police do not understand. It is the Spearfinger witch. It is Utlunta."

Sal smiled a little. "What I meant, Little Elk, is that the murders are being committed by someone who is using her legend, her methods of attack—to get inside our heads."

"No, Sa-lo-li. You are like many of our younger Cherokee. You know of our stories, our traditions, our words, but you do not believe them. You do not know how they work in our world. It is Utlunta that you seek."

"I'm sorry. I don't understand."

"Centuries ago, many brave warriors sought out the witch to end her terrible reign against our people. Much had to be sacrificed; she was eventually driven away to live in the tree shadows and the black smoke of the fire. But true evil never dies. It is a battle we must always face. Always."

"Yes, but I don't think…"

Little Elk stood and looked down on Sal. "Seek the Spearfinger, Sa-lo-li. Seek the witch and you will find your killer."

5:28 PM

Kate and Johnny climbed the stairs to the second level of the Cherokee Inn, a fifties style motor court on the southside of Cherokee. They stopped in front of room 202. Johnny gave the door a quick knock, but there was no response.

"Not here," Kate said.

"He's probably still at Runningdeer's office, playing chief. Let's take a peek anyway."

Kate frowned. "Might need a warrant for that."

Johnny smiled. "Look the other way, Agent Wilcox." He then popped the door open with a bump of his shoulder.

They both entered. It was a simple room; neatly maintained: clothes on hangars in an open closet, the queen-sized bed fastidiously made. Kate looked in the adjoining bathroom as Johnny focused in on the ordered desk next to the bed.

"Anything?" Kate called out.

"No, just your fairly standard-looking motel room," he said checking the desk drawer. Johnny then rifled through the man's clothes in the closet and then took a quick peek under the bed. "Got something. A briefcase," Johnny said, as he brought it from underneath the bed. "But it has a lock."

Kate reentered the room and joined him at the desk in studying the black leather case. "Combination lock. Any guesses?"

"We could start at zero-zero-zero."

"Or..." Kate began. She grabbed a paper clip, straightened it, and worked it into the tumbler.

"What about that search warrant, Special Agent?"

Kate kept her attention on the tumbler but grinned at the question. "Let's just say your discovery methods seem to be way more time-efficient, Lieutenant."

After a few more seconds, the tumbler latch sprung open, and Kate dumped the contents on the desk. They scanned through various paper elements: addressed envelops, file folders and a cache of Bureau forms. Johnny found a map and spread it out on the end of the bed.

"Whatcha got?" Kate asked.

"Mitchell County map. It's in the upstate—about two hours away." He studied it further. "Large area circled near the town of Bakersville—several numbers and notes in a shorthand I'm unfamiliar with. How about you?"

"Kate brought several of the papers over and sat on the edge of the bed. "Lots of official-looking paperwork, but I don't know what it is. Some kind of application. Tribal forms. What is the Toe River Valley Tribe?"

"Toe River? That's in the upstate too. It's the headwaters of the Nolichucky River. Eventually flows into the French Broad."

"Is there a Cherokee tribe there?"

"No…."

"Says Cherokee on this form."

Johnny sat down next to Kate and perused the paper for a moment. He then looked up at Kate and grinned. "I think you may have found the tipping point."

10:16 PM

Captain Mitchell rubbed his hands together as he paced back and forth behind his desk. He paused momentarily and then turned to the others gathered in his office. "That's a very interesting development, Lieutenant. But I need to know what it means."

Johnny, who was standing near the office door with Kate and Sal, moved between the guest chairs in which Chief Runningdeer and his father were sitting. "We aren't sure of everything, Cap, but it seems to all of us that this may have been the reasons for the murders in the first place: disrupt the Boundary, throw everything into chaos, give this other group time to organize into tribal status."

"They have caused chaos exponentially, that much is certain. But for what purpose?" Mitchell followed.

"Thievery, Captain," Runningdeer offered. "If our hands are tied for the next several months, this new group could get at the head of the line for the development money for expansion, create a new reservation, perhaps even set up a casino as we were doing. Build hotels, new access roads, restaurants, and the like around it. We're talking tens of millions in possible revenue that should be going our way."

"Still, that wouldn't stop us from having our own casino eventually, would it?"

"The Bureau's grant money is earmarked for a certain period," Runningdeer said. "Plus, we have several other loans tied into our completing the casino project. Needless to say, we would have to start all over. It may be years before we could get that kind of investment together again."

"And by that time," Eddie jumped in, "the new tribe would be well-established, exceeding our success in a fraction of the time, stealing our thunder, so to speak."

"And who are they?" Mitchell asked. "What tribe are we talking about?"

Johnny looked briefly at Kate and then his father before answering. "They're a non-established group, seeking confirmation now."

"But under what lineage?"

"Cherokee, Captain. At least that's what we saw on the form."

Mitchell shook his head. "No. They would need to establish historical bias, be on the Baker Roll. You can't just claim to be a Cherokee and open your own Boundary."

"What is the Baker Roll?" Kate asked.

"It was an act of Congress in 1924 which established an enrolling commission to determine membership in the Eastern Band," Mitchell stated. "This group would have to be on it in order to be considered Cherokee."

"Unless you are Cherokee, Captain," Johnny said. "At least in your DNA."

Mitchell's eyes lit up at the realization. "Our long-lost clan? The Tlameha?"

"Which would explain a whole helluva lot if true," Eddie said. "They would know the Spearfinger story, for sure, and perhaps their own part they played in its history."

"Unbelievable..." Mitchell said. "And exactly who is the lead claimant for these newly discovered Cherokee?"

"Someone named Vernon Early from Bakersville—owns a rock quarry near Roan Mountain," Johnny said.

"I've asked the FBI to look into him," Kate added. "See what else we can find."

Mitchell paused for a moment as he processed it all and then looked directly at Runningdeer. "What do you think, Chief?"

Runningdeer managed a smile. "It seems a bit of a stretch, doesn't it? But at the same time, it makes a lot of sense: a wayward clan with a grudge, symbolically killing their fellow Cherokee to halt our progress, with a pot of gold waiting for them if they succeed. All I know, Captain, is that we can't let that happen."

"If any of this turns out to be true," Kate said, "you'll have the full backing of the FBI; that I promise."

"Thank you, Agent Wilcox," Mitchell said. "I would like for you and Lieutenant Whitetree to come up with a contingency plan for engaging these brothers of ours. We have every right to confront them, but I want to do it in the correct manner with the law on our side."

Kate and Johnny both nodded.

"And what of our witch problem?" Eddie asked. "As far as we know, Spearfinger is still out there."

"Maybe we've been doing that part wrong, Captain," Sal said, leaning up from off the wall and finally engaging in the conversation. "We've been waiting around for the witch to come to us. Maybe it's time we went after her."

OCTOBER 30, 1995

6:23 AM

Johnny and Sal came out of the station doors in step and headed for the parking lot. Sal had his leather chaps back on and held his bike helmet under his arm. Both had on their heavy Tribal Police jackets as the mountain temperature had dipped below freezing.

"Are you sure you want to do this alone?" Johnny asked.

"I travel faster alone, Johnny. I can cover more ground."

"Whiteside Mountain has a lot of ground, Squirrel. Even more than you can cover. And I doubt Spearfinger is gonna leave out any this way signs pointing you to her doorstep."

"I'm just gonna poke around, Lieutenant. According to the history and your father, it was her home during the ancient times. We have nothing else to go on right now. Who knows? Maybe I'll get lucky," Sal said as he jumped on his Harley and fired it up.

"This person has proven to be extremely dangerous, Sal. Do not engage if you do come across something," Johnny said above the bike's roaring engine.

Sal rolled his eyes to the unsolicited advice. "Yes, Mother, I promise." He slid on his helmet, gave the throttle a quick punch and peeled out of the lot.

Johnny laughed to himself and shook his head. Typical Sal.

A few seconds later, Kate pulled up in her Crown Vic, stopped near Johnny, and powered the passenger window down. "Ready?"

"Yeah. Let's do this," Johnny said as he climbed in.

Kate pulled the search warrant from her coat and flashed it for Johnny to see. "Good for forty-eight hours. Had to bend a lot of arms and convince a lot of minds at the US Attorney's office just to get probable cause."

"If we're right about this, a lot of heads are gonna roll."

"Let's start them rolling," Kate said as she brought the car onto the street, heading north from the sleepy town.

9:13 AM

Eddie Whitetree and Mary Ellen Runningdeer walked into the Tribal Council House and discreetly made their way to the chief's private office.

Ken Wilkes pushed his glasses further up the bridge of his nose as he looked up from behind the desk. "Chief Runningdeer, Mr. Whitetree, I am surprised to see you."

"Bet you are," Eddie said.

Wilkes smiled and stood. "What can I do for you two?"

"Well, for one, you can get out from behind that desk; give Chief Runningdeer her office back."

Wilkes smiled and then cleared his throat. "I think I made it clear to our esteemed chief yesterday that we had to make drastic changes to the Eastern Band's operations. Because of recent events, of course." He turned his attention to Runningdeer. "Did you not tell Mr. Whitetree what transpired?"

"Oh, yes, I told him," Runningdeer said. "But that wasn't quite the truth, was it?"

"Excuse me?"

"You failed to mention that this was all a ruse for our supposed long-lost brothers on the Toe River," Runningdeer said.

"Quite the plan actually," Eddie added. "Distract the Eastern Band with all this Spearfinger business while pushing through the North Toe River Tribe as an official bloodline—a Cherokee bloodline. So, they can then claim tribal property and start their own reservation. Maybe build a casino up there and get the jump on us? Was that the endgame?"

"I don't know what the hell you two are talking about. I was ordered by the National Bureau to take…."

"Save it," Runningdeer spit out. "We know all about it, Wilkes. You manipulated the BIA so you could take over in Cherokee. And you pushed the Toe River application quickly to the front of the line. The FBI and the Cherokee Police are on their way to the Early Quarry as we speak."

"This is insane. I don't have to listen to this."

"You betrayed the Cherokee people, our history, our blood," Eddie said. "You have invited a murderous line back into our fold." Eddie leaned on the desk. "You took a vow to support our heritage. What happened?" He added, "How much does your integrity cost anyway?"

"Get out of this office. I have jurisdiction here. I have orders from the Bureau."

"You are a fool, and a disloyal one at that," Runningdeer said. "You get out."

Wilkes snorted a laugh. "Right. And who's gonna make me? You two?"

"No, I will," Captain Mitchell said as he stepped into the office with armed Patrolmen Allan Grogan and Maury Tobias behind him. He pulled out handcuffs from his belt. "Deputy Director Wilkes, you are under arrest."

10:32 AM

Kate floored the Crown Vic up the squiggly mountain highway toward Spruce Pine, North Carolina, taking what little pavement the curves allowed. Johnny sat in the passenger seat and was skimming the FBI's file on Vernon Early.

"Ten years in the Marines as an explosive ordnance disposal tech—honorable discharge. Some questionable business practices and a few squabbles with the IRS, but not too much criminally on Mr. Early," Johnny said.

"Check out the family history," Kate said. "That's where things get interesting."

"Why? What's up?" Johnny asked, while flipping back through the file.

"On his father's side, he had a great uncle named John Early. Like most of the family from previous generations, he was just a poor, dirt farmer who had settled near the creek lands of Roan Mountain. But this uncle had a couple of screws loose. Hacked a bunch of the locals' farm animals, raped some poor girl, and nearly wiped out an entire family with an axe. Back in the day, the papers called him the Roan Butcher."

Johnny furled his brow. "Hmm. Yeah, I remember hearing something about that."

"Strange case. I studied it in one of my behavioral analysis courses at the Academy."

"So, a little craziness runs in his blood, but what about the

Cherokee connection?"

"That we have nothing on. We were able to trace back four generations but that's where things get hazy."

Johnny mused on the information. "My guess is that, if he is indeed a Cherokee descendant from the bat clan, there are other families in the area with the same genes. It would give their claim greater validity."

"If everything is going according to plan, Captain Mitchell should be putting an end to those claims as we speak."

"Yes, but its more than that, Kate. It's a four-hundred-year-old grudge that this group harbors. They aren't likely to give up on this so easily."

"We'll be ready for them no matter how they react. Our Critical Incident Response Group is meeting us in the town of Spruce Pine. The CIRG team is highly trained; they'll be ready for anything."

Johnny looked out the window as they passed another dangerous curve. "I sure as hell hope so."

10:45 AM

Sal had driven to Cashiers, North Carolina, in under an hour; but once he passed the Whiteside Mountain sign and turned toward the Georgia border, he slowed down considerably. He was not sure what he was looking for, but he kept his eyes peeled, nonetheless. He made many side trips down dirt road annexes and stopped at plenty of scenic overlooks to summon his intuition, but nothing was coming to him. The whole Nantahala Forest seemed empty, like an old, abandoned house. No signs. No indicators.

She's not showing herself.

He finally pulled in at the trail head to Whiteside Mountain. Even from where he parked his bike, he could make out the sheer cliff faces of the mountain. They embodied their namesake as a brilliant whiteness gleamed from the massive stone surfaces. Sal had learned at early age that these were the highest cliffs on the eastern side of the Mississippi River, and he had heard many tales of rock climbers who had challenged those slick cliffs and lost.

Momentarily, he felt foolish for even thinking he could find anyone hiding out in this vast wilderness, but he had come this far, so he decided to give it a go. He secured his weapon in his side holster, grabbed his canteen, and headed down the rocky trail.

The main loop was a two-and-a-half-mile trail that took hikers through lush forests, filled with towering hemlocks, white snakeroot, and speckled wood-lily, to ascend to the cliff views at the top. He and his brother had camped there several times before, so he knew the layout well. He marched up the headway's steep incline and crossed a small split-log bridge until the path flattened out a bit. Sal went at a snail's pace, checking around every boulder, fallen tree, rain sluice, and black bear path along the way.

Eventually, he made his way to the top of the loop trail and went out on the precipice of the highest cliff. Elevation at the top reached nearly 5,000 feet, and he took in the impressive view, looking back at what had at one time been all Cherokee land. The fall leaf colors rolled like ocean waves in the forest canopy below. He felt the connection that most Cherokee do—the natural world was a part of him—as much a part of him as blood and bone.

He pulled out his canteen and leaned against an oddly shaped boulder. The winds were wicked and were biting through his heavy coat. As Sal took another quick sip from his canteen, he thought about all that had transpired over the past few days. It seemed so impossible, and yet it was very real. And now here he was, on top of Whiteside Mountain, looking for the Spearfinger witch.

Where are you, Utlunta?

And then, in a moment of infinite improbability, she appeared before him.

2:30 PM

Agent Kyle Crabb, the leader of the FBI's Critical Incident Response Group, hopped out of the black Tahoe and was the first to be seen by Johnny and Kate, who were standing patiently in the Ingles Grocery parking lot in the mountain town of Spruce

Pine. Crabb was an impressive sight in his military fatigues, a six-four athletic type with dark hair, beard, and dark sunglasses. Five other agents from CIRG soon joined behind him, exuding the same success through readiness vibe that their leader possessed.

"Good to see you again, Agent Crabb," Kate said, shaking the man's hand.

"You too, Agent Wilcox. Been a while."

Kate indicated Johnny behind her. "This is Lieutenant Whitetree of the Cherokee Tribal Police. He's been handling the investigation in the Boundary."

Crabb gave him a brief nod but refocused on Kate. "We've got a scout team already at the quarry. We're ready for whatever play you have in mind."

"We've expedited a warrant to search the quarry offices," Kate said. "Lieutenant Whitetree and I will make the call on Early. Just have your group in position in case we need backup."

"Expecting any fireworks?" Crabb asked.

"If our theories are correct," Johnny jumped in, "and Early is the man behind the madness in Cherokee, he has motive, money, and enough fireworks, as you put it, to come out swinging hard. So, yeah, it's a possibility."

"There's a stability question, too," Kate added. "We're not sure how he is going to act when confronted."

"Understood," Crabb said. He pulled a walkie-talkie from his belt and held it up. "We'll only be a call away. Give us the signal, and we'll come running."

2:57 PM

Thinking he had spotted the black cloak and hood of Spearfinger darting around the base of the cliff, Sal had thrown down his canteen and had gone to a prone position. He army-crawled to the edge of the precipice and surveyed the 750-foot rockface below. He held this position for hours awaiting some type of confirmation. As time wore on, he began to doubt himself; perhaps it had just been some type of large prey bird, maybe a falcon, as they were known to habitat there. But then it happened again: He saw the black tip of the hood sticking out from a protruding ledge in the middle of the white cliff.

Gotcha!

Sal quickly traversed back down the trail and made a stealthy approach, forging his own path. He was now crouched deep in the underbrush of the cliff. He could hear Johnny's words in the back of his mind admonishing him not to confront the witch alone, but this was an opportunity too good to pass. He pulled his Sig 9mm and crept forward through the entangling mountain laurel and other dense foliage, keeping his eye on the bottom ledge of the cliff. His movements were slow and methodical, but he could not prevent the occasional rustling of the leaves.

He finally made it to the base, a narrow ledge with jagged rocks, a few sparse, weedy plants and a harrowing drop off to the forest floor below. Above him was 100 yards of the cliff face that looked damn near impossible to climb, but that was the general area where he had seen Utlunta. He searched along the bottom looking for the best avenue to the top. As he maneuvered to the far-left side of the rock face, Sal spied a climbing rope tucked away in one of the crevices of the giant rock.

No broom needed for this witch.

But as he moved forward to grab the grey nylon rope, Sal was unaware of the taut trip wire hidden at his feet.

3:11 PM

"Here he comes," Kate said to Johnny.

The guard at the entrance to the Early Quarry just outside the small town of Bakersville, North Carolina, walked back from his small post hut to Kate's car. He leaned his meaty form into the open window. "Mr. Early said to send you through." He pointed across the quarry. "Follow this road to the main office building. It's at the top of the next hill, right on the river."

Kate gave a quick nod and sped off in the office's direction. Stacks of stone slabs in wire cages and piles of loose rock surrounded industrial warehouses as they navigated the dirt road.

"Kind of surprised he agreed to speak with us," Johnny said.

"He doesn't know what we know," Kate said. "I imagine he'll change his tune soon enough."

Kate followed the guard's instructions and they arrived at the office building. It was tastefully constructed, built with stone material from the quarry but with only two scrawny crepe myrtle trees, loose sod and several boxwoods comprising the otherwise barren landscaping. The Toe River did indeed snake past the back side of the building, contrasting with the harsh look of the quarry.

Early's assistant, Andrew Connors, led them to the grand office in the back. Kate and Johnny took in the stately room, noting the wealth of Native American sculptures and paintings throughout. Johnny zeroed in on the dark tribal mask behind the desk, where the man sat signing papers.

"Mr. Early? Special Agent Kate Wilcox, FBI," she said, approaching his desk and offering her hand.

Early stood and shook her hand, but he eyed Johnny warily. "What's this all about, Agent Wilcox?"

"We understand you are filing a tribal application with the Bureau of Indian Affairs to establish a presence here on the Toe River."

"Yeah, so…" Early said to Kate but kept his eyes squarely on Johnny. "Nothing illegal about that."

"No, sir. Are you aware of a Mr. Ken Wilkes? He's the Bureau's deputy director of the Eastern Region—he covers tribal matters for North Carolina."

Early stiffened, frowned and then shrugged his shoulders. "I have had dealings with him. He's handling our application, as a matter of fact. Why? What's going on?"

"Cut the shit," Johnny finally said. "You know exactly what's going on."

Kate stopped Johnny with a raised hand and continued, "Mr. Early, are you aware of what has been happening in the Boundary of the Cherokee's Eastern Band? The murders that have taken place down there?"

Early, still triggered from Johnny's tone, took a moment to settle himself and then said in a calm voice, "Has nothing to do with me. Nothing to do with the Toe River Tribe."

"Sir, it is our belief that Mr. Wilkes was acting under your direction to take over in Cherokee—to delay their establishment of a tribe run casino so that you and your interests could formulate your own reservation here."

"Nonsense, Agent Wilcox. What would we care what happens in Cherokee? Why would that have anything to do with us?"

"It is believed that the land grant money that was earmarked for the Boundary's expansion plan would be redistributed to you if the Cherokees waivered and the Toe River were to soon receive established status."

"That's crazy. What evidence do you have to make such a claim?"

Kate pulled several papers from her jacket and placed them on Early's desk. "The Toe River Tribe application, Toe River's request for the same expansion money, and correspondence from you to Mr. Wilkes—all but outlining your takeover plan of Cherokee."

Early laughed, turned his back to them, and moved to the antique serving table near the window to pour a glass of whiskey. "This is ridiculous. I had nothing to do with what's happening down there. I work and live here in Bakersville—never even been down to Cherokee. And I have plenty of witnesses to that fact. Our attempt at tribal establishment is based on family history."

"And what history is that exactly, Mr. Early?' Kate asked. "It's my understanding that tribal formulation is a rigorous process. It requires quite a bit of evidence."

Early turned back to face them and sipped his whiskey. "We have our histories and traditions—passed down through generations. And we have the most important evidence of all, our blood." He then emphasized, "Cherokee blood."

"You mean the tainted blood of the tlameha," Johnny shot back, pointing to the clan mask on the wall.

Early glared at Johnny, downed the rest of his drink, and stepped toward him in an imposing manner. "And just who the hell are you anyway?"

Johnny held his position and looked him dead-on. "Consider me the wolf at the door, Mr. Early. I've come to finish the job."

Early fumed in silence for a moment, then dismissed Johnny with a muffled laugh, and turned back to Kate. "This is beyond absurdity, and my patience is gone. I want you two out of my office."

"Can't do that, sir. This is a warrant from the US Attorney's office to search your offices and all buildings here in the quarry. I would advise that you adhere to it," she said, handing him the paper.

He looked at it briefly, shook his head and handed it back to her. "Okay, Agent Wilcox, you win. Have a look around. Look in our files and warehouses. Go through it all. I won't stand in your way. But you'll just be wasting your time."

Vernon Early walked confidently past Kate and Johnny and out the office door.

In the front reception room, Early saddled in next to his assistant and whispered, "Call all the brothers now. Tell them to prepare for war."

3:41 PM

Sal came to. He tried to move but was unable. His back was broken—he was sure of it. His internal organs were ruptured; he could feel the blood pooling in his body. He blinked the blood and dust from his eyes and tried to focus on his surroundings, but all he could see were hints of the cloudy sky through the brush and rock which had impacted him.

He then remembered Utlunta and reaching for the rope, but there had been a flash of white light and an explosion which lifted him off the ground and sent him careening to the forest floor some three hundred feet below the cliff face. More rock and debris followed on top of him, adding to his torment.

Sal's breathing became quick and shallow. He lay as still as possible, hoping that death would take him soon. But then he heard someone approaching. He managed to look down toward his broken legs and saw the witch towering over him.

At first, Utlunta showed him the sharp rock finger from underneath the black robe, but then it recoiled. The witch held still for a moment and then used the opposite hand to reach up and remove the black cowl.

Even in his weakened state, Sal recognized the person in front of him—the thin, greasy hair, the wiry but muscular physique, the scruffy beard on his chin. "Rob Conroy," he managed.

"Glad you remember me, Corporal Beck. And, of course, I remember you," Conroy said. "You got me twice for possession and once for B and E, ain't that right? Busted my brother's nose once too as I recall."

Sal winced in a moment of pain and then, "Why?"

Conroy laughed. "Why? Why do you think? Money, of course. Some Injun wannabe in the upstate paid me a ton to dress up in this Halloween costume. Trained me for weeks. Gave me all kinds of weapons and toys to screw with y'all—made my two years in the Army time well-spent. He also sent me a list of those he wanted out of the picture. But truthfully, I couldn't stand you red niggas to begin with, so killing Cherokees was an easy choice."

"You're going down," Sal said weakly.

Conroy laughed again. "Not likely. I got one more payment coming and then I'm gone. You won't see my white ass around these Smoky Mountains ever again. Tribal police should never have messed with us—should never have messed with us Conroy boys. We gonna be your undoing."

Conroy knelt near Sal's head. He pulled out the nine-inch spear-finger from beneath the cloak; a hideous apparatus attached to his hand via a series of leather straps on his wrist and forearm. He held it up so Sal could see. "Tell me one thing before I rip open your gut and snatch out your liver, Mr. Policeman. You wouldn't happen to be from the Wolf clan, would ya?"

Sal had no strength left to muster words, but his eyes burnt right through Rob Conroy's soul.

"I'll take that as a yes," Conroy said.

6:15 PM

"And what is this one?" Kate asked.

Andrew Connors had just entered Early's office with another box of files and put it with the other stacks. "More transactions, receipts, billing—that sort of thing."

Kate marked the box and wrote down his response on a clip board. "And don't forget the company's computers. The FBI will be taking those as well."

"You'll have to give me a little more time for that," Connors said.

Kate shook her head. "Ready or not, they're going with us."

"This is all bullshit," Johnny said, leaning against Early's desk. "Receipts, billing… we're not gonna learn anything from this. We've got to tie him in with Spearfinger somehow. There must be some private files somewhere. A diary of some sort or a day-to-day journal. Where would your boss keep those?"

Connors turned up his shoulders. "I have no idea what you're talking about. This is all our company's information." He then exited the room.

"He wouldn't keep it out in the open," Johnny said to Kate. "We're not looking in the right place."

The realization came to them at the same time as both looked to the Tlameha's ceremonial mask. Johnny moved to the wall and removed the mask from its mount—a combination safe was hidden in the recess of the wall.

"Bingo," Johnny said.

As he placed the mask on the desk, Kate joined him, and they both tried to open the safe.

"Locked," Johnny said. "I don't think your paperclip trick is going to work on this one."

"That's okay," Kate said. "The warrant will cover the contents of the safe as well. We'll pull the whole damn thing from the wall if we have to."

At that moment, the lights in the office building went out, throwing them into complete darkness. "Shit," Kate said as she instinctively dropped to one knee and grabbed her radio. "Crabb? What's happening?"

"The whole quarry just went down," Crabb said over the com. "And it looks like several trucks and vans are heading through the south gate."

Early sat in the passenger seat of the lead van—a loaded .38 in his right hand. "Get in and get it done as quickly as possible," he commanded to the three Tlameha clan members behind him.

"What do we do with the bodies?" one of the hulking figures asked.

"Throw them in the van. Evan can take the fed's car. We'll take 'em to Roan—stage a little accident on the mountain road. Some gas and a match should do the trick."

184

"Others will be coming," another warned. "They will press for a full investigation into the deaths of two cops."

Early nodded. "By that time, we will have sealed the cave and separated ourselves from Wilkes. We'll leave no trace."

Despite the darkness, Johnny and Kate worked quickly and efficiently. They jammed the antique table up against the door and flipped Early's desk on its side to act as protection. As they crouched behind the impromptu barricade, Kate went to her walkie-talkie.

"Crabb, if any shit goes down, we are in the main office in the back of the building."

"Copy that," he replied. "We've got a team approaching the back from the riverside, but we won't be able to cut them off from the front entrance in time. They should be coming… any second now."

Johnny and Kate heard the squeal of tires and the slamming of the vehicle doors. Heavy footsteps in the connected hallway were next and then someone rattling the locked office door.

Kate reached out and lightly touched Johnny's shoulder. "Get ready," she whispered.

Within seconds, bullets from the blowback-operated TEC-9s whistled through the office door, shredding the antique table. Each successive blast of rapid fire lit up the room. The weapons went silent as two of the Tlameha began kicking away the frame of the shattered door and remnants of the table. Johnny took advantage and rolled over to the left side wall of the office and popped up into a kneeling position. He then sensed the two men enter and opened fire—head high. As they returned fire, Kate stood and joined in with her .40 Smith & Wesson. The two intruders were confused by the source of fire and the hesitation cost them as they both crumbled to the floor.

"Kate!" Johnny barely got out as a third man broke through, spraying his bullets all over the office.

Kate dove behind the desk and managed a floor-level shot toward the assailant. His knees buckled as he grabbed his ankle. She fired again hitting the man in the chest and ending his life.

Two more rushed the room and fired. A bullet caught Johnny

in the shoulder sending him spinning to the floor. Before the two had a chance to do any more damage, red laser dots emanating from outside the window crisscrossed the intruders' targeted chests. In no time, an array of bullets penetrated the window glass and found their marks, cutting the men down.

Kate held her position behind the desk, holding her breath, straining to listen for any other movement in the building. A few more seconds ticked by, and then she heard more glass from the office window shatter. As she rose, she saw flashes of three CIRG members hoist themselves through the opening. Each had weapons raised and was equipped with night vision goggles. A penlight came on and the beam fell on Kate's bruised and bloodied face.

"Agent Wilcox?" CIRG member, Agent Hank Seaton, called out.

She nodded. "I'm okay." She turned to the darkness. "Lieutenant? Johnny?"

"I'm here," he said as he appeared beside the desk.

"Sir? Are you injured?" Agent Seaton asked.

"My shoulder, but I'll live. What do we do now?"

"We wait here until we get the all-clear." Seaton handed his penlight to Kate and joined his two other team members guarding what used to be the doorway.

Kate shone the light on Johnny's shoulder and lifted a flap of his tattered shirt. "Looks bad, Lieutenant. But don't worry; we'll get you fixed up now that the cavalry is here."

"Well, generally speaking, that's not something you ever want to say to a Native American, Agent Wilcox."

They both managed a laugh despite their exhaustion.

"What's happening? What's taking so long?" Early said from inside the van. The driver just shook his head.

A round of fire shattered the window of the truck next to them. "What the hell? Who's shooting at us?" Early craned his neck in all directions, looking for the source. "Something's gone wrong! Let's get outta here!"

The driver cranked the engine and threw the van in reverse but then held his position. Slowly, he raised his hands from the steering wheel.

"What are you doing? Didn't you hear me? Let's go!"

But then it too became clear to Early as red dots crisscrossed his chest. He raised his hands as Agent Crabb swung open his door and pressed the nose of his Colt M4 assault rifle into Early's cheek.

OCTOBER 31, 1995

5:25 AM

Paramedic Jan Stephenson of the Mitchell County Emergency Management team re-wrapped the bandage on Johnny's shoulder. She took her time, making sure the blood had stopped seeping through the cotton and heavy gauze. "It looks okay for now. But like I told you earlier, you'd be better off getting this checked out at the hospital. You're going to need stitches."

Kate handed Johnny his shirt and watched as he slipped it on. "She's right you know. We can handle things from here. Why don't you go to the hospital? Get that taken care of."

Johnny hopped off the long table in the conference room which they had been using for triage after the night's events. "And miss out on all the fun? No way."

He and Kate walked out the conference room and into the hallway of the quarry's office building. Shattered glass, bullet casings, destroyed furniture, fallen ceiling tile, chunks of drywall, and shredded lumber littered the hallway. To them both, it looked like a scene from some over-the-top war movie.

"What's the final count from last night?" Johnny asked.

"Five dead. Thirteen arrested. All transferred out except for Early. It could have been so much worse though; those boys were packing a lot of heat."

"What's the inquiry process on shootings with the FBI?"

"Long and slow. We'll be doing interviews and paperwork for the rest of the year, I'm afraid."

"Where's Early now?"

"He's in his office. We're keeping him here until we can get into that safe."

"Good. Let's go have a word."

As Kate and Johnny entered Early's wrecked office, they found the man sitting in a folding chair in the middle of the room, his hands cuffed, and two deputies from Mitchell County warily watching over him. At the wall safe, two tech agents from the

FBI's Science and Technical Branch were working the locks and hinges with an array of drills and prying tools.

A bit dazed, Early looked up at the approaching cops and growled, "I want my lawyer."

"She's been in contact," Kate said. "She said she'll meet you at the complex just as soon as we are finished here. And you don't have to say a word until then." Kate paused and leaned over—nose to nose with Early. "But maybe you'd like to do yourself a favor and help yourself out now."

"What do you mean?"

"Attempted murder of two law officers is not going to go well for you," Kate said.

"We heard there was a break-in in the building," Early hastily explained. "That's why…"

"No, Early, that's not going to fly, and you know it. But tell us what you know now and maybe we can help you out later."

"Tell you? Like what?" Early demanded with bitterness.

"Like who the hell is Spearfinger?" Johnny jumped in, taking Kate's position. "And how did you know about the Tlameha clan in the first place?"

Early narrowed his eyes at Johnny. "Go to hell."

"Listen, Early, there's twelve people dead in Cherokee because of you. Five of your people from last night are also gone. You better start talking or you're gonna pay the ultimate price for all of them."

"I've got nothing to say to you."

"Agent Wilcox…" one of the FBI techs began. Everyone turned their attention to the wall safe. "We've got it."

The safe had been cracked; the opened door hung off its hinges. The blood in Early's face drained, and he lowered his head.

Kate moved to the safe, donned gloves and began inspecting the contents. Wrapped in a white cloth, she found several large pieces of pottery, arrowheads, a worn battle hammer, a stone necklace and even a deteriorated wooden blowgun—all significantly aged. She carefully bagged the items and handed them off to the techs. She then pulled out the last item in the safe, an eighteen-inch, slender tube. She held it up to the light.

"What's this?" she wondered aloud.

Early looked over but then almost immediately hung his head again.

Johnny moved closer. "Looks like an anti-degradation cylinder." He put on gloves and took it from Kate. "My dad has a few of these in his museum. He uses them to store writings from long ago—those that might become oxidized and are in danger of falling apart."

"Should we open it?" Kate asked.

"If we do, we may lose whatever is inside." Johnny thought about it for a moment and then walked over to stand in front of Early. "I've got a feeling I know what's in here, but maybe we should just go ahead and open it anyway. Is that what you want?"

Early cut his eyes up at Johnny—his hatred was pronounced, but he maintained his composure. He finally stood, rousing the deputies behind him. "There is no need," Early said with resignation. "I will show you."

9:45 AM

Captain Mitchell stopped at Allan Grogan's desk; the young patrolman was once again manning the phones and had the receiver pinned to his ear. He covered the mouthpiece with his hand.

"Yes, sir?"

"Any further word on Lieutenant Whitetree, Patrolman?"

"He's still at the quarry, helping with the FBI's interrogation of the quarry owner. He's refused to go to the hospital for his wound," Grogan laughed. "Sounds like our Lieutenant, eh Captain?"

Mitchell shared a quick smile with Grogan. "Keep me informed, Patrolman."

"Yes, sir."

Mitchell continued past the desks in the control room and past the offices in the back. He came to the end of the hallway where a holding cell, complete with bars and locked cage door, was used to hold temporary prisoners. Ken Wilkes stood upon the captain's approach and met him at the cell door.

"You asked to see me, Deputy Director?"

"Yes, Captain Mitchell, thank you."

"You are being treated well, yes?"

"Yes, it's not that. I just wanted to talk. And I realize I'm giving up my rights to do so."

Mitchell nodded. "The attempts on the lives of the FBI agent and my Lieutenant have failed, thankfully—still, you have much to answer for."

"I swear I had nothing to do with those attempts, Captain."

"Perhaps not," Mitchell said, drumming the cell bars with his fingers. "So, tell me, what part did you play in all this?"

"I was contacted by Vernon Early nearly two years ago. He had me start the verification process for tribal recognition for the Toe River Tribe—said he had proof of Cherokee blood in several family lines. Once we were on our way to establishing the tribal line, he contacted me again. He offered me a significant percentage if I would switch the grant money from Cherokee to his proposed tribe in Roan. He wanted what you were to have here—a thriving reservation with casinos, hotels, and the like."

"He could have waited. The BIA offers many grants, helps native peoples in many ways."

Wilkes conceded a nod. "True, but it was more than that, Captain. Early has a deep resentment for the people here in Cherokee. He knew, if he could establish his tribe and develop Toe River as the tourists draw that the casinos and attractions provide, Cherokee would lose much of its reputation as a place to visit and vacation. Without the income of the casino, he hoped the Boundary would grow stagnate and die."

"But too much progress had been made in our goal of expansion," Mitchell surmised.

"Yes, I told him there was nothing I could do at that point to slow Cherokee down. So… enter the witch."

"Spearfinger was his last straw, his last attempt to disrupt our progress, to confuse our people, to take Runningdeer out of office. But also, to ceremoniously murder members from each of our clans as a taunting form of revenge."

Wilkes bumped his shoulders. "I guess so. Believe me, Captain; I had no idea about that part of plan. I would have never condoned murder."

"And yet, as it happened, you said nothing."

Wilkes squeezed his eyes shut and dropped his head at the

thought of what he had done. "Again, I am very sorry, Captain."

"Do you know who Spearfinger is? How he operates in the Boundary? Where he might be found?"

Wilkes looked back up and shook his head that he did not.

"Then pray he is found quickly, Director Wilkes. For the sake of the Cherokee and for your sake as well."

11:10 AM

Johnny and Kate entered the cave opening which had apparently been hewed by heavy machinery at some point in the past. The dampness of the cave made the airy temperatures inside the mountain feel that much colder. As they progressed, the cave walls drew in tighter into a more natural formation. The access eventually zigzagged into the darkness beyond.

"We stumbled upon it seven years ago," Early said, his voice echoing. He continued into the cave followed closely by the two deputies. With the safe in his office compromised and his plans now in ruin, Early felt compelled to provide information to the two law officers in the hope of receiving some form of leniency. But he did so with a thinly veiled contempt. "We were stripping this hillside when one of my men noticed the cavern. Much of the entrance was under the Toe River, and we had to pump the subterranean water out before we could get to it. The cave was rich with deposits and had smooth stone for cutting, but obviously we found so much more buried inside."

Johnny looked all around. "This is where they lived—the Tlameha. These caves are where they went to after leaving the Boundary."

Early simply nodded as he came to a stop.

"So, could this place be what the ancients called hilltop fire?" Johnny asked.

"Perhaps," Early admitted. "Roan Mountain is known for many things but especially the fiery flowers of the rhododendron plant which grows near the top in summer. From a distance, it could look like flames near the mountain's pinnacle."

Johnny moved face to face with Early. "What else do you know about this? What do you know of your ancestors?"

"They remained here in these caves, hiding out for many years. Eventually, they moved out, mixed with the white race, and settled the creek lands of Roan. They farmed the valley for many generations after, coming very close to losing their heritage."

"See, that's what I don't understand. How could someone in this century even know about the Tlameha clan? How did you find out about it?" Johnny questioned.

"You hold the answer in your hand," Early said, indicating the anti-degradation container in Johnny's possession. "It is the history of our people."

"But how?"

"Sequoyah. It is his words—his syllabary—his alphabet." Early paused and cut his eyes to all angles of the cave as if his betrayal of the Tlameha's secrets might somehow summon vengeful ghosts. "In 1839, after the forced migration, Sequoyah traveled from the Boundary in Cherokee to Roan. He was the only one at the time to know what happened between the Tlameha and the other clans. He hoped to find descendants of the Bat, convince them to return and reunite with the Eastern Band. He told them what had happened and wrote it down for them. But Tlameha leaders feared what the Cherokee would do to them if they found out how they helped the Spearfinger witch during ancient times. So, in order to cut off any remaining ties to the mother clans, they buried Sequoyah's history in the old caves and sealed them off forever."

"Until your company stumbled upon them," Kate finished.

"Yes. Amazingly preserved."

"Why not leave the recording as a significant archeological find?" she asked. "Why corrupt your heritage in such a way?"

Early's eyes narrowed at the question. "You see, Agent Wilcox, Roan is a community of diggers, farmers, and more to the point: the poor. The clans in Cherokee were on the cusp of a great fortune." He looked to Johnny. "A great fortune that should have been ours as well."

Johnny shook his head in disgust. "So that's it? That was the reason for all this? You would murder innocent people just to fill your pockets?"

Anger rose in Early's eyes. "Fill our pockets? Tell me, Tsalagi, tell me why a crook like Ranshaw wanted in on your operation so much. Tell me how much your people will gain monetarily from the casino. Tell me about the new schools, businesses and development coming your way. Tell me how much you will benefit while we are left with nothing but dirt under our fingernails."

"Nothing is worth taking a life, especially that of a brother, a fellow Cherokee," Johnny said.

Early's laugh dripped in sarcasm. "A brother? You are no brother of mine. The Tlameha is its own clan, its own tribe, its own brotherhood. The rest of you Cherokees can rot in hell."

"And which of your brotherhood, did you send as your assassin? Who is Spearfinger?"

Early held his tongue for a moment but then decided it no longer mattered. "I would not have any of the Tlameha soil his hands with your clans' blood. I hired someone who had equal amounts of hate for you Cherokee."

"Who?" Johnny and Kate both demanded.

"His name is Conroy. Rob Conroy."

"What?!" Johnny fired back.

"Who is Rob Conroy?" Kate asked.

"A punk criminal," Johnny answered. "A three-time loser in the judicial system—lives on the outskirts of the Boundary. He and his low-life, piece of shit brother have been a pain in the ass for the tribal police for many years."

"I trained him for some time," Early said. "I taught him the ways of the Tlameha, gave him what he needed to be Spearfinger. He was not ideal in many ways; I had to get him out of jail twice in the last six months, but he got the job done. And he was easily motivated. He hated you as much as I."

"How could you do this?" Johnny asked.

Early shrugged his shoulders. "No skin off my nose. If he had been caught, there would not have been a connection—just another disgruntled member of your community who had had enough of the Cherokee."

Johnny lashed out, backhanding Early in the face, dropping him to his knees, and causing blood to gush from his nose. The deputies moved to restrain Johnny, but he got in Early's face.

"Now, there's a little skin off your nose! Tell me where we can find Conroy!"

Seething, Early looked up at Johnny, spit blood. "Where do you think you'd find the witch? The answer has been in front of you all this time."

Johnny looked perplexed until it came to him, "Whiteside Mountain?"

Early's hateful silence confirmed everything for Johnny.

2:00 PM

The Bell UH-1 transport helicopter landed dead-center of the Whiteside Mountain parking lot with pinpoint precision. Johnny, Kate and the CIRG team disembarked and made their way to the trailhead where the Jackson County National Guard unit had set up a large tent to act as a command base. Captain Mitchell, Major Hector Gonzales of the National Guard, several of his guardsmen, and a few of the Jackson County deputies came out of the tent to greet them.

"Any word on Corporal Beck?" Johnny hurried out.

"Nothing yet, Lieutenant," Mitchell replied. "They found his bike in the parking lot but no other sign of him. National Guard has been rotating troops through the trails and surrounding forest so hopefully they will find something soon."

"What about Conroy?" Kate asked.

"Two of our tribal police searched his trailer near the Boundary and came up empty. Neighbors reported not seeing him for several weeks."

"That would fit the timeline Early told us, if he is indeed hiding out here at Whiteside," Kate said.

Johnny moved away from the group for a moment to view the mountain. He turned back quickly. "Have the Guard checked around the cliffs? Several have deep crevices and protruding handles that Conroy could use as his base."

"We have not as of yet," Major Gonzales said. "Difficult to get to."

"We can search those for you," Agent Crabb volunteered. "Our group is well-trained in rock-climbing."

"Go," Kate ordered. She held up her walkie-talkie. "But stay in contact."

Crabb nodded and, after gathering some additional equipment, headed off with five other CIRG agents toward the trailhead.

Mitchell took the moment to pull Johnny aside. "Lieutenant, how's the shoulder?"

"It's fine, Captain, the bullet just dug at the skin a little. I'm more worried about Sal right now."

Mitchell shared his concern but got to the point. "Tell me about this man, Early, that the FBI arrested. He is definitely a Cherokee descendent?"

"It looks that way," Johnny said. "He has proof of his connections to the Tlameha clan—blood samples, artifacts. But he is not a stable person. He shares nothing that the Cherokee value."

Mitchell nodded. "Still, as the old saying goes, 'my blood, my brother, my heart.'"

"He will have to look to the evil in his own heart, Cap. His hatred has destroyed any connection to us forever."

3:17 PM

Chief Runningdeer sat in her comfortable chair behind her desk. She had only been ousted from her office for a day, but it seemed like a lifetime, so she just sat there and soaked it back in—her antique book collection, the Native American dolls the local school children had made for her which were standing guard among those books, the tribe's autonomy verifications and numerous civic awards, the pictures of her with different local organizations within the tribe.

As she continued to look around her office, she noticed the cutouts of a smiling pumpkin, a dancing skeleton, and a witch riding a broom taped to her door. She realized for the first time that today was Halloween, but she understood there would be no trick-or-treating this night, no little kids in costumes, no haunted trails in the local forest. These past few weeks had ironically turned the Boundary into a veritable ghost town, and she longed to have her people return and bring it back to life. She knew that it was not over yet, but she prayed that Mitchell and the police would bring an end to this nightmare soon.

It suddenly dawned on her that, with all that had happened, she had never spoken with Eddie Whitetree about what exactly he may have found in ka-i-e-le u-de-li-da. She wondered about its significance in solving the case, how it tied into the Tlameha clan. *As chief, I should know such things.*

She stood, locked her office door, and retrieved the book of secrets from the wall safe. Once in her hands, she carefully laid out the ancient text on her desk. Although she never had the opportunity or desire to look through it before, she felt an overwhelming sense of importance in   opening the seal. As if by magic, she happened to turn right to the section on Spearfinger's story.

She marveled at Sequoyah's calligraphy and had little problem interpreting his words. She read of the grotesque history of the witch's predatory antics and paused as she noted the help Spearfinger received from the forgotten Tlameha. Like Mitchell, she felt a weird sense of loss about those who had descended from the bat clan, but she could not find it in herself to forgive them.

She clutched at her spirit beads as she read with a sense of urgency the final entry. It told of the Cherokee warriors who braved the treacherous climb of Whiteside Mountain and how they, with the help of the Great Spirit, were able to rid the world of Utlunta's evil.

Upon reading the final words, Runningdeer carefully closed the aged text and leaned back in her chair. *History is daring to repeat itself,* she thought. *And if that's true, then this was meant to happen. Utlunta will always find a way to return to our people. We must always be prepared. We must always be vigilant.*

Mary Ellen Runningdeer stood and turned to the pictures of the Eastern Band chiefs hanging on the wall. She ran a finger across the sixth one from the end and smiled. "I have listened, Grandpa, and now it's your turn to hear me," she said aloud. "I promise you this: I will not be caught unaware again; we, as a people, will not be caught unaware. From now on, we will always be ready for whatever comes our way. The world will forever know the strength of the Cherokee people."

4:04 PM

Agent Crabb held up his right hand in a closed fist, bringing his team to a halt. They were spread out in five-yard increments, keeping a tight line as they followed their leader through the underbrush of the cliff sides. The wind continued to howl and push wispy clouds all about them.

"Watch your step," Crabb said. "Looks like a recent slide happened here." He indicated the crushed laurel under broken rock and slag.

"There's a ledge about a hundred yards up," one of the other agents called out. "Could be enough cover to hide a man."

Crabb agreed with the assessment, radioed in the team's position to Kate, and then led the team to the base of the cliff. They split up into three teams of two and attacked the cliff at different starting points. As they free climbed toward the protruding ledge, they were slow and methodical, inching their way up the slick rock face.

As they climbed, Conroy was watching. He had several natural view spots in the rock ledge from which he could scan the trails and forest below, and he had made the FBI group early in their ascent. He scurried to the other rock openings in the white cliffs, watching the team's climb from different vantage points with a powerful Barrett .50 caliber sniper rifle in hand. The rifle had plenty of range to pick off the FBI team, but he wanted to wait until they were in their most vulnerable position in the climb.

Later, still watching from his perch, Conroy smiled as two of the CIRG came within near striking range at a dihedral angled part of the cliff. He leveled the rifle and focused the scope on the top plane of the formed rockface. All he needed was for the unwitting climbers to clear the curvature for a clean shot.

"C'mon… c'mon," Conroy whispered.

Agent Crabb and his climbing partner, Hank Seaton, had made the best time of the three groups and were a mere twenty yards from the open shelf.

"We can rest on that next level, Hank," Crabb said to his

weary second. "Can you reach that hold to your upper right?"

Seaton glanced above him and weighed the move. He outstretched his right arm, found a temporary hold within the rock fissure, and grimaced as he pulled his 220 pounds to his new position.

He had good footholds and was steady again, but now his head was exposed above the rock plane. Seaton glanced at the targeted ledge above him. "Not much further," he surmised.

His last utterance was followed by an explosive shot from the sniper rifle which nearly decapitated him and tore him away from the rock face. Another shot immediately fired and caught another exposed CIRG agent below, also knocking him from the cliff.

In the Whiteside parking area, the lawmen rushed forward at the echoing of the powerful blasts from the rifle. Most stood with their mouths open, binoculars in hand, watching in horror.

"Mayday! Mayday! Agents down! Repeat… agents down! We are under fire!" Crabb's voice crackled through the walkie-talkies.

Another shot fired and echoed across the lot.

Johnny took off for the trailhead but was blocked by Mitchell. "No, Lieutenant! That's what he wants!"

"But the CIRG agents… Sal…"

"You'll be running blind up to that cliff. We know he has substantial firepower—he'll pick us off one by one."

"Damn it, Cap, we've got to do something," Johnny pleaded.

"We must be patient," Mitchell stressed. "We will not provide any additional targets for this madman."

"But there has to be a way we can get to him," Johnny said. "We can't just let those men die up there."

Kate expressed a look of confusion herself but then caught sight of the Huey at rest in the lot. She shot a look at Johnny. "What if we approach from a different way? From the top, maybe."

Picking up on her thinking, Johnny glanced over at the copter. "Rappel down?"

"It would take away his height advantage. And I don't think he would have IEDs planted in the rock above him—that would be suicidal."

Mitchell dismissed the idea with a wave of his hand. "Too risky. We'll wait him out. He can't last up there forever. I will get the Asheville Negotiation Unit down here. Maybe they can talk him into surrendering."

"It won't happen, Captain, and you know it," Johnny said. "The only thing that's going to stop Rob Conroy now is a bullet. Besides, we don't know how long Agent Crabb and his men can hold out. And if there's a chance Sal is up there…."

"Captain Mitchell," Major Gonzalez interrupted as he continued to survey the cliff side with high-powered binoculars. "You're going to want to see this."

Mitchell, Johnny, and Kate grabbed binoculars of their own and joined the others.

"What is it, Major?" Mitchell asked.

But there was no need for explanation as they were all able to see what was happening. In Conroy's final taunt of the Cherokees, Sal's body, tied at the feet with climbing rope, was being lowered from the cliff's ledge. Sal's arms were outstretched above his head, a gaping hole in his midsection continued to pour what was left of his blood onto his face. The bat had the last word; the wolf had been slayed.

5:22 PM

Johnny sat leaning against the cold, rattling bulkhead inside the Huey as the chopper's blades thumped the harsh mountain air outside. His eyes were open to everything around him, but all he could see was the image of his best friend splayed open, hanging upside down, dangling from that cliff side. His anger had morphed into a form of vengeance bordering on possession—a feeling Johnny had never experienced before. He was not going to wait on a negotiating team; he was not going to listen to his captain or take advice from the National Guard. It was his play now, his call, and no one was going to stop him.

"Johnny… Johnny…" Kate tried.

"Lieutenant," she said with more force. Johnny snapped out of his trance and looked at the FBI agent. "We're nearing the target. Time to strap in."

Johnny stood and joined Kate near the bay door. Courtesy of the CIRG team's tactical equipment, she was decked out the same as Johnny with a body armor flak jacket, double-leather gloves, a rappel harness, a leg strap for her Smith & Weston, and a Colt M4 carbine slung over her shoulder. Two volunteer Guardsmen who had some experience in these types of rappelling maneuvers helped clip the ropes to the rings on the harnesses.

"Any further word from the CIRG team?" Johnny asked.

Kate shook her head. "Nothing in the last thirty minutes. Communication has gone silent."

"You know you don't have to do this, Kate."

"Yes, I do. I want the bastard as much as you."

"It's gonna be dangerous as hell—a true long shot."

"Believe me, I know. It was my idea, remember? We just have to be careful and smart. He's a caged animal now with nothing to lose."

"Just his life...."

Kate nodded and forced a grin. "Ever rappel out of a helicopter before?"

"Never even been in a helicopter before today," he said with his own nervous grin.

The pilot of the Huey said something into his headset and a green light came on over the bay door. The two Guardsmen slid the hatch open allowing Johnny and Kate to take their first look at their daunting task. The protruding ledge from where Sal's body continued to hang was a little over half-way down from the top of the cliff. Crabb and whoever else was left of CIRG were somewhere below Sal, hopefully still hanging on.

The plan was for the Huey to maintain its current position with the Guardsmen providing cover while Johnny and Kate lowered themselves to just above the ledge. From there, they would scale down the remainder of the rock and attack Conroy from above. The Huey would then circle back and help get the remainder of the CIRG team from their position. Beyond that, the only plan was to reassess as they went.

SPEARFINGER

The Guardsmen threw out the ropes making sure the ends marked the landing near the center of the cliff. Johnny and Kate got in a seated position and swung their legs to the outside of the Huey. They pivoted 180 degrees and placed their feet against the right skid of the chopper. They pushed away from the skid at the same time allowing the rope to pass through their guide hands and their brake hands behind them.

The high elevation winds that greeted them pushed them around, making the task seemingly that much more impossible, but they fought for stability and continued their descent. They both felt their abdomens tighten and their arm muscles burn as they tried to maintain their targeted speed and angle of approach. They were but twenty feet from the landing when the first shot sounded off the cliff. Johnny dared a look below.

Conroy, still wearing the black cloak of the witch, was standing on the outer most part of the ledge, aiming his .50 caliber rifle right beneath them. The Guardsmen returned gunfire from the cargo bay but to no avail. Conroy was then able to fire a second shot, this time striking its intended target—the fuselage of the Huey. A third shot followed, again striking its target. The copter dipped, then pitched wildly, slamming Johnny and Kate up against the face of the cliff. The impact ripped at them both. Johnny hit hard on his back, and Kate spun and bounced off her right side twice, losing her assault rifle in the process. They furiously clawed at the slick rock, trying to grab hold.

"Hold on!" Kate screamed as she lashed at the rock.

The rotors spat and sputtered for a moment and then the Huey sunk quickly, smashing its blades up against the rock and tilting the chopper back away from the mountain. The rappel ropes zipped back through the harness rings, slashing at Johnny and Kate. They both managed to unclip from their harnesses before the ropes yanked them completely away from their holds.

The Huey pitched again, its blades coming within feet of them. It then turned out and tilted on its side as the rotors stopped spinning. To Johnny it felt like everything at that moment was happening in slow motion. He was able to see inside the open bay hatch—the shock of life's final moments on the Guardsmen's faces. He then watched the helicopter turn completely over and drop into the valley below.

Mitchell felt the Huey's explosion echoing in his chest and then steadied himself as he watched the flames in the distance. He shook his head in disbelief as he searched the cliff face, looking for any signs of life. In the dying sunlight, he had no way of knowing if Lieutenant Whitetree or Agent Wilcox had completed their descent, but given the circumstances, it didn't seem likely. More lives lost, more tragedy. To lose Beck, Whitetree, Wilcox, the Guardsmen, and all those FBI agents in the same hour was too much. This day from hell was finally breaking him.

National Guard troops ran about the parking lot like scattering ants, following their leaders' barking orders. But it all seemed surreal, like a nightmare of sorts.

Major Gonzalez finally saddled up next to the captain and forced his attention. "Captain Mitchell," Gonzalez said. "We've got a bead on the entrance. We could knock a hole in the cliff side and end this right now."

"Not yet," Mitchell said. "On the chance…" He paused trying to convince himself. "Just give our people more time."

Gonzalez confirmed with a nod, but his eyes belied Mitchell's assessment.

Mitchell walked a little further up the Mountain trail, eyesight straining through the binoculars, hoping against hope.

6:14 PM

Johnny returned to his foothold in the craggy face of the cliff and secured a new spot for his hands. Although the high winds hammered at his and Kate's positions, he felt confident in the path he had just sussed out below him. He knew that plenty of rock climbers had performed free climbs of these mountain's cliffs in the past, and that if they took their time, did not panic, and were not shot at again, they could possibly make it to the ledge.

Kate remained frozen in her position, having re-injured her damaged right knee after slamming into the rock. She kept her face pressed against the slick wet cliff and tried her best not to look down.

"Kate," Johnny yelled. "I think I found an avenue for us. There is a vein running to the ledge just below me. It has enough jug-holds for us to scale down. I think we can make it all the way."

"What about Conroy?"

Johnny took another brief look down. "Getting dark, but no sign of him now. He probably thought we fell with the chopper."

Kate scanned to her left and caught her breath. "I don't think I can get to your position."

"You can. Just go up a few feet and then cross."

"It's my knee, Johnny. I think I messed it up for good this time."

"There's no other option. We've got to do this."

Kate did not say another word. Although doubt was ever-present, she knew Johnny was right. Summoning every bit of her physical and mental strength, she grabbed at the holds above her and climbed upward, fighting the fire-like pain of her injured leg.

"Good, Kate. Now, work your way over."

With her right knee damaged beyond use, she depended solely on her left leg as the brace for her movements. She alternated between resting on that leg and then making the sideways moves with just the strength in her arms. She felt every strain, from her back muscles to the tips of her fingers, but she endured and eventually made it across.

"Great. Now come on down. I've got you."

Once in position, Johnny began guiding them both down through the vein in the cliff. The sun was on the verge of completely setting, and they utilized the darkness to help cover their movements.

7:22 PM

Night had fallen. The harvest moon periodically poked its face through the swirling, misty clouds as Johnny made the final step down onto the partial ledge. He slung his assault rifle into his hand while helping to secure Kate's landing as well. Kate grimaced with every movement of her right leg, but she was thankful to at least have a somewhat flattened surface to rest upon. She leaned up against the rock wall and gently slid down into a sitting position. He knelt next to her as both took a moment to catch their breath.

In the intermittent moonlight, Johnny noticed that the barrel of his Colt M4 was severely bent. He surmised his earlier impact into the cliff had done the damage. Kate ran her finger down the barrel and simply frowned, giving her opinion. He laid the useless weapon against the rock. They were now down to just their two handguns—her .40 S&W and his SIG P228. It would have to be enough.

"Stay here. I'll go flush him out," Johnny whispered.

Kate checked her weapon, cocked it, and nodded to Johnny's plan.

With no sign of Conroy lurking about the ledge, Johnny began scoping out the wall of the cliff. As he ran his hands along the rock face, he found the rope Conroy had used to hang Sal and traced it to the outer rim and over the side of the cliff. He knew it was too risky of a move to bring his friend's body up now, and he did not have time to emotionally deal with seeing his friend like that anyway. *Forgive me, Squirrel. I'll be back; I promise.*

The other end of the rope snaked behind a curvature in the cliff and into a four-foot high and one-foot-wide opening. It had to be where Conroy had disappeared. Johnny knew he would not be able to get through with his harness and flak jacket, so he unbuckled them and tossed them aside. He turned sideways, and with a flashlight in one hand and his weapon in the other, he squeezed and scraped past the rock opening.

Three yards in, the access opened slightly, and the sound of the mountain winds died down considerably. Johnny had to crouch to keep from hitting his head, but it was wide enough for him to move about. He paused, looking around. In all the years of hearing about the Spearfinger Witch, he never imagined that her hideaway cave was real, hidden in the middle of Whiteside Mountain's largest cliff face.

A few more feet inward, it opened up even more and Johnny spied a rectangular box leaning against the cave wall. As he progressed, he saw four more of the boxes. They were slender, a yard long, painted an army green. He opened the lid on one— sawdust mixed with .50 caliber bullets. Conroy's cache. His war chest. He imagined the IEDs and other expensive ammo used against his people had come from Vernon Early—another reason to lock that man away forever. Beyond the boxes: an unlit kerosene lantern, beer cans, assorted trash.

Johnny moved in slowly, scanning with the flashlight and weapon in tandem. Among the bits of trash, he picked up several discarded pieces of paper. A sense of dread overcame him as he realized it was Conroy's hitlist: the names of the clans and potential victims under each clan—those who were accessible, where they worked and lived. Among the names scratched out were both Attle and Lynnette Armstrong, Amadahy and Sherry Simpson. On the last piece was a crudely drawn map of Cherokee and the planned points of attack. It sickened Johnny to his core.

He stuck the paper evidence in his back pocket and continued his search. Perplexing enough, there was no sign of Conroy's presence anywhere in the tiny cave, but he did see another weapon, a rifle, leaning against the back wall. He pocketed his Sig Sauer, walked slowly over to the weapon, and picked it up. It was the Barrett M-82 sniper rifle, the one Conroy used to bring down the Huey. It was still warm to the touch, but it was not loaded.

Why leave the weapon here?

It then dawned on him—*To draw me in.*

The thought came too late. Johnny dropped his flashlight and the rifle, screaming out as he felt the spear-finger puncture his back. The razor-sharp point ripped through his skin and buried deep under his rib cage. His nerve endings were set aflame, and he immediately tasted his own blood in his mouth. Johnny dropped to his knees and fell against the cave wall. After the spear was pulled from his back, Johnny managed to turn over to face his assailant. As he did, he fumbled for the pistol in his pocket. But Conroy was on top of him and swatted it away.

"Forgot to check above you," Conroy said in an icy voice. "There's a little overhang right in the cave ceiling. I was watching you the whole time."

Conroy grabbed the flashlight and shown it on Johnny's face. "Well, well, this must be my lucky day—Lieutenant Whitetree, ain't it? Two of Cherokee's finest coming to pay ol' Rob a visit. That's mighty white of you boys." He laughed. "Maybe I should get paid double for taking the two of you out. What do you think?"

Johnny sputtered his words between breaths, losing blood fast. "You're not getting outta here, Conroy. You're going to die today."

"Like I told that other redskin pig: I think you've got that reversed."

"Johnny?! Johnny?! Can you hear me?!" Kate called out from the cave entrance. "Are you okay?"

Conroy furled his brow and turned briefly. "Somebody else knocking on my door. Now who could that be?"

Johnny winced in pain. He was fading and could only manage, "Don't...."

"Hang on, Whitetree. I'll be back for you in a minute."

Conroy grabbed Johnny's pistol, took out the magazine, threw the empty weapon against the rocks, and disappeared toward the entrance.

Leaning against the cliff next to the cave opening, Kate had both hands around her Smith & Wesson. The wind whipped hard against her. She took a deep breath, leaned in, and yelled again, "Johnny?!"

With no reply, she knew he was in trouble, so she did as Johnny did before and took off her harness and protective jacket to get into the opening. With her weapon in her right hand, she maneuvered into the cave with her left side first. But like a coiled viper, Conroy sprung towards the opening and struck at her with the deadly spear-finger. The slice went through her left hand, taking off the tips of her middle and index finger.

Kate fell back out and onto the ledge. She dropped her weapon and cupped the injured left hand with her right. Blood poured from the severed fingers. Before she could even think of her next move, Conroy was there. She reached out for her weapon, but he reacted quicker and kicked the pistol off the ledge.

From her knees she looked up at Rob Conroy. The wind wildly blew the black cloak and his thin hair all about him. A wicked smile etched across his face at the thought of another victim. As their eyes met, Kate sensed she was looking directly into the eyes of madness.

Conroy paused as the recognition came to him. "The waterfall girl," he said. "Yeah, we've met before."

He moved closer, showing her the hideous spear-finger, covered in blood. Kate managed to get on her feet but was unsteady. She backed up more as he swung the spear in her direction.

"No getting away this time," he said.

Johnny grabbed at the sniper rifle with trembling hands. He continued to lose blood and his eyesight was becoming blurry, but he used his elbows and began a slow crawl across the cave floor. He had heard Kate yell out and could only hope that she was still alive.

As he inched forward over rock and dirt, the pain began to throb and spread throughout his body. He felt like everything inside of him was shutting down. He had to grit his teeth now to keep from passing out. He finally managed to reach the open rectangular box. He tipped it over and a solitary .50 caliber bullet rolled next to his hand.

Kate was backed up as far as she could go. She held her injured hand against her bloody shirt. Conroy continued his slow approach, toying with her, swinging the spear-finger back and forth. The fight or flight adrenaline kicked in for Kate, lessening the pain in her hand and knee and increasing her bravado. She knew it was now or never. She yelled out, rushed him, grabbed him around the wrists, and pushed him back.

Forging a strength from deep within, Johnny managed to rise to his feet. He leaned against the cave wall and, using only the thinnest of rays of moonlight as a guide, aimed the sniper rifle toward the cave opening. He put his finger on the trigger, closed his left eye, and held his breath.

Conroy regained his footing and threw Kate against the cliff wall. "Enough! Time to die!" He raised the spear-finger high in the air and thrust it down toward her throat.

Mere moments from collapse, Johnny heard a voice: "Now, Crossing Bear, now!" He pulled the trigger.

The bullet ripped through Conroy, blowing off his arm at the elbow. He bellowed a tortured scream as if drowning in the fiery pits of hell itself. The spear-finger weapon and the severed remains of his arm dropped at his feet.

Kate seized the moment and rushed him again, this time throwing her shoulder into the stunned man's chest. It was enough to force Rob Conroy to tip backwards, lose his balance and slip off the ledge where he fell through the darkness to his death.

MARCH 2, 1996

10:10 AM

Kate pulled her Crown Victoria into the parking lot of the Cherokee Indian Hospital and found a spot. She exited the car and winced a bit as she stood favoring her left leg. Despite the bright sun on this early spring day, it was still cool in the Smoky Mountains, so she wore her heavy blue pea coat over her jeans. A knee brace covered over her right pants leg, and she still had bandages wrapped around her injured left middle and index fingers.

She opened the back door of her car and grabbed a small plastic bag and flowers from the backseat. She had a slight limp as she carried the items into the hospital.

A young Cherokee woman met Kate at the reception desk. "May I help you?"

"Yes. I'm here to visit a patient," Kate said.

"And the name, please?"

"Whitetree."

The woman looked through her patient index. "Yes, Whitetree. Room 227. Take the elevator to the second floor. Take a right by the nurses' desk. It is the second room on the right."

Kate nodded and followed the young girl's instructions to the second floor and easily found the room. The door was closed, so she gave a singular knock.

"Come in," Johnny said.

As Kate entered, she saw Johnny standing beside the bed, a huge grin on his face. Daya was in the bed holding her newborn, and Grandpa Eddie was sitting in a chair next to the window—he too with an enormous smile on his face.

"Hello. Hello. Hope I'm not intruding," Kate said as she entered.

"Not at all. Come in," Daya said.

Johnny gave Kate a brief hug. "Hey, Kate. How are you?" he asked.

"Getting better. You?"

Johnny simply nodded his okay.

Eddie stood and briefly waved from across the room. "Welcome back, Agent Wilcox. Good to see you again."

Kate smiled. "Good to be back." She refocused on the baby. "And how's the newest Whitetree doing?"

"She's doing great," Daya said leaning up and offering Kate the opportunity to hold her. "She just finished her second breakfast."

Everyone laughed.

Kate handed Johnny the flowers and the bag and took the baby in her arms. The child was beautiful with dimples and a head full of the blackest hair. Kate gently swayed her back and forth as Johnny placed the flowers on a cart and handed the bag to Daya.

"What's this? You didn't have to get us anything," Daya said.

"Just a little something I picked up at Bearmeats Indian Den on the way over here," Kate responded.

Daya unwrapped a box she found in the bag and smiled. "Aww. Her first pair of moccasins." She held them up for everyone to see. They were handcrafted with tiny red and blue beads sewn into thread of the soft leather. "Thank you so much. Very thoughtful."

Kate nodded and looked at Johnny. "By the way, the owner, David Smith, said he'd be by here later to welcome her to the world as well." She looked down at the baby and then back to Johnny. "What's her name anyway?"

Johnny paused, looked to Daya who nodded, caught a wink from his father, and then looked back at his daughter. "Sa-lo-nee-ta. It means young squirrel." Johnny smiled but his eyes misted over. "We're going to call her Sallie."

11:11 AM

"Thanks for walking me out," Kate said to Johnny as she reached her car in the lot.

"Yeah, no problem. Needed to stretch my legs after being cooped up in the hospital for two days anyway," Johnny said. He paused and then, "Any word on Agent Crabb and the remaining team members?"

"They have fully recovered and are already back in action. I saw him two weeks ago. He said to give you his best. He thinks your resourcefulness that night should be given special commendation."

"You're the resourceful one. Your triage on my back wound and using the flashlight to signal Mitchell for help really saved our lives that terrible night."

"Believe me, you did plenty of saving that night, too. And plenty of times before. Maybe we should just call it even."

Johnny agreed with a laugh.

"Still don't know how you managed that shot from inside that cave," Kate wondered. "Truly one in a million."

Johnny shrugged. "I'm not sure either. Something kept pushing me… told me where to line it up and when to pull the trigger. Cherokee intuition, I guess."

"Well, whatever you call it, it was perfect timing." She then added in a softer voice, "You were there when I needed you most."

Johnny nodded but said nothing. Kate reached out and grabbed his hand. She blew out a heavy sigh, summoning the courage.

"I lied to you, Johnny. I'm sorry, but the truth is I never got over you."

"Kate…."

"No, let me finish. We worked great as a team through all this. And that couldn't have happened unless you and I had a connection. I know you felt it too. But you couldn't; you wouldn't because you're an honorable person. And I think that's another reason why I felt so attracted to you." She paused again and laughed. "Leave it to me to fall for a man who was already in love."

"You said it yourself, Kate, when people are in the trenches together it's hard not to share body and soul. Ultimately, our connection paid off—we stopped the madness—got the bad guys. Everything else will fade away in time."

Kate nodded and dropped Johnny's hand. "I assume you're right. I just had to let you know how I felt."

"My father always said that letting the world see your heart is the best way to free your spirit."

Kate smiled. "Wise man that father of yours." She looked past Johnny to the hospital and then back to him. "Go to them, Johnny. Take good care of Daya and Sallie. And take good care of yourself."

"I will," Johnny said. He leaned over and kissed Kate on the cheek. "Goodbye, Kate. You will find your happiness. It's out there."

11:58 AM

Kate drove her car up the twisty turns of Soco Road, heading out of the Boundary. She found her thoughts were all over the place. She realized that not only was she giving up her connection with Johnny but with all of Cherokee as well. She thought how it might be one of the last times she would ever travel this way. Though the case had been complete hell from start to finish, there was so much in this corner of the world that she would desperately miss, from the beauty and majesty of the Smoky Mountains to the generosity and hopefulness of its people.

As she rounded a particularly sharp curve, she saw someone on the side of the road. It was an elderly man, a Cherokee. As she neared him, Kate noticed that he wore traditional Cherokee buckskins and had red and white paint covering his face. She slowed considerably and even thought about rolling down her window to ask if he needed help. But he did not seem in need of any kind of assistance, and in fact, he seemed to be standing there for some larger purpose.

Kate passed by, and as she did, the old man lifted his hand to acknowledge her. She gave the man a brief but respectful nod in return. In that moment, Kate took a deep cleansing breath and felt an immediate sense of peace and clarity. She knew that somehow everything was going to be all right. She then refocused on the road and continued on her journey homeward.

The old man watched until Kate's car was no longer in sight. He then turned and disappeared into the lush, green forest behind him.

ACKNOWLEDGEMENTS

The late naturalist, John Muir, once famously said, "The mountains are calling, and I must go." It is a sentiment to which a great many people can relate, a simple yet astute expression of the connection with mother earth and all that she has to offer. For me, the mountains in question are the Great Smoky Mountains in Western North Carolina. When I hear that voice beckoning me, that's where I go to hit the trails. From Asheville to Sylva from Maggie Valley to Roan, my footprints, as well as my family's, can be found there and all spots in between. I have always enjoyed my time camping and hiking about the Blue Ridge Parkway or in the Great Smoky Mountain National Park. As a writer, it has provided the greatest of inspirations, and I found myself excited to be using the area again as the setting for this new mystery.

On a deeper level, this story is more Cherokee-centric. The Eastern Band of the Cherokee Nation, who live in the Qualla Boundary near the corner of the parkway and the park, provide the legends and cultural references that are so prevalent in *Spearfinger*. There is a sense of spiritual awe and wonder that the Tsalagi people hold in their world view that, again, is very inspirational and the reason why this novel is dedicated to them. I have used many of the roads, sights, and attractions that can be found in Cherokee and surrounding areas, but I do so hope the locals will forgive a few slight changes made for creative concerns.

I would also like to acknowledge the many people who have helped contribute to this novel's development. Although the story elements are formed from many sources, I must signal out the contributions of David Smith, Phil Webster, Sean Keefer, Russ Fender, Jeanna Reynolds, Suvajit Das, and Joni Thackston for their invaluable input, creative eye, and sage advice. And please note that any factual errors in content and storytelling fall strictly on my shoulders.

SPEARFINGER

I would like to thank my family, friends, colleagues, students, and former students who have been such a big part of my life. You keep me sane every day, even when it appears that I'm not.

And finally, to my readers and supporters, thank you for staying with me on this journey. The trail lies ahead. Let's see what's around the next bend.